COPY    63

4

388.420  Cudahy, Brian J
C           Under the sidewalks of New York : the
        story of the greatest subway system in
        the world / by Brian J. Cudahy. --
        Brattleboro, Vt. : S. Greene Press,
        c1979.
           176 p. : ill.

           ISBN 0-8289-0352-2  16.95
        L S C A  TITLE I

        1.Subways--New York (City) 2.New York
        (City)--Transit systems.

19

                          19899    79-15221 Je80
                                      MARC

# UNDER THE SIDEWALKS OF NEW YORK

*New York City Transit Authority photo*

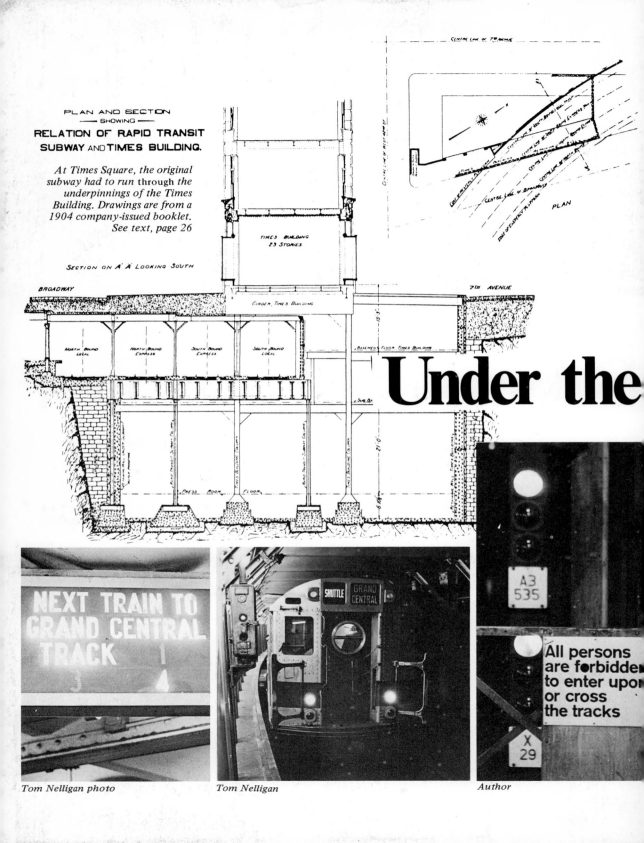

PLAN AND SECTION
— SHOWING —
**RELATION OF RAPID TRANSIT
SUBWAY AND TIMES BUILDING.**

*At Times Square, the original
subway had to run through the
underpinnings of the Times
Building. Drawings are from a
1904 company-issued booklet.
See text, page 26*

SECTION ON A'A' LOOKING SOUTH

TIMES BUILDING
23 STORIES

PLAN

CINDER, TIMES BUILDING

BROADWAY                                        7TH AVENUE

NORTH BOUND LOCAL    NORTH BOUND EXPRESS    SOUTH BOUND EXPRESS    SOUTH BOUND LOCAL    BASEMENT FLOOR TIMES BUILDING

PRESS ROOM FLOOR

# Under the

NEXT TRAIN TO
GRAND CENTRAL
TRACK
1
4

SHUTTLE    GRAND CENTRAL

A3
535

All persons
are forbidden
to enter upon
or cross
the tracks

X
29

*Tom Nelligan photo*          *Tom Nelligan*          *Author*

NYCTA-IRT collection     Author     John J. Cahill     Author

# Sidewalks of New York

*The Story of the Greatest Subway System in the World*
*by* **BRIAN J. CUDAHY.** *The Stephen Greene Press*
*Brattleboro, Vermont 05301*    Publishers of the Shortline RR Series

NYCTA         NYCTA

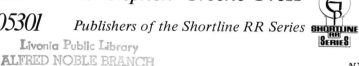
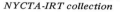

This book has been produced in the United States of America. It is designed by R. Dike Hamilton and published by The Stephen Greene Press, Brattleboro, Vermont 05301.

**Library of Congress Cataloging in Publication Data**

Cudahy, Brian J.
    Under the sidewalks of New York.

    Includes index.
    1. Subways—New York (City)  2.  New York (City)—
Transit systems.  I.  Title.
TF725.N5C8        388.4'2'097471        79-15221
ISBN 0-8289-0352-2

PUBLISHED SEPTEMBER 1979
*Second printing February 1980*

*"Through these portals...." In the photo on page i, a bank of six turnstiles invites passengers to take a ride on the subway. Following illustrations (pages ii-v) are of the 42nd Street shuttle terminal at the Times Square end, an interlocking signal displaying "double green" at the end of a platform together with a sign reminding patrons of one of the subway's no-nos, and station scenes typical of the daily comings and goings of subway trains and their riders throughout the system.*

*At the top of page iii: Signs and symbols that have marked station kiosks at various stages in the subway's history—IRT's illuminated globe, BMT's*

(continued on next page)

# Contents

v

*"flag sign," the TA's design and a still newer set of graphics: MTA's big blue "M" with "New York City" and "transit" lettered much smaller above and below it.*

*Below, left, a Lexington Avenue local at 33rd Street, having passed through the Lexington Avenue tunnels shown in the construction drawing at center. Right, the subway's celebrated A train, here comprised of R-10 units, pauses at 59th Street just prior to its express dash under sixty-six city blocks to 125th Street. Passengers homeward bound for apartments in the Isham and Inwood park areas will stay aboard right to the end of the IND's tunnel at 207th Street and Broadway. (Tom Nelligan photos)*

# Chronology

## Personalities

SPRAGUE

BELMONT

HYLAN

WALKER

QUILL

RONAN

LINDSAY

| | |
|---|---|
| 1863 | World's first subway in London |
| 1870 | First Manhattan el |
| 1870 | Beach pneumatic subway |
| 1883 | Brooklyn Bridge opens; cable railway begins service |
| 1885 | Brooklyn Elevated Ry. begins service |
| 1887 | First successful electric streetcars in Richmond, Va. |
| 1892 | First elevated railway in Chicago |
| 1893 | Proposal to expand Manhattan els turned down |
| 1894 | Rapid Transit Commission formed |
| 1896 | Electrified service across Brooklyn Bridge |
| 1897 | America's first subway in Boston |
| 1897 | Rapid Transit Commission recommends building a subway |
| 1897 | Sprague perfects m.u. control |
| 1898 | Amalgamation of five boroughs into the City of New York |
| 1898 | Through BRT el service over Brooklyn Bridge |
| 1900 | Contracts signed and ground broken for subway |
| 1900 | Brooklyn els electrified *in toto* |
| 1903 | Belmont acquires Manhattan els |
| 1903 | Manhattan els fully electrified |
| 1904 | First New York subway opens |
| 1905 | Interborough-Metropolitan merger |
| 1906 | Elsberg Bill |
| 1907 | Rapid Transit Commission dissolved; state PSC assumes control of subway matters |
| 1907 | Trial runs through Steinway tunnels |
| 1908 | Interborough service to Brooklyn through East River tunnel |
| 1908 | H & M service between Hoboken, N.J., and Manhattan |
| 1908 | BRT el service over Williamsburg Bridge |
| 1909 | Manhattan Bridge opens |
| 1909 | Ground broken for Fourth Avenue (Brooklyn) subway |
| 1910 | Penn Station opens for business |
| 1911 | Construction begins on upper Lexington Avenue line |
| 1913 | Dual Contracts signed |
| 1915 | First Dual Contracts lines in service |
| 1917 | Last New York (and U.S.) horsecar line |
| 1918 | Malbone Street wreck |
| 1918 | BRT receivership |
| 1921 | Transit Commission created |
| 1923 | BRT reorganized as BMT |
| 1924 | First Triplex delivered to BMT |
| 1925 | Ground broken for Independent subway |
| 1925 | Walker defeats Hylan |
| 1928 | IRT loses fare case in U.S. Supreme Court |
| 1931 | Final link of Dual Contracts completed |
| 1931 | New IND cars run tests on BMT |
| 1931 | IRT in receivership |
| 1932 | IND opens |
| 1932 | Walker resigns; O'Brien becomes mayor |
| 1934 | La Guardia takes office |
| 1938 | Sixth Avenue El first Manhattan el to be abandoned |
| 1939–40 | New York World's Fair |
| 1940 | Manhattan's Second and Ninth, Brooklyn's Fulton and Fifth els abandoned |
| 1940 | BMT and IRT under municipal ownership and operation |
| 1941 | Service inaugurated over former New York, Westchester & Boston right-of-way in the Bronx |
| 1941 | Queensboro Bridge el service abandoned |
| 1944 | Brooklyn Bridge el service abandoned |
| 1947 | Fare raised to 10 cents |
| 1953 | TA formed; fare raised to 15 cents |
| 1955 | Third Avenue El abandoned |
| 1956 | Rockaway line opens |
| 1957 | Last streetcars in New York |
| 1960 | First mechanical car washer |
| 1964 | Federal grants available for mass transit |
| 1964–65 | New York World's Fair |
| 1966 | Lindsay takes office; 13-day strike begins on New Year's Day |
| 1966 | Fare raised to 20 cents |
| 1967 | Chrystie Street connection |
| 1968 | MTA assumes control |
| 1969 | Last BMT Standard withdrawn from service |
| 1969 | Myrtle Avenue El abandoned |
| 1970 | Fare raised to 30 cents |
| 1972 | Fare raised to 35 cents |
| 1972 | Boston subway celebrates 75th anniversary |
| 1972 | Ground broken for Second Avenue Subway |
| 1975 | Fare raised to 50 cents |
| 1977 | All prewar IND cars withdrawn from service |
| 1979 | 75th anniversary of IRT |

# Introduction

HOW CAN ONE BEGIN to speak about the New York subway, an urban railway network of almost unfathomable dimensions? Daily it carries four million passengers. If the subway tokens these people drop in the turnstiles in one day were stacked one on top of another, they would tower 21,000 feet into the air—a genuine menace for aerial navigation. Placed edge-to-edge along the ground, they would extend from Times Square to Bridgeport, Connecticut. The system provides work for over 20,000 employees, requires a fleet of 6,500 subway cars to meet daily schedules, and spends about 100 million dollars each year just for electricity! The police force that patrols the New York subway—just the subway *alone*—is the fifth largest in the country. Furthermore, as it is in no other city on earth, the subway of New York is intimately woven into the fabric and identity of the city itself. The number of Hollywood films with a New York setting that feature subway footage, for instance, includes several Academy Award winners. How many movies shot in London or Paris give us scenes on the Underground or the Metro?

New York's subway is not the oldest in the world—London's had been operating underground transit for forty-one years before New York opened its first line. The New York system lacks the electronic complexity of such modern operations as the Washington DC Metro, or San Francisco's BART, and New Yorkers have few qualms in admitting that theirs is not the world's most beautiful subway. Indeed, it isn't even the biggest in terms of route miles; London beats out New York in this respect, 252 miles to 231. But New York carries more passengers than London—although fewer than Tokyo or Moscow—and it operates more subway cars than any other subway system, almost as many as London, Moscow and Tokyo combined! The busiest day ever on the London Underground, on authority of the prestigious Guinness *Book of World Records,* was May 8, 1945, VE Day, when 2,073,134 passengers were accomodated. The New York single-day record is 8,872,244—the author among them, incidentally—achieved on December 23, 1946. Though not yet memorialized by Guinness, this is a record not likely ever to be broken, by New York or any other city.

Herewith a brief caveat: The generic term "subway" correctly and strictly refers to an underground urban railway. Nevertheless, precision in much New York terminology is apt to be subject to perpetual qualification. Thus there are instances when New Yorkers call an elevated transit line a subway; then again there are times when they don't. . . .

By whatever terms, New York's rapid transit system is an enterprise of appropriate magnitude for the city it serves, a city where things superlative have long been regarded as ordinary—the Empire State Building, Grand Central Terminal, the 1927 Yankees, Tin Pan Alley, the Great White Way. And also the IRT, the BMT, and the IND.

# PROLOGUE: The Secret Subway

THERE IS AN ODD AND INTERESTING "PREFACE" to the subway saga, an episode that took place under the sidewalks of New York many years before the 1904 inaugural of today's subway system, and which forms a counterpoint to the city-wide proportions that are the normally perceived attributes of Gotham's rapid transit. In February 1870, during the presidential administration of Ulysses S. Grant and less than a year after the country's first transcontinental railroad was completed, a small subway car began offering demonstration trips under Broadway between Warren Street and Park Place, a distance of 312 feet. In 1870, Thomas Edison was a twenty-three year old struggling inventor, and the vehicle was powered not by electricity, but by pneumatic pressure. The twenty-two-passenger car was "shot," in effect, through the tunnel like a projectile.

This minuscule forerunner of the world's preeminent subway system was financed and built by one Alfred Ely Beach, an individual of some historical significance who was, among other things, the publisher of *Scientific American* magazine. He did important research on hydraulic tunneling, but perhaps the most intriguing aspect of Beach's subway was that he was unable to obtain a conventional franchise for the line, and so he built the project in total secrecy. Transit planners today, who must ply their trade in an atmosphere of intensive public participation, can be forgiven any envy they feel for Mr. Beach.

At any rate, Beach's construction crews worked in the dead of night and began their tunnel through the *basement* of Devlin's clothing store on Broadway at Murray Street. Dirt from the bore was smuggled out through the store in a manner not unlike that associated with the digging of escape tunnels in World War II prisoner-of-war movies.

The underground road was opulent—wall frescoes, a fountain, fine upholstery. But the secrecy surrounding the construction spoke eloquently of New York's political climate during Beach's day. William Marcy Tweed—the "boss" of New York politics—was outraged at what he saw as an affront, namely, Beach's initiative. Municipal approbation for a project such as Beach's subway was not difficult to come by. But it had to be obtained "according to Tweed," and in tune with Tweed's designs. Meanwhile, the independent-minded Mr. Beach was already talking about expanding his system into a city-wide transit network.

Tweed would have none of this. Although Beach's expansion plans received approval in the state legislature, Governor John Hoffman—Tweed's man— vetoed the proposal. Promptly thereafter the short demonstration tunnel was closed. Out of sight became out of mind, and the pneumatic subway was soon forgotten.

Beach was a perceptive man. He recognized the emotional strain subway passengers might experience when traveling beneath the ground, and he sought to allay their anxiety by providing a grand piano in the waiting room of his underground railway. Too bad his system didn't survive another sixty-two years! For if it had, Beach's piano player could have added a most appropriate tune to his repertoire. Written by Billy Strayhorn of the Duke Ellington orchestra, it celebrated a major public work of *its* day, and quickly became Ellington's theme song. The song was called *Take the "A" Train.* Beach's piano recitals aside, Strayhorn's composition represents the only musical note in the entire history of the New York subways, whose initial seventy-five years of operation are the subject of the story that follows—

# UNDER THE SIDEWALKS OF NEW YORK

*In 1912, workers building the Broadway subway (a segment of the Triborough System that was eventually absorbed into the BRT) exhumed the old Beach pneumatic subway near Warren Street. This photograph shows the brick-lined tunnel of New York's first, albeit forgotten, subway. (Robert L. Presbrey collection)*

*A latter-day view of City Hall station, unquestionably the most ornate in the entire system. Although the loop track is still very much in service, the station itself is now closed and passengers must walk a short distance to Brooklyn Bridge to board trains. (NYCTA)*

*Much of the ornate design work that went into the city's first subway is still visible today. Here we see a bas relief of the Santa Maria, which identifies the Columbus Circle station. (Tom Nelligan)*

# 1 "I Declare the Subway Open!"

IT WAS AUTUMN IN NEW YORK and the year was 1904. John McGraw's Giants had won the National League pennant with a very respectable 106–47 record, although they had to forego a crack at the American League champs since the World Series was not played that year. The Russo-Japanese War raged in the Far East. Theodore Roosevelt was re-elected as the nation's twenty-sixth president.

The union totaled forty-five states, and there was great national interest in a major public works effort which the country had just taken over from a failed French attempt—the completion of a canal across the Isthmus of Panama. The population of the City of New York was approaching the four million mark in 1904, and it was the seventh year since the five boroughs[1] had been amalgamated into a single city.

In the first decade of the century New York was also beginning to assume a distinctive style of life. Tammany Hall, an organization with roots back in pre-Revolutionary days, had become an important mechanism within the Democratic Party and thereby within the city itself. Many people justifiably link Tammany with unholy corruption and graft, but the organization managed periodically to purge itself of its sins and become a vehicle for genuine political reform. The days of Grand Sachem William Marcy Tweed, who plundered the city to the tune of between 30 million and 200 million dollars, depending on who is counting, were followed by the regimes of such respected Tammany leaders as Samuel Tilden, August Belmont Sr., and Horatio Seymour.

In 1904 John Wanamaker was selling player pianos—"makes everyone a musician"—for $485, and Stern Brothers store on West 23rd Street advertised "women's velveteen walking costumes" for $28.50. Quarter-acre lots in Merrick, Long Island, sold for $89.

On June 15, 1904, New York suffered one of its worst tragedies. The excursion steamer *General Slocum* burned near Hell Gate, killing 1,030 persons.

One of the problems city planners faced in 1904 was that Manhattan was becoming critically congested. The city's population had increased by almost five fold during the last half of the nineteenth century and getting into town from such fashionable residential sections as Brooklyn Heights or Harlem was a tedious and time-consuming task. The Brooklyn Bridge opened for traffic on May 23, 1883. Its construction, first under the guidance of John A. Roebling, and then his son, Washington, took fourteen years and cost 15 mil-

lion dollars. In 1903 the Williamsburg Bridge was opened. Linking Brooklyn with Manhattan, both bridges offered a swift alternative to East River ferryboat travel. But land was the limiting factor in lower Manhattan, and travel within the city was becoming more and more hampered as New York's population continued to swell and its business and commerce continued to grow. Streets were hopelessly clogged; horsedrawn buggies, foot traffic, pushcarts, wagons, and even an occasional horseless carriage, competed jealously and aggressively for maneuvering room.

Thus in 1904 New York took a bold step that would face up to these several problems and promote the orderly growth of the city thenceforward. At precisely 35½ minutes after two o'clock on the afternoon of Thursday, October 27, with Mayor George B. McClellan[2] at the controls, a subway train pulled out of a terminal and carried passengers under the sidewalks of New York for the first time. Things haven't been the same since.

### A HOT TIME IN THE OLD TOWN

The day that subway service opened in New York was filled with unabashed revelry. Ceremonies began in the Aldermanic Chamber of City Hall with some 600 special guests present. After the oratory had run its course, McClellan stepped forward and said: "Now I, as Mayor, in the name of the people, declare the subway open."

*Opposite page: The elegant kiosks that marked entrance and exit points to the original subway. These ornate structures lasted until the mid-1950s, when they were replaced with a simplified design. This 1906 photo was taken at City Hall. Note the old Post Office building in what is now City Hall Park. If you look sharp you'll see that graffiti already adorns the kiosk! (NYCTA-Interborough collection)*

*Top hats, derbies, and a contingent of helmeted New York City police head for the kiosk and the entrance to the subway. The oratory is over; service is about to begin! (Brown Bros.)*

The various speeches inside City Hall lasted beyond the scheduled 2 P.M. departure for the first train. As the official party of bewhiskered and silk-hatted dignitaries proceeded out of the building and down into the sparkling new subway station located adjacent to the seat of municipal government—and called City Hall station—whistles, bells and sirens already were proclaiming the opening of the new line. Cynics, of course, may think it fitting that the city's first subway train was a half-hour late.

Up and down the route New Yorkers clustered around the subway entrance kiosks. It was an unusual kind of celebration, since most could not see what was happening. Few, however, were unaware of the historic significance of the day.

Mayor McClellan was presented with an inscribed, Tiffany-made solid silver control handle by the president of the Interborough Rapid Transit Company, the proud host of the event, to use on the inaugural trip.[3] With company officials keeping a careful eye on the neophyte motorman, His Honor latched back the controller and fed 600 volts of direct current into the cars' traction motors. Subway service began.

Original plans called for the mayor to operate the inaugural train only a short distance, then let the Interborough's motor instructor take over. But McClellan did not surrender the handles until the train reached 103rd Street, so thoroughly did he enjoy his task. A single minor incident marred the trip.

After leaving Brooklyn Bridge Station, and before crossing onto the express track from the local track, the train came to a noisy and abrupt stop, "as if it had hit some large stationary object," as one journalist put it. The fancy silver controller being used for the ceremonial trip did not fit properly. Consequently it had hit the air brake valve, throwing the train into an emergency stop. Interborough technicians made adjustments and the incident was not repeated.

THE ORIGINAL ROUTE

The city's original subway line began as a single track turnaround loop* under City Hall in downtown Manhattan, but quickly expanded into a four track line at the Brooklyn Bridge Station, less than a mile away. Four tracks permitted the operation of both local and express service. The line proceeded north from Brooklyn Bridge under what were then known as Park Row, Center Street, New Elm Street, Elm Street, Lafayette Place, Fourth Avenue and Park Avenue to East 42nd Street. A more practical line from downtown, in the opinion of some, would have been a tunnel under Broadway, New York's most famous and important thoroughfare. Property owners on that avenue were unconvinced of a subway's merit, and managed to kill construction proposals in the courts. At 42nd and Park, the site of Grand Central, a major express station was located, and the line turned west under 42nd Street. The Grand Central of 1904 was not the current railroad terminal building, which was not completed until 1913. Cornelius Vanderbilt started running his New York Central and Hudson River Railroad trains out of what was originally called Grand Central Depot in 1869. His sanity was seriously questioned at the time for building his New York terminal on 42nd Street, so far away from what was then the heart of the city.

Proceeding crosstown under 42nd Street, the original New York subway line took another 90 degree turn at Times Square and headed north under Broadway. The name Times Square was coined just prior to the subway's opening when *The New York Times* opened its new office building at the site.[4] Previously called Longacre Square, the area adjacent to 42nd Street and Broadway was becoming a major focus of the city's theatrical activity in 1904. Many enterprising showmen bought up property in the area and moved their operations uptown from such older theatre districts as 23rd Street and 14th Street.

The Interborough failed to anticipate the traffic potential to Times Square, though, and in 1904 it was a mere local stop. Eventually it would become the second busiest subway station in the city, and one of the busiest in the world.

From Times Square the four-track line continued north under Broadway to 145th Street. With the exception of a fifteen-block stretch of track near 125th Street, the entire line was built underground. At 125th Street, a geo-

*See plan, page 16

*October 27, 1904. The city's very first subway train is about to leave City Hall station on its historic inaugural run. In the center is Mayor George B. McClellan, who handled the controls. Frank Hedley, who would one day become president of the Interborough, is the man on the left; E. P. Bryan is on the right. (Brown Bros.)*

logical formation called Manhattan Valley cuts across the western portion of the island. Rather than tunnel below this depression, engineers let the subway emerge from below ground and vault across the valley on a viaduct.

One of the line's four tracks stopped just north of 96th Street, but the other three continued north to 145th Street. A junction of importance was also located at 96th Street where a two-track subway cut eastward, then north under Lenox Avenue, eventually reaching West Farms Square in the Bronx after tunneling under the Harlem River and onto an elevated viaduct. But neither this route, nor a two-track line north of 145th Street, were ready for service on October 27. The contract for the construction of New York's first subway called for considerably more trackage than that which opened on inaugural day; the City Hall-145th Street section was simply the first segment to be completed. The first addition to the original nine-mile route—an extension beyond 145th Street to 157th Street—opened a scant two weeks after the October 27th gala. Formally opened, that is. On Saturday, October 29, a temporary service was operated to the incomplete 157th Street station to accommodate fans attending the Yale-Columbia football game (which the Elis won, 34–0).

The inaugural special ran express to 145th Street, where it arrived at 3:01½ P.M., twenty-six minutes after leaving City Hall. The return trip ran as a local, making all stops, to allow dignitaries a chance to examine the beautifully executed station details. This took forty-one minutes.

Immediately after the first train left City Hall, additional trains which had been backed up along the southbound tracks followed it into the loop terminal and went into service for a select group of 15,000 invited guests. These riders sampled the line until 6 P.M. Then, after an hour's breather, the general public was allowed aboard. Some 150,000 New Yorkers tried out the line on its first evening of service, while dignitaries from the afternoon's ceremony retired to Sherry's for a testimonial dinner.

For the record—and it is an oft-repeated story—on one of the early "invitation only" trains a gentleman from Philadelphia named F. B. Shipley became the first man to offer his seat to a woman on the New York subway. Later, after the general public was allowed aboard, Henry Barrett of 46th Street noticed his $500 diamond horse-shoe pin was missing after he paid his fare at the 28th Street station, the first recorded incident of a passenger being separated from his property on the subway. Mr. Shipley's chivalry has been repeated in diminishing proportions, and Mr. Barrett's misfortune in increasing proportions, in the years since 1904.

Indicating how quickly the subway melded into the fabric of New York life, many of the 15,000 invited guests on the early trips decided to forego the return trip to City Hall, and instead get off at the stations nearest their homes. The ensuing scenes at the various subway exits comprised an ordinary evening rush hour, as passengers emerged from the underground stations and headed home to supper in a manner that would be commonplace from then on.

Heavy crowds came to inspect the new subway on its first weekend of op-

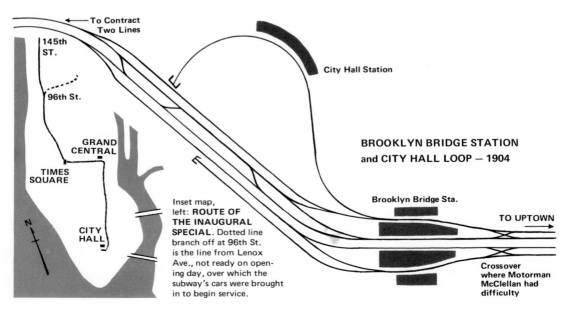

To Contract Two Lines

145th ST.

96th St.

GRAND CENTRAL

TIMES SQUARE

CITY HALL

City Hall Station

BROOKLYN BRIDGE STATION
and CITY HALL LOOP — 1904

Brooklyn Bridge Sta.

TO UPTOWN

Inset map, left: ROUTE OF THE INAUGURAL SPECIAL. Dotted line branch off at 96th St. is the line from Lenox Ave., not ready on opening day, over which the subway's cars were brought in to begin service.

Crossover where Motorman McClellan had difficulty

eration, and complaints immediately surfaced. At several stations built on curves, a large gap developed between the platforms and the subway cars. This problem was eventually rectified by the installation of a mechanical "sliding platform" which moved out to fill the gap as soon as the trains stopped. Another criticism concerned the advertising signs which, in the view of some beholders, defaced the beauty of the stations. There were frequent complaints about crowding in the trains and stations, a problem the New York subways have yet to solve.

The stations were attractive in their design and appointments. The construction contract was most explicit: "The railway and its equipment as contemplated by the contract constitute a great public work. All parts of the structure where exposed to public sight shall therefore be designed, constructed, and maintained with a view to the beauty of their appearance, as well as to their efficiency." Critics agreed these goals were amply met. A trade journal of the transit industry called the subway stations "dignified and artistic efforts of the highest order." One journalist called them "architecturally superlative executions."

In that weekend of service, the subway had to cope with the first of its "problem" passengers, of a kind. According to the records of the Yorkville Court, Magistrate Breen presiding, one Michael Pollack was charged with being drunk and disorderly in public on October 29th, a Saturday. He had been arrested the previous evening, and thirteen others were brought in on the same charge as well. Said Pollack to the judge: "Please, your honor, I rode from the Bridge to 145th Street and back in the tunnel. The dust was terrible, horrible, your honor. I had to take a drink to get it down."

The judge then asked if a single drink was responsible for the man's condition at the time of his arrest, to which the resourceful Pollack replied: "Oh, no. But one wouldn't do for that dust. I had to take six."

The case was dismissed with the suggestion that, in the future, the el might prove to be less dusty than the subway. The other thirteen, impressed by Pollack's performance, had exactly the same story to tell. And all won acquittal from the amused magistrate.

*Notes to Chapter 1*

---

[1] The City of New York is composed of five "boroughs"—Manhattan, the Bronx, Brooklyn, Queens and Richmond, the latter more popularly known as Staten Island. A borough is a unit of city government, and the elected president of each borough is an *ex officio* member of the City Council. Each borough is also a separate county, a county being a unit of state government. To make matters slightly more confusing, in some cases the boroughs and counties have different names. Thus the Borough of Brooklyn is also known as Kings County.

[2] Son of the Civil War general.

[3] Read the inscription: "Controller used by the Hon. George B. McClellan, Mayor of the City of New York, in starting the first train on the Rapid Transit Railroad from the City Hall station, New York, Thursday, Oct. 27, 1904. Presented to the Hon. George B. McClellan by August Belmont, President of the Interborough Rapid Transit Company."

[4] The building survives today and is known as the Allied Chemical Tower. It enjoys a brief moment in the limelight once each year on New Year's Eve, since it is atop this building that the famous "lighted ball" descends to mark the start of the new year.

# 2 From Steam to Electricity

THE SUBWAY LINE THAT OPENED IN NEW YORK in the autumn of 1904 was not the first of its kind to operate in the world, nor even the first rapid transit line to traverse Manhattan Island.

The world's first subway opened on January 10, 1863, in London, a steam-powered line that carried Queen Victoria's subjects on a 3.7-mile track between Farringdon Street and Bishop's Rock, Paddington. "The line may be regarded as the greatest engineering triumph of the day," commented the *London Times.* The New York subway doesn't even rank as the first subway in the United States. That honor belongs to Boston where, on September 1, 1897, trolley cars of the West End Street Railway began operating into the Tremont Street subway, adjacent to historic Boston Common. On June 10, 1901, the Boston Elevated Railway began running elevated trains into the same Tremont Street subway.[1] The New York press, while sufficiently laudatory of Boston's initiatives, was visibly annoyed that any other city could accomplish such a major effort ahead of New York.

The Beach effort aside, the first practical rapid transit line on Manhattan was a section of single-track elevated railway that opened for passenger service on February 14, 1870, almost thirty-five years before the first subway run. The line boasted a grand total of three wooden passenger cars that were propelled by a moving cable. When the line opened in 1870 it ran from Dey Street to 30th Street. Eventually it became part of the Ninth Avenue el.

Cable operations quickly proved unsatisfactory, and the elevated company turned to the technology of standard railroading and began hauling trains behind diminutive steam locomotives. These little engines became a permanent fixture on the New York scene for more than twenty-five years. Both the cars and the locomotives of the elevated lines were essentially scaled-down versions of regular railroad equipment, although they ran on the standard track gauge of 4 feet, 8½ inches. At one time the elevated lines even interchanged freight cars with conventional railroads.

By 1880 elevated lines had been built by various companies down Ninth, Sixth, Third and Second avenues. All were powered by steam locomotives, and all eventually ran from various points in the Bronx down the length of Manhattan Island to South Ferry at the southern tip of the island, where an armada of ferryboats made connections for points in Brooklyn, Staten Island and New Jersey. Various steam-powered el operations were started across the river in Brooklyn and Queens at about the same time.

In addition to the four elevated lines, several networks of street railways criss-crossed Manhattan prior to 1904, but as these had to compete directly with street traffic, they can scarcely be called true rapid transit. The els, however, were a major-league operation. In the last full year before the subway opened, they carried over 250 million passengers.

Steam power on the elevated lines, though, even in the 1890s, was a pronounced civic liability. The engines were sooty, messy and noisy. They started fires in awnings, startled teams of horses, and in general wreaked havoc with efforts to lead a quiet and tranquil life. The press was vocal in decrying these conditions. "A major city should not suffer such indignities any longer," scolded one reporter.

Despite their drawbacks, the little engines had a definite charm. An 0-4-4 type, developed by—and named after—M. N. Forney, was especially appealing. It carried fuel in a bunker behind the cab, water in on-board tanks, and could operate equally well in either direction. The cab roof was decorated with a pair of colored discs by day, and lanterns at night. By knowing the proper color codes, passengers could determine a given train's destination and tell whether it was a local or an express before it entered the station. The stations themselves were jewel-box masterpieces of Victorian gingerbread. Light danced into the waiting room through stained-glass windows. In winter months the ticket agent was kept busy scooping coal into a potbellied stove to keep waiting passengers warm.

As the turn of the century drew near many sensed that an effective replacement for steam power on the els was not only necessary but near at hand. This new power promised to be clean, efficient and silent, a type of energy that would truly fulfill the concept of urban transit: electricity!

At the Berlin Industrial Exhibition in 1879, Dr. E. Werner von Siemens demonstrated what is generally regarded as the first practical use of electricity to haul passengers. A series of experiments and demonstrations followed, as

*Congestion in the 1870s! Steam-powered el trains contribute sparks, soot and clatter to the brouhaha at street level. Horse at the head end of the street car at lower right is the most placid figure in the scene: Franklin Square on the Third Avenue line, according to the caption of this* Harper's Weekly *1878 woodcut.*

*Top: An 1872 view of the Ninth Avenue el. Note drop-belly sides on the cars to insure a better center of gravity, and small steam engine on the far end of the train. (Smithsonian Institution) Below: The crew of No. 173 poses for posterity at the northern terminal of the Sixth Avenue line. In the background can be seen, just barely, the grandstand of the original Polo Grounds, home of John McGraw's New York Giants. The elevated structure where the engine sits survived, by a strange quirk, to become the final segment of the original elevated lines in Manhattan to remain in service. (NYCTA)*

in 1880, when Thomas Edison built a 10-h.p. narrow-gauge electric locomotive at his Menlo Park, N.J., laboratory.

Through the final two decades of the 19th century continual efforts were also underway to develop an efficient replacement for the horsecar which was then the standard vehicle of the street railway industry. Naptha engines and other exotic ideas were tried—unsuccessfully. Here, too, electricity would eventually win the day. Electricity would put the horses from the street lines out to pasture and send the steam locomotives from the els to the scrap heap.

Many complex engineering problems remained to be solved, however, before electricity could be successfully employed in a heavy-duty, multi-car transit operation such as an elevated line. An Annapolis graduate named Frank Sprague did more than any other individual to upgrade the state of the art. Years later, Frank Hedley, who was president of the Interborough after

*Manhattan in the age of the el! Steam gave way to electricity on the els by the turn of the century at the same time horsecars were being replaced by electric-powered streetcars. Here is a vintage scene shortly after the changeover, showing the intersection of Sixth Avenue, Broadway and West 34th Street. The el and the streetcars are long gone but the location, today, is perhaps the greatest concentration of electric railways anywhere on the planet – all underground! See text, page 159. (Smithsonian Institution)*

World War I, said of Sprague: "It has rightly been said that he bears the same relation to electric transportation that Thomas A. Edison bore to electric illumination."

In 1887 in Richmond, Va., Sprague designed and built the first successful electric streetcar installation. But the innovation of Sprague's that was most significant in paving the way for electric-powered elevated trains and subways was the development of "multiple-unit control." Multiple-unit control, as the name suggests, allows the motorman in the lead car of a multi-car train to operate the motors of all cars from a single control station. By today's space-age standards, m.u. control may not seem notably outstanding, but in 1895 when Sprague began work on the project, it was a technological breakthrough that was desperately needed. Sprague's success meant that trains could be lengthened or shortened at will and as traffic warranted. Only simple cable connections were needed to make, say, an eight-car train as easy and efficient to operate as a single-car train. In short, multiple-unit control made the change from steam to electricity a genuinely radical one. It was not merely a case of replacing steam locomotives with electric locomotives; instead, each car contained its own power unit. And furthermore an eight-car train required only one motorman, not eight.

On July 16, 1897, on an experimental track outside the General Electric plant in Schenectady, N.Y., Sprague successfully demonstrated the first workable m.u. lash-up. Later in the same year, the method was tested on the South Side Elevated in Chicago.[2]

Thus the way was cleared for the most daring and, ultimately, the most successful attempt to solve the growing congestion of New York streets. With electric power and multiple-unit control an underground rapid transit line suddenly became more feasible than ever before.

Electric traction advanced with amazing speed. In 1900 the management of the Second Avenue el made the decision to electrify their entire operation. By early 1903 all four Manhattan elevated lines were converted from steam to electric operation with m.u.-controlled cars.

Electricity progressed in other areas of the transportation industry, as well. A serious rear-end collision in the New York Central's Park Avenue tunnel in January 1902, caused by obscured visibility from steam locomotive exhausts, prompted state legislation prohibiting steam operation in the tunnels. Even prior to the accident, New York Central had begun to study the possible electrification of its Manhattan operations. In late 1906, electric equipment was phased into service. Meanwhile New York Central's longtime rival, the Pennsylvania Railroad, was planning its own assault on Manhattan Island via a Hudson River tunnel and with electricity as a source of propulsion. With none but steam engines in its roundhouses, PRR was forced to terminate its trains from the west across the Hudson in Jersey City, and transfer New York-bound passengers by ferryboat, a decided competitive disadvantage. Electric power brought the railroad smack into midtown Manhattan.

Westinghouse and General Electric, then, would be the prime movers of a transformation that would soon shape the way of life of millions. Neither corporation was the giant it is today, of course, but each was dealing with an idea whose time had arrived. At the turn of the century, the harnessing of raw electrical energy was a significant and dramatic development.

*Notes to Chapter 2*

[1] The full story of the Boston subway is told in the author's book *Change at Park Street Under* (Brattleboro, The Stephen Greene Press, 1972).

[2] Following the 1897 test, the South Side Elevated was totally converted from steam power to electricity, the first commercial deployment of Sprague's m.u. control. Other elevated lines in Chicago began electrified service with a different technique—motorized power cars hauling non-motorized trailers. All eventually converted to multiple-unit operation.

# 3 The Birth of the Interborough

NEW YORK WAS DETERMINED to build rapid transit underground, and even flirted with the possibility of steam-powered lines. As early as 1868, serious talks were underway concerning such projects. In 1872, Cornelius Vanderbilt incorporated something called the New York City Rapid Transit Company to build a "sub-surface rail road" in Manhattan, but the plan was dropped. Something of a formal move came on April 9, 1890, when Mayor Hugh J. Grant appointed a Rapid Transit Commission to study the matter. This commission eventually recommended that a steam-powered line be built on a viaduct from the Manhattan end of the Brooklyn Bridge as far as Astor Place, and then through a tunnel to 42nd Street. Underscoring the determination to go beneath the streets, in 1893 the Manhattan Railway was rebuffed in a bid to construct additional elevated lines, despite an urgent need for new routes. Before any steam-powered subway line was built, of course, electric power had become a reality.

In 1894 a new Rapid Transit Commission was formed by state legislation. It included the city's mayor and comptroller as *ex officio* members, and such other distinguished citizens as Seth Low and William H. Steinway. William Barclay Parsons was retained from the staff of the older commission as chief engineer. Public hearings were held throughout 1896, and in 1897 Parsons presented plans for what would eventually become the 1904 Manhattan-Bronx subway. Many obstacles had to be overcome in the courts, such as the borrowing limit of the municipal government. But on January 15, 1900, bids were opened for the construction of the subway.

There were only two contending contractors. The company of John B. McDonald bid 35 million dollars for basic line work and an additional 2.7 million dollars for stations, beating out the Andrew Onderdonk organization. McDonald was experienced in tunnel work. He had constructed the Baltimore tunnels for the B&O Railroad, the nation's first mainline railroad electrification. But McDonald ran into unexpected trouble obtaining security bonds, supposedly because certain street railway interests, who saw the subway as a threat, used their influence with the banking community to block approval. In order to obtain the necessary bonds, McDonald was forced to seek out a man whose imprint on the New York subways was to be firm and lasting.

McDonald formed a partnership with August Belmont, son of the North American representative of the Rothchilds, who had access through his father (August Belmont, Sr.) to virtually unlimited funds. Belmont capitalized the

*On March 14, 1903, the first spike was driven in the new subway at Columbus Circle and a suitable ceremony was held to commemorate the event. Presiding were (left to right) John B. McDonald, William R. Wilcox, a man who would later become chairman of the state Public Service Commission, William Barclay Parsons and Mayor Seth Low, who is holding the mallet he used to drive home the silver spike. (NYCTA)*

*On the left (inset) is August Belmont, the guiding influence behind the early Interborough. After the subway opened, Belmont, McDonald and Parsons teamed up on another transport venture — the construction of a canal across Cape Cod! (Brown Bros.)*

newly formed Rapid Transit Subway Construction Company at 5 million dollars. On February 21, 1900, the firm signed a construction contract with the city through the Rapid Transit Commission. Of note is the fact that the city only undertook the construction of the subway in 1900; the question of operating the trains was not raised. The general assumption along Park Row[1] was that an existing elevated or street railway company eventually would be franchised to run the trains.

Early in March of 1900 construction began in Washington Heights, and on May 24th of the same year, Mayor Van Wyck broke ground officially in front of City Hall. McDonald separated his own contract into fifteen subcontracts, which were then opened to bid by other firms. Different construction companies had responsibility for different sections of the line, and the McDonald-Belmont organization functioned as a sort of holding company supervising the entire effort. Before construction was even close to completion, however, financial and political maneuvering took place that greatly influenced the future development of subways in New York.

The first hint of clandestine activity appeared in the newspapers of April 1, 1900. Belmont announced that the vice-president and general manager of the Terminal Railroad Association of St. Louis, a gentleman named E. P. Bryan, would become the general manager of a company being formed to operate the subway, and would advise the construction company on matters pertaining to operations. Until this time, neither Belmont nor McDonald had expressed any interest beyond mere construction. But in 1902 the Interborough Rapid Transit Company was formally organized and incorporated. Its president was August Belmont. Its purpose was to operate the new subway.

Belmont was not finished. Later in 1902 McDonald's firm was awarded an 8 million dollar contract to extend the still unfinished subway down lower Broadway, under the East River, and through downtown Brooklyn to the Long Island Rail Road terminal at Flatbush and Atlantic avenues. This addition was referred to as the "Contract Two" segment of the subway, while the original work was known as the "Contract One" segment. In the same year the Interborough signed a 999-year lease for all properties of the Manhattan Railway Company, by then the operator of all four elevated lines. The lease, which guaranteed a seven per cent return each year on the el company's stock, took effect on April 1, 1903. It meant the Interborough would become the operator of all rapid transit on Manhattan Island, both new subway and old elevated, enabling the company to plan integrated operations, especially in the less densely settled residential sections of the Bronx. A combined subway and elevated network would also offer stronger competition to the street railway lines. Belmont's action provided the Interborough with extensive rapid transit experience before the subway itself opened, and eliminated by consolidation whatever competitive threat the elevated system represented for the new subway.

## How to Build a Subway

Meanwhile, construction of the Manhattan-Bronx line had begun. The trade press of the day described the construction as the "shallow excavation type," a technique similar to that which had been used on the Glasgow Central Railway, and also the subways of both Boston and Budapest. Crews dug out the right-of-way from street level, built a concrete and steel subsurface structure for the trains to run in, then rebuilt the surface thoroughfare atop the tunnel. Tunneling methods varied, of course, according to the geography or the geology of a particular section. At times mole-like deep bore tunneling—perfected on the London Underground—proved to be more practical than shallow excavation. Deep bore tunneling had the advantage of not disrupting surface activity. If the ground through which a deep bored tunnel was cut proved to be firm, the work was routine and the finished bore merely had to be lined with concrete. But if the ground was soft, crews were forced to work in an artificially pressurized atmosphere within an airlock, and the tunnel was built with iron rings bolted together to form a secure, and even watertight, structure.

Shallow excavation work, or "cut-and-cover" construction as it later came to be called, was by no means a simple procedure, even if less complex than deep bore work. Sewer and gas mains had to be temporarily diverted, then rebuilt as the work moved along. Often there were no maps showing the precise location of these utility lines. The texture of the soil also presented a variety of problems. Quicksand was discovered in the Canal Street area, while at other places construction crews had to blast through solid rock. On the west side of Fourth Avenue at Union Square, engineers found nothing but rock from street level on down, while on the east side of the same avenue, the first fifteen feet of work merely required the removal of soft sand.

One of the most troublesome problems was the shoring and protecting of existing construction along the subway route; the elevated structures of the Manhattan Railway particularly caused trouble for Belmont's engineers. One ingenious solution of such problems was at the curve from 42nd Street into Broadway at Times Square. *The New York Times* was erecting its new headquarters building at that site. The Interborough tunnel was literally run *through* the foundation of the newspaper building,* although the supporting work for each is totally independent of the other.

A typical four-track section of tunnel, built by the cut-and-cover method, was fifty-five feet wide. Tracks—100-pound rail laid in thirty-three-foot sections—were spiked to conventional hard pine crossties embedded in broken stone ballast. All curves were fitted with guardrails on the inside of the turn,

*See drawing opposite title page

and an outside third rail was mounted on top of insulators affixed to extra-long crossties. A wooden guard was installed over the third rail following a style developed by the Wilkes-Barre & Hazelton Railway in Pennsylvania, an added safety feature to insure against accidental electrocution.

Track and ballast were installed atop a poured concrete floor, a slab generously treated with waterproofing compounds of several varieties. Between each set of tracks, as well as along the tunnel's outside walls, rows of steel "I" beams were erected on five-foot centers, providing a reserved corridor for each of the four tracks, and firm support for the roof beams. Tunnel sidewalls were finished off in concrete, and the stand of beams separating the two express tracks, on which trains would pass in opposite directions, was cemented to provide the additional safety of a "crash wall" in the event of an accident or derailment.

The construction project endured its share of tragedy. On January 27, 1902, six men were killed and 125 hurt in a dynamite explosion. A tunnel cave-in on the east side of Park Avenue between 37th and 38th streets caused such damage to nearby property owners that an exasperated August Belmont found it easier to buy out the entire block for a million dollars than to attempt to indemnify specific liabilities. Ten men died in another cave-in during the fall of 1903.

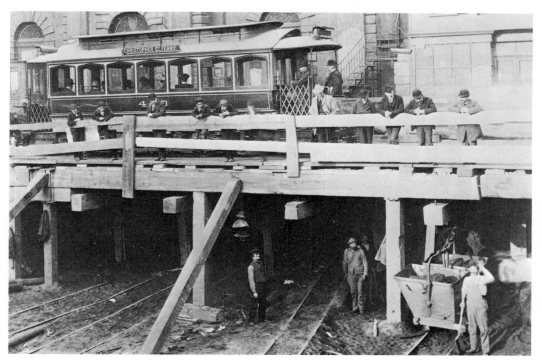

*The year is 1902 and the location is Astor Place. A crosstown street car heads for the Christopher Street ferry slip, and workers have begun to excavate the right-of-way for New York's first subway, as "sidewalk superintendents" look on. (Robert L. Presbrey collection)*

*Subway construction was a vexing problem all along the new line's route. This view from the Brooklyn Bridge el station looks south along Park Row. Subway excavations are visible on either side of the street. Note the underground conduit for the street cars. The gentleman in white to the left of center is cleaning up after an equine indiscretion. (Robert L. Presbrey collection)*

Progress, though slow, was steady, and New Yorkers never grew tired of hearing about their new subway. Rolling stock was of special interest to potential passengers. The Sunday supplements devoted endless copy to describing the cars that would soon roll along the underground railway.

The first two subway cars to arrive in New York were experimental vehicles built by the Wason Manufacturing Company of Springfield, Mass. One was called the *August Belmont,* later to be designated No. 3340 in the Interborough numbering sequence, and the other was the *John B. McDonald,* listed on the roster as No. 3341. Although neither car would ever run in regular passenger service, they established design features not only for the earliest production-model subway cars, but for subsequent Interborough car orders, until 1925, of more than 2,500 vehicles. Wason delivered the first batch of regular cars to the Interborough in the summer of 1903. Thanks to the lease of the elevated lines, the company had a full-fledged test facility at its disposal. On September 14, 1903, a five-car train of new subway cars took a demonstration run over the Second and Third Avenue elevated lines. By late fall more than 200 of the original order of 500 cars were delivered

*One of the Interborough's early experimental cars, the John B. McDonald. (NYCTA-Interborough collection)*

from Wason and three other manufacturers who were sharing the order. They were quickly pressed into service on the Second Avenue el to test their mettle through the harsh winter months.

These cars came to be called the "Composites" because they were built of both wood and steel. Frames and structural members were all made of steel, but car sides were of wood. Officials repeatedly called attention to the layers of asbestos and other materials that made the cars "virtually fireproof." Good looking cars both inside and out, their white ash exteriors were finished in a deep rich wine color. The sides of the cars were slightly tapered, making them narrower at the top than at the bottom. They measured fifty-one feet, two inches in overall length, eight feet eleven and seven-eighths inches wide at the windowsills, and just a fraction of an inch over twelve feet high. Each car was equipped with fifty-two seats made of attractive rattan. To allay the qualms of passengers unaccustomed to riding through the darkness of underground tunnels, officials never failed to emphasize that each car was illuminated by twenty-six electric light bulbs. The most distinctive feature of the Composites, however, was a copper sheathing overlay that protected the lower reaches of the wooden car sides.

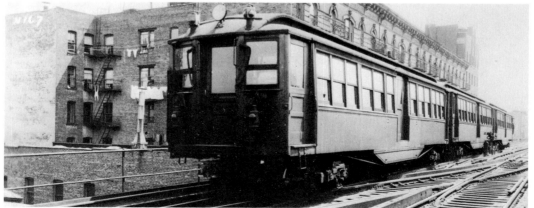

*IRT Composites shown in 1930 after they had been removed from subway service and placed on the els. Center door and fish-belly girder are later additions. (E. B. Watson collection)*

**30** *Construction scenes at right and below are at the curve at Dyckman Street and where the Interborough vaults across West 125th Street. The city's original subway made frequent use of elevated construction, much cheaper than tunnel work, in the then "wilderness" areas of the Bronx and upper Manhattan. (Photos on this page are from author's collection)*

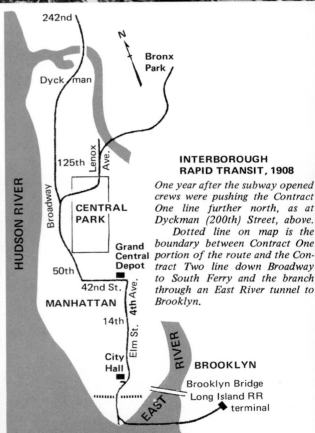

### INTERBOROUGH RAPID TRANSIT, 1908

*One year after the subway opened crews were pushing the Contract One line further north, as at Dyckman (200th) Street, above.*

   *Dotted line on map is the boundary between Contract One portion of the route and the Contract Two line down Broadway to South Ferry and the branch through an East River tunnel to Brooklyn.*

*"Cut-and-cover" construction scenes at left, reading uptown, are at Chambers Street and West 50th Street, where the steelwork for the station is in place.*

Following the design pioneered in Nos. 3340 and 3341, the Composites featured enclosed end platforms, or vestibules, and manually operated sliding doors. Actually, No. 3341 had a trolley car-style folding door on one end, but it proved to be less desirable than the sliding variety and was never thereafter repeated. Something of an advance in the design of the Composites was the location of the motorman's station on the end platform, with the control apparatus protected by a full-length door when a given car was coupled into the middle of a train. Previously, as on the els operating open platform cars, the cab was squeezed inside the car behind the platform. To be certain the motorman's vision was not obstructed, admonitions were posted everywhere on the els: "Passengers Not Permitted to Ride on Front or Rear Platforms."

## FIRST ALL-STEEL SUBWAY CARS

The Interborough toyed with another idea before signing the contract for the Composites in December of 1902—an all-steel car. Electrical engineer George Gibbs, the resident genius on the Pennsylvania Railroad, was retained by Belmont to design such a vehicle. Gibbs later designed the Long Island Rail Road's first multiple-unit electric cars, and almost all the electrical installations on the Pennsylvania itself. But car builders were reluctant to commit themselves to the idea. An all-steel passenger car had never been built before, and the industry was unwilling to experiment at a time when it had a heavy backlog of orders for conventional cars.

So the Composites were ordered to insure that the new subway would have some rolling stock on opening day. But the Interborough refused to let the all-steel idea die. Thanks to Gibbs' good offices with the Pennsy, that line's Altoona Shops turned out No. 3342 and delivered it to the Interborough in February 1904, eight months before the subway opened. The car carries the distinction of being the first all-steel passenger car ever built.

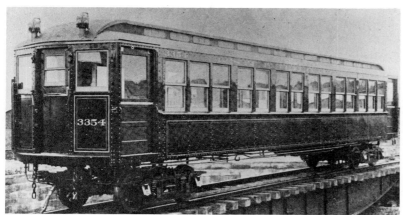

*One of the Interborough's early all-steel cars, the design developed by George Gibbs, at the Berwick, Pa., plant of the builder, A.C.F. Electrical components were yet to be added and, in later years, its appearance would be significantly altered by the introduction of a mid-car center door over a fish-belly center sill, which compensated for the structural loss to the carbody. (James E. Tebbetts collection)*

Officials needed to assure a wary public that there was no more danger of electrocution in a steel subway car than in a wooden one, and a fleet of 200 additional "Gibbs cars" was quickly ordered from the American Car and Foundry Co. Opening day saw 103 of them on the property, and the inaugural special that Mayor McClellan piloted was made up of the new all-steel rolling stock. With the exception of the original fleet of 500 Composites—which saw service only until 1916, when they were transferred to the elevated lines—wooden equipment was never again ordered for subway service in New York.

The Gibbs cars were basically like the Composites. They featured the same enclosed end platforms, manually operated doors, and a convertible motorman's cab. They were powered by a pair of 200 hp motors, both mounted on one truck. The steel cars lacked, of course, the copper sheathing of the Composites, and they did not have tapered sides. Neither the original Gibbs cars nor the Composites were equipped with center passenger doors, a feature which would become standard on the Interborough in later years. Consequently these cars lacked the typical Interborough "fish belly" side, which was necessary to give structural strength to a car whose side wall is cut out for a door. Because of the absence of a center door, eight sets of transverse seats were installed in the middle of the original subway cars. Expectedly, the all-steel Gibbs cars outweighed the Composites by two tons each. Both types were equal in length although the Composites were a few inches wider. Performance statistics were impressive for the time. Both cars could attain a maximum speed of 45 mph. Electrical components were designed to permit a fully loaded train to accelerate at 1.25 mph per second on level track.

As opening day drew closer, interest in the subway gathered momentum. On January 1, 1904, Mayor McClellan took a group of VIP's on a handcar tour over the new line. Photographs taken of this trip have often been incorrectly captioned as the October 27th opening, and many journalists commented that the handcar operators, who were drafted from the ranks of subway construction workers, appeared unexpectedly dapper in the uniforms Belmont provided for the occasion. However, instead of using the term "construction workers," newspapers usually identified the men simply as "Italians," and presumed readers knew who they were talking about. Such was the extent of ethnic consciousness in New York in 1904.

On April 15th, Belmont and other officials toured the line behind a small steam engine rigged to burn oil instead of coal. On September 1st, power was fed into the entire system from the Interborough's huge new Manhattan generating station at Eleventh Avenue and West 58th Street, and Belmont led an official party on an inspection tour in a regular subway train. By September 6th as many as twenty trains were running simultaneously in the subway, testing the new line. Meanwhile personnel were being instructed in equipment operation.

*New Year's Day 1904, and a group of dignitaries tours the subway "by handcar." Mayor McClellan is seated on the right in the front row. This photo, often reproduced, has at times been incorrectly captioned as the first real subway operation on October 27, 1904. (NYCTA)*

*During the summer of 1904 — straw hat season in New York — August Belmont took a group of VIPs on a tour of the abuilding subway and its associated elevated routes. The special was powered by a steam engine from the el lines, and here it pauses for a formal portrait at 125th Street and Broadway. (NYCTA)*

During construction the Interborough repeatedly claimed the new line would get one from downtown Manhattan to Harlem in fifteen minutes. Initial test runs were held to slow speeds until October 3, 1904, when a run was made from City Hall to 96th Street, with 150 newsmen aboard, in ten minutes, forty-five seconds. The promise had been kept.

A curious editorial prior to opening day suggested that wooden cars would prove to be more popular with passengers than the steel ones. One reason stated was the clearly superior decor of the Composite cars; by contrast, the Gibbs cars were almost Spartan. Another reason was perceived as safety. In the event of an accident, it was argued, rescue workers with axes could more easily gain access to a passenger trapped in a wooden car. A later disaster in Brooklyn proved, however, that the greater collision protection provided by steel equipment at the moment of impact is a much more important consideration.

As the inaugural drew near, many New Yorkers grew curious about rolling stock logistics. The Composites were providing almost all service on the Second Avenue El through the summer of 1904, but there was no physical track connection between the elevated line and the new subway. How would the cars get from the el into the tunnels? The solution: The cars were taken to the north end of Second Avenue, at the Harlem River, and placed aboard barges. They were then floated to the head of Lenox Avenue and run down a temporary ramp into the Lenox Avenue tunnel. Although this section of line did not open for regular service until November, trackwork had been installed and the cars reached the City Hall-145th Street line via the Lenox Avenue branch.

After the gala opening, remaining segments of the original Contract One work were opened piece by piece. Service was extended to Bronx Park over the Lenox Avenue line and the Harlem River tunnel on November 26, 1904, and trains began to run to 242nd Street and Broadway on August 1, 1908—a departure from original plans which called for the northern terminal to be at Bailey Avenue adjacent to the Kingsbridge Station of the New York & Putnam Railroad. Service was extended down lower Broadway on the Contract Two phase of the project to South Ferry on July 10, 1905, and through the new East River tunnel to Brooklyn in January of 1908. Trains reached Flatbush and Atlantic avenues by May that same year.

*A contemporary view on the IRT Broadway subway at 137th Street. The train of R-21 units is on a part of the Contract One line that opened for service on October 27, 1904 (Tom Nelligan)*

*Notes to Chapter 3*

[1] The street in Manhattan, adjacent to City Hall, where many newspapers then maintained their offices.

# 4 Competition for Mr. Belmont

THE SUBWAY RAN UP IMPRESSIVE STATISTICS during its first year of operation. A total of 106 million passengers rode at five cents a head. Brooklyn Bridge, expectedly, was the busiest single station, recording some 18 million fares. But Times Square, rather unexpectedly, became a very busy station, the most popular local stop on the line, with five million fares paid. A group of area theatre owners unsuccessfully petitioned the Interborough less than a month after the line's opening to install crossover switches between local and express tracks near the station so express trains could also stop there.

The Interborough was hit with an unpleasant strike of a week's duration during March 1905, the first of many work stoppages over the years. The 500 Composites were overhauled, emerging from the shops with larger end doors and other alterations. Effective ventilation of the tunnels was a minor but continuing problem, especially in warm weather. Advertising posters on the station walls annoyed many sensitive New Yorkers who appreciated the finely done mosaics of the underground railway stops. Some even tried to imply that the bad air, such as it was, was actually caused by the presence of the advertisements.

Few issues in New York fail to admit of conflicting opinions. The advertising franchise for the Interborough stations was held by Artemas Ward, great-grandson of General Artemas Ward, the Revolutionary commander at Dorchester Heights. Defending the concept of subway advertising—and Ward, too—in a speech before the Spinx Club in New York in early 1905, when the debate was raging, one Max Wineburgh delivered the following rebuke to the ad critics: "The worthy and eminently respectable gentlemen who are making all this outcry are simply out of touch with the times. The masses who struggle for existence, who produce the money upon which their leisurely critics live, get much of their information about what is going on in the business world through reading the signs arranged for their entertainment upon the walls of the subway."

From the beginning, there was the problem of loading and unloading the subway trains, especially during the busy rush hours. This was later corrected by the addition of remotely controlled doors cut into the center of the cars. In time, the end, or vestibule, doors were also equipped with remote controls, a departure from original Interborough practice. When the subway opened, a separate conductor, or guard, was stationed between every two cars to open the doors manually and oversee the entry and exit of passengers. Once the doors were remotely controlled, the number of conductors on Interborough trains was reduced. Interestingly, in 1905, when the whole problem of remotely controlled doors was under discussion, one highly respected scientific journal examined the problem in detail and announced that it was totally impossible, could never be done!

When the extension down lower Broadway was opened as far as South Ferry in July 1905, the Interborough was able to improve its terminal procedures at the southern end of the line. The South Ferry station was built on a turnaround loop, which allowed inbound trains to be dispatched back uptown with greater flexibility. The South Ferry loop, however, was an engineering horror to construct. It came to within a few feet, literally, of Manhattan Island's shoreline, so that pumps ran continuously to keep the waters of Upper New York Bay out of the works. To add to the woe, the entire complex was directly under a large and busy elevated terminal which had to be carefully shored up throughout.

The new subway tunnel under the East River ran 1.2 miles from the Battery to the foot of Joralemon Street in Brooklyn. At midpoint it was ninety-five feet below mean high water, and forty feet below the silty river bottom. Trains had to descend and then climb a maximum grade of 3.1 per cent, a stiff one by railroad standards, but no great effort for a multiple-unit electric train. The tunnel was the first long tube to carry any kind of regular passenger vehicles beneath tidewater in New York. The city's first major river tunnel of any kind was the Ravenswood Gas Company's eight-foot-high tunnel under

the East River between Long Island City and Manhattan, completed in 1894 as a conduit for gas mains. It was largely chiseled out of solid rock, while the subway crossing used the shield method of tunneling. The shield method involves a huge circular cutting bore through the soft material under the river, and then lining the tunnel with iron rings from the inside. The entire operation must be carried out under a pressurized atmosphere.[1] While the subway tunnel was being built, three eminent engineers made public a statement warning that the tunnel would collapse like a deflated balloon when it was completed and depressurized. It hasn't yet!

Had fortune been kinder to an earlier venture, a Hudson River tunnel might have been the city's first major underwater tube. A group headed by a man named Dewitt Clinton Haskin began work on a Jersey City to Morton Street (Manhattan) tunnel in 1874, but after a serious accident the half-finished bore was abandoned and remained thus for over a decade. Eventually the tunnel was completed. It became part of William Gibbs McAdoo's Hudson & Manhattan Railroad and opened for passenger service in late February 1908, a few weeks after the Interborough's East River crossing was placed in service.[2] In another early effort a trolley car tunnel was built under the East River between Manhattan and Queens in 1907 but, for reasons to be discussed in a later chapter, it did not open for passenger service until 1915, and even then not as a trolley car tunnel. The Interborough's own Harlem River tunnel opened in 1904—it was considerably shorter than the East River crossing and was built using a system of caissons.

*At 66th Street station, guard and "chopper box" await some business on the Interborough's Contract One line. And there are two examples of advertising signs from which patrons can "get much of their information about what is going on in the business world." (NYCTA-Interborough collection)*

*On Joralemon Street in downtown Brooklyn there's a row house that looks a little different from others on the block. No windows, for instance, just heavy shutters. In actuality it isn't a house at all, but a cleverly outrigged air shaft for the Interborough's East River tunnel which passes directly underneath. (Author photo)*

The success of the Manhattan-Bronx subway prompted talk of more lines. Groups and syndicates were rumored to be seeking financial support for all manner of new routes. As a matter of course, the Interborough continued to profess its own interest in handling future construction and operation, taking great pains to point out that the original line was a compromise on the city's real subway needs—a compromise dictated by the city's rigid debt ceiling, which restricted the amount of construction bonds that could be issued. If the audience was appropriate, Belmont did not hesitate to speak of what he called the city's "moral obligation" to award future construction and operation rights to the Interborough and the Interborough alone.

Belmont gave priority to a spur up Lexington Avenue from the Grand Central area and to additional construction along the lower West Side, especially after it became known that the Pennsylvania Railroad would build its huge New York terminal on Seventh Avenue at West 33rd Street. And the Interborough could well hanker after more subways for, in 1905, it appeared to be a truth beyond question that operating rapid transit in New York was a very lucrative business.

(Something else happened in 1905 that would later impinge on the destiny of the New York subways. In County Kerry, Ireland, John Daniel Quill and his wife, Margaret, had their seventh child, whom they named Michael Joseph.)

Finally, in 1905, one group did present a serious challenge to the Belmont interests for construction and operation rights to future lines. The Metropolitan Street Railway had managed in the years prior to 1900 to gain control of almost all surface car lines in Manhattan and a goodly number in the Bronx, too, either directly or through its parent corporation, Metropolitan Security. The only large surface operation to elude its grasp prior to 1900 was the Third Avenue Railroad. When that system went into receivership in 1900, it too was taken into the Metropolitan family. So, in 1905, the Metropolitan moved to get for itself the additional subway lines the city unquestionably would soon build.

The Rapid Transit Commission looked favorably upon the Metropolitan's proposals, principally because there was growing uneasiness with Belmont's de facto monopoly of Manhattan rapid transit. Both corporations soon presented roughly similar plans for additional subway lines. The Interborough was able to propose an expansion and extension of its original line, while the Metropolitan had to build a brand new system from scratch. Another difference was that the Metropolitan was reconciled to having the Interborough as a competitor. Belmont was not amenable to grant a similar concession.

That March, when details of the two rival plans became known, the press took sides. Some newspapers favored allowing Belmont to continue as the city's sole subway entrepreneur; others thought competition from the Metropolitan would benefit both the city and the Interborough in the long run. From still other quarters came a different cry—municipal operation. The subways are an essential public service, like fire and police protection, it was reasoned, and private interests should not be allowed to profit from them.

Another Belmont competitor emerged in April of 1905 when a streetcar and elevated railway company named the Brooklyn Rapid Transit Company submitted a proposal to the Rapid Transit Commission outlining a much greater penetration of Manhattan by lines from Brooklyn. The BRT, an unsuccessful bidder for the Contract Two lines in 1902, suggested it was prepared to bid on the construction and operation of such routes. Amid strong rumors of a BRT-Metropolitan alliance, the commission agreed to report favorably on almost all of the BRT's suggestions, and include them in its master plan for transit expansion.

Some saw the commission's action as a body blow to the Interborough. Belmont's chief argument in his head-to-head battle with the Metropolitan for new construction rights was that his was the only system that would and could offer through service from the Bronx to Brooklyn. The Interborough already had one line into Brooklyn under construction—it would open in 1908*—and its expansion plans included additional mileage in Brooklyn. The Metropolitan, by itself, had no desire to build into Brooklyn, and presented as its trump card transfer privileges between its new subways and its existing network of street lines. Belmont thought he had the leverage he needed when he threatened not to operate any lines in Brooklyn unless the Interborough got exclusive rights in Manhattan. But the BRT's rumored consortium with the Metropolitan, coupled with the decision of the Rapid Transit Commission, dulled Belmont's bargaining edge in his efforts to stop the Metropolitan.

In mid-December, trading in both Interborough and Metropolitan stocks assumed irregular patterns, a reaction to rumors of high-level negotiations. Then on Friday, December 22, 1905, Belmont issued a simple, factual announcement. He had purchased the Metropolitan—lock, stock and streetcars. As he had three years earlier with the lease of the elevated lines of the Manhattan Railway, August Belmont demonstrated himself to be as resourceful as he was rich. He responded to challenge with a classic maneuver; he crushed the upstarts, emerging from combat without a scratch. Of note was a rumor, circulated earlier, that the BRT had been involved in the Wall Street dealings. Yet the Brooklyn firm was not a party to the final agreement and retained its autonomy, a matter that would later prove to be most important.

Belmont's bold stroke gave the advocates of municipal operation added

*See map, page 30

fuel, and they began to speak out more strongly against private operation of the city subways. Publisher William Randolph Hearst, perhaps the most vociferous foe of private operation, went so far as to petition the New York State Attorney General to file suit to block the Interborough-Metropolitan merger. But Attorney General Mayer refused to bring action against Belmont, ruling that existing anti-monopoly statutes were inapplicable to rapid transit firms. Belmont, on the other hand, expected no serious problems to arise from the merger: "There need be no public anxiety occasioned by the adjustment of transportation matters in New York City," he said.

## SOUND AND FURY

August Belmont had firm views on the question of private vs. municipal subway operation. Speaking before the Chicago Real Estate Board in January 1905, he proclaimed ". . . if associated with municipal ownership there is municipal operation of these properties, then I think the justifiable line of municipal activity has been overstepped."

Among Belmont's staunchest supporters was *The New York Times*. It continually backed the concept of private subway operation, even suggesting that the truest test of the real need for any proposed subway route was the "reasonable certainty of profit" by a private operator. The advocates of total municipal operation, spearheaded by the Hearst organization, made the counter argument that only subway construction in advance of actual need would be able to spur the development of outlying areas, adding needed valuation to the city's real estate tax rolls, and allowing municipal growth to take place in an orderly and planned fashion. Growth rate figures of the Bronx after the original subway opened were often cited by municipal operation advocates. In pre-subway 1903, 6.5 million dollars in building construction was begun in the borough. In 1905 construction had ballooned to 38 million dollars, with the bulk of the increase credited to the presence of the subway.

In 1906 all arguments on private and municipal operation became largely academic. The Interborough-Metropolitan marriage was consumated on March 6, 1906. Later that year the state legislature enacted something called the Elsberg Bill.

The original subway was *owned* by the city and *leased* to a private operator under a long-term agreement: the Interborough, which held a fifty-year lease for the Contract One lines and a thirty-five-year agreement on the Contract Two segment. The leases stipulated that the Interborough was to finance its own rolling stock. Both leases contained identical twenty-five-year renewal options. The Elsberg Bill, named for a state senator from the 15th district of New York City who was a strong municipal operation advocate, greatly shortened the length of lease the city could sign with private operators. The

*Before the original subway opened in 1904, a second contract was signed to extend its route down Broadway to South Ferry, then under the East River to Brooklyn. In this 1906 view, we see two of the ornate kiosks at Broadway and Rector Street on this portion of the route. (Author's collection)*

*Above, car No. 3815 is a 1910-built unit that was delivered before automatic doors became commonplace. When the center door was later added it was installed as an automatic, but the end doors remained manually operated on these old Hi-Vs until they were retired from service in the 1950s. (Author's collection)*

*Left, an early view of a Gibbs Hi-V deck roof car on the IRT. Note that the original Van Dorn coupler has yet to be replaced by an automatic version. (Brown Bros.)*

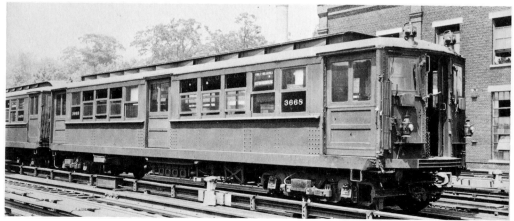

*A highly distinctive car on the Interborough was a fleet of deck-roof units first placed in service in 1907. No. 3668 was built by A. C. F. (Author's collection)*

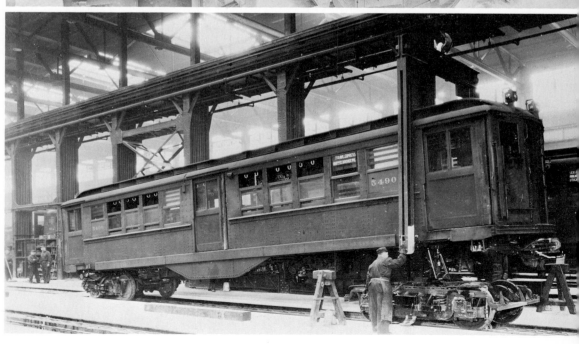

*Opposite page: Action in the Interborough's shops! In the top view, rows of cars undergoing repairs. The bottom photograph shows how basic components, such as a motor truck, can be removed from a car for maintenance. Meanwhile the car itself can be re-equipped with a substitute truck and returned to service. (NYCTA-Interborough collection)*

*A derby-hatted spectator observes the activity in an Interborough repair shop during the early years. It is likely that the cars shown here are being outfitted with new automatic couplers, replacing the original Van Dorn models. (Brown Bros.)*

maximum term under the new law was twenty years, with a single twenty-year renewal option. Economically, the new measure meant that any equipment investment would have to be amortized over a shorter term than before, so that profits would be reduced by the expense of meeting payments on equipment bonds.

Belmont was quick to denounce the new law, saying it was designed to force municipal ownership and operation. The Rapid Transit Commission likewise stood adamantly and unanimously against it, but for a different reason. Instead of leading inevitably to municipal operation, the commission reasoned, the short term leases meant that only the city's existing subway operator could afford to bid on new lines. The Interborough could risk the short term lease because it already owned power houses, repair shops and storage yards. George L. Rives, counsel for the commission, said: "It is manifest that under such provisions the city would get only such future subways as the Interborough Rapid Transit Company sees fit to build."

In the end, the Elsberg Bill resulted in neither municipal ownership nor any new Interborough routes. Belmont continued to express interest in new lines, but the restrictive features of the Elsberg legislation, coupled with unfavorable economic conditions brought on by the panic of 1907, effectively discouraged any firm commitments by Belmont or anyone else. Total municipal operation was ruled out on practical grounds by the city's rigid debt limit, on theoretical grounds because public opinion was not yet ready to accept it.

Thus passed 1906, the year not only of the Elsberg Law, but also of the destructive San Francisco earthquake and of one of New York's more notable murders—the shooting of architect Stanford White by Harry Thaw, a Pittsburgh millionaire who claimed he was avenging the honor of his wife, the international beauty and *femme fatale* Evelyn Nesbit.

Out of the Elsberg dilemma eventually emerged a highly detailed proposal for new rapid transit construction—the Dual Contracts, or Dual System, which would account for the building of the major portion of today's subway network. The Dual Contracts were signed in March of 1913, seven years after the passage of the Elsberg Bill and eight and one-half years after Mayor McClellan notched out the silver controller on the city's first subway.

The Dual Contracts were negotiated over a period of years and involved all the complexity, intricacy and diplomacy of a major treaty between nations. The New York State Constitution had to be amended, legislation had to be passed, old regulatory agencies abolished and new ones created. After the contracts were drawn up, two private transit companies and several arms of government had to adjudge them to be in their own best interests. Further-

*Left: One of the original Gibbs Cars has survived. Here is No. 3352 at rest on a storage track at the Seashore Trolley Museum in Kennebunkport, Me., idle for a while after years of IRT service. (R.T. Lane photo)*

*At right, owner James E. Tebbets of Manchester, N.H., works at restoring No. 3352 to like-new condition. The center door and center sill have been removed and, except for the trolley pole —necessary for operation on Seashore trackage—the veteran car will look just as it did in 1904! (R.T. Lane)*

more the advocates of total municipal operation either had to be won over to the Dual Contracts idea, or be politically outflanked in some other way. Court tests were complex and involved; at many stages the Dual Subway System seemed destined to become just one more good idea that would never materialize. But the contracts were completed, thanks principally to the long and patient work of such people as William R. Wilcox, who headed up the state Public Service Commission during most of the Dual Contracts talks, and former mayor Seth Low, who is credited with rescuing the negotiations on numerous occasions. If any single man can be called the prime mover behind the Dual Contracts idea, it is Wilcox. He began the six years of talks when it became clear that the city's debt limit clearly ruled out large-scale municipal subway operation, and the Elsberg Law prevented the construction of new privately run lines adequate to the city's needs. Borough President George McAneny of Manhattan was also a key participant, as was Alfred Craven, chief engineer of the PSC, whose expertise on technical matters helped resolve critical moments in the talks.

Throughout the years of negotiation—1909, 1911, 1912—history-shaping events, too, kept right on happening. Claiming that he got there first, Admiral Peary "discovered" the North Pole; C. P. Rogers made the first transcontinental airplane flight, taking only six weeks longer than if he'd gone by train; and the *Titanic* both sailed and sank. Inexorably, through it all, subway plans continued to simmer in New York.

---

*Notes to Chapter 4*

[1] In 1905, while the Interborough's East River tunnel was under construction, a weak spot developed in the roof of the tunnel. Since the bore was pressurized, the weak spot became not a cave-in, but a blowout. One of the sandhogs working in the tunnel was sucked up by the developing cyclone, and propelled upward through mud and water to the surface of the East River. He had survived, and was hale and hearty—but scared and wet—when pulled aboard a passing tug boat.

[2] The story of both the Pennsylvania RR tunnels and the Hudson & Manhattan RR is told in the author's *Rails Under the Mighty Hudson* (Brattleboro, The Stephen Greene Press, 1975).

Above: Sands Street station at the Brooklyn end of Brooklyn Bridge. Here it was that bridge cable cars terminated before the BRT's elevated lines were electrified. Today the site is merely part of a roadway complex leading to the bridge. (Edward B. Watson collection)

A three-car train of open-platform el cars curves gently from the Lexington Avenue line onto the three-track Broadway line. Both avenues – Lexington and Broadway – are names of thoroughfares in both Brooklyn and Manhattan. This is Brooklyn! (NYCTA)

Although the Manhattan els have garnered more fame, the BRT operated an extensive network of such lines in its home borough of Brooklyn. Many were upgraded and became extensions of the Dual Contracts subways in the years after 1913. Others, such as the Myrtle Ave. line, continued to operate older open-platform type cars long after such equipment had gone out of general style. (Author's collection)

Riders on the els sat in rattan-upholstered seats (left) and were informed of routings from metal plate destination signs. (NYCTA)

# 5 The BRT, the Triborough System
## and the End of Interborough Dominance

ONE OF THE DUAL CONTRACTS traction operators was, naturally, the Interborough. August Belmont relinquished the line's presidency in 1907 to become chairman. (He would die in 1924 at the age of 71.) The company was then run by Theodore P. Shonts, a distinguished-looking gentleman who wore pince-nez glasses and sported a fine white moustache. Shonts was a long-time railroad man who came to the Interborough in 1907 after a stint as chairman of the Isthmian Canal Commission, the group responsible for building the Panama Canal. The other traction company to sign the Dual Contracts, the firm that was able to convince the city government, and the Interborough, too, that more than one firm should run subway trains in New York, was the Brooklyn-based BRT.

The BRT traced its roots to the late 1880s on the western end of Long Island—today the boroughs of Brooklyn and Queens. The area was crisscrossed by sixty separate horsecar, trolley, elevated and short-haul steam railroad companies. The Interborough always operated in comparatively built-up urban areas, but the territory in which the BRT germinated included densely populated sections of downtown Brooklyn, suburban residential areas such as Ridgewood and Flatbush, the rural precincts of Canarsie, and ocean-front resort communities at Brighton Beach and Coney Island. As time passed, the sixty transit firms began to amalgamate and merge. Senselessly competitive routes were eliminated. The result of the evolution was the BRT. Two distinct kinds of transit operation were involved, elevated lines and streetcars. The els, originally steam powered but converted to electricity at the turn of the century, funneled from outlying districts into two different sections of what can best be described as old Brooklyn. In outlying districts BRT "elevated" lines often ran on ground level right-of-way much like a conventional railroad. Sometimes they actually rolled onto Brooklyn streets and trundled alongside ordinary traffic like streetcars. Trains drew electricity from a third rail while on the el structure, but often switched to an overhead trolley wire as a safety precaution when they descended to surface running. BRT el cars also were equipped with steps to use at suburban stations with no high platforms.

The BRT reached into the Borough Hall section of Brooklyn with trunk elevated lines along both Myrtle Avenue and Fulton Street. Feeder lines for these two els reached downtown from as far away as Ridgewood and Coney

Island. After they were electrified, both lines ran trains over the Brooklyn Bridge to City Hall and Park Row.[1]

Another BRT operation focused around the el which ran along Broadway (Brooklyn's Broadway, not Manhattan's) from East New York. The line terminated at an East River ferry, a maritime service that would be rendered obsolete by the opening of the Williamsburg Bridge in 1903. Like the Myrtle-Fulton complex, the Broadway trunk line had several feeder routes.

By 1910 the BRT had become a stable and prosperous operation. It had rebuilt and standardized its fleet of hand-me-down el cars and supplemented them with new equipment. Its car barns were all tastefully decorated with whitewashed rock gardens that drew praise from the trade press—"this is how a railway should be managed." Its stock was the kind of issue conservative bankers and rich widows looked to with supreme confidence, although early in its history the company was anything but highly regarded on Wall Street. In the teeth of the panic of 1907, the BRT had the financial muscle to float 60 million dollars in bonds to underwrite capital improvements.

Despite the Elsberg Law, some limited subway construction was begun after 1906 and prior to the Dual Contracts. A loop line linking the Manhattan terminals of the three East River bridges—the Williamsburg, the Manhattan and the Brooklyn—was one such project. As early as September 1906, the Rapid Transit Commission was considering two proposals, one a subway and the other an el on the Manhattan portion of the route. The BRT lacked experience in subway operation and owned no genuine subway equipment. Since its Broadway el was already projected to run over the Williamsburg Bridge, through the loop, and back over the Brooklyn Bridge, the BRT recommended an el. Brooklyn residents, anxious to obtain rapid transit service into Manhattan, were impressed by the fact an el could be built more quickly than a subway. But the city government had the last word and it wanted a subway. Thus, on September 16, 1908, the BRT reluctantly started running Broadway elevated trains from East New York and Canarsie across the Williamsburg Bridge and into a terminal at Delancey Street, a bona fide subway station. Once again Mayor McClellan handled the controls as the first official train left the underground Manhattan terminal at 9:55 A.M. In celebration of the event, bands played, firecrackers exploded, and orators decried the sorry state of New York subway expansion. The BRT had joined the Interborough in the subway business on Manhattan Island after a fashion, although in fact it was the *third* company to operate underground rapid transit into Manhattan. The Hudson Tubes had been running trains between Hoboken, N.J. and Manhattan since February 25, 1908.

The BRT's connection over the Williamsburg Bridge to Delancey Street was hardly a major accomplishment. Some purists would even argue that the

BRT never really became a subway operator until it extended this line inland some years later. But it was the third transit line to cross the East River and link Brooklyn with Manhattan, and in due time it became a route of major importance. In 1908, however, it left "its passengers from Brooklyn at a point in Manhattan where almost nobody wishes to go," to quote the caustic words of a newspaper reporter.

Construction of the loop line continued at a very sluggish pace so that not until August of 1913, five months after the Dual Contracts were signed, had service been extended slightly over a mile to a new station under the Municipal Building near the Brooklyn Bridge. Even in 1913 the BRT had no steel subway cars and continued to use wooden elevated equipment in the Centre Street loop subway, much to the company's embarrassment.

### A Jolt for Mister B.

The BRT's real coup in the years before the Dual Contracts came when it was awarded operating rights for the Fourth Avenue subway in Brooklyn. As long as subways were discussed in New York, a line out to Bay Ridge seemed inevitable. The obvious move would then be to tunnel under the Narrows, and link Staten Island with the rest of the city. In October 1909, the Board of Estimate approved construction of the Bay Ridge segment of this route with an appropriation of 15.8 million dollars, after a complex court action had determined that the city's debt ceiling was somewhat higher than previously thought. (The debt limit was, essentially, a percentage of the city's taxable real estate valuation, and the court ruled that a more liberal formula could be used in calculating a precise figure.) The Interborough appeared to be solidly entrenched for operational rights over the new line. After all, wasn't its Brooklyn line already a proven success? Interborough officials were understandably jolted when the BRT won the contract.

Brooklyn's Fourth Avenue subway was conceived as part of a master plan developed within the state Public Serivce Commission and called the Triborough Subway System. This was a network of new lines envisioned to connect Manhattan, the Bronx and Brooklyn. Since construction was to take place under the limitations of both the Elsberg Law and the city's debt ceiling, it was not the kind of robust and complete subway system most observers felt the city needed. The Triborough System did not necessarily intend to exclude the Interborough from consideration as operator of the new lines; however it clearly did not intend to link up with the older subway either.

Eventually the Triborough was absorbed into the more comprehensive Dual System. Yet two interesting aspects, conceived during the planning of the Triborough System, survived to influence the subways for decades.

First, a line to cross the East River, as decided by Triborough officials, should be by way of the new Manhattan Bridge. This span had been proposed even before the Triborough concept emerged, at which time the BRT had stated that it could connect the Brooklyn end of this bridge with its existing elevated network, an idea patterned after the Brooklyn and Williamsburg bridges. Specifications were drawn up for a massive four-track el structure down Flatbush Avenue Extension to the bridge plaza. But the city fathers wanted no old-fashioned els for their new span. Thus the Public Service Commission turned down the bid, proclaiming that Flatbush Avenue Extension was to be "a fine avenue, which the construction of the [elevated] railroad would frustrate." The timing was perfect. The Triborough plan was adapted so that its subway tunnels could bring trains onto the new bridge, through a connection with the new Fourth Avenue line.

The second hand-me-down from the Triborough System was the tunnel dimensions specified for the rail network. Trains would run on standard gauge track, as on the Interborough lines, but tunnels were to be built wider, higher and with broader curves to allow suburban-type equipment from standard railroads to connect with the subway. Standard railroad cars simply could not squeeze into the restrictive confines of the original subway. The Triborough decision was reached in part on the strength of the operational flexibility it would permit—through service someday between the city and suburbs, so it was hoped. Still, the key reason was economic. The Public Service Commission,[2] where the decision to go with the larger tunnels was ultimately made, aimed at persuading a conventional railroad company to take over the entire operating responsibility for the new system. This was clearly spelled out by the PSC in a letter to the city's Board of Estimate in January of 1908.

Such visions of the PSC were never realized. Actually, the "big railroad" dimensions for the Triborough System served only to freeze two different sets of specifications into the New York subways, and it prevents to this day total interchangeability between the various lines. No railroad company became a serious candidate for operation rights, and no through city-suburb service ever developed.[3]

There were authorities who thought (out loud) that the larger dimensions were *very* unwise, among them Frank Sprague, of multiple-unit fame. On October 17, 1910, he delivered a paper to the American Institute of Electrical Engineers in which he harshly criticized the Triborough plan, foreseeing that it would rule out integration of the new lines with the old 1904 subway. A pity that Sprague's arguments were ignored!

BRT's victory in clinching operating rights for the Fourth Avenue line was a choker for the Interborough. Once its line crossed the East River on the Manhattan Bridge, the BRT would have additional access to Manhattan Island, territory the Interborough regarded as its private turf. And the BRT was destined to win again. In the midst of the Dual Contracts discussions, it was suggested that the BRT's Fourth Avenue line should not only cross the East River and serve downtown Manhattan—as conceived in the Triborough scheme—but also swerve and tunnel north up Broadway to the Times Square area, eventually to operate into Queens via another East River crossing. The Interborough immediately threatened to break off all negotiations. The older line, by then, grudgingly conceded the BRT its foothold in downtown Manhattan, but the proposed Broadway line would be too painful an intrusion into Interborough country.

Nevertheless, the days were over when an August Belmont could call every shot. City representatives responded to the Interborough break-off threat by blandly asking the BRT if it would be willing to assume operation of *all* the subway lines then up for consideration, including such obvious Interborough links as the upper Lexington Avenue spur. When the Brooklyn company responded "Yes!" the Interborough swallowed hard and gave in to the idea of mid-Manhattan competition.

*Relic of a bygone day—metal sign advertising the BRT's Dual Contracts plum, its Broadway line in Manhattan! (Author photo)*

*Notes to Chapter 5*

---

[1] A conventional view held that vibrations from reciprocating steam engines could weaken and even destroy a suspension bridge. Washington Roebling, the Brooklyn Bridge's chief engineer, disagreed. He said the small elevated steam engines could certainly traverse the bridge without damage, and he pointed out that conventional railroad steam engines regularly plied the suspension bridge his father, John Roebling, had built over the Niagara River. Nonetheless, Roebling was ignored and the Brooklyn Bridge ran cable car shuttles, and never steam-drawn trains. Steam-powered el trains of the BRT and its predecessor companies terminated their runs at the Brooklyn end of the bridge. Through service over the bridge from the BRT elevated system did not begin until the lines were electrified.

[2] The 1894 Rapid Transit Commission—which supervised the construction of the city's first subway—was disbanded in 1907. The State Public Service Commission then assumed regulatory powers over city transit matters.

[3] When the new—and current—Grand Central was built in 1913, it was designed to permit an eventual connection between the lower level of the railroad terminal and the Interborough's Contract One subway. The connection was never made.

With two young subway buffs at the head-end door, a train of contemporary equipment heels into the curve at Dyckman Street, some three-score years after Mayor McClellan inaugurated service on this Contract One line. Apartment buildings flank the tracks, evidence of New York City's emergence as a vast metropolis due, in no small measure, to the availability of convenient, efficient rapid transit. Compare this with the construction scene on page 30. (Tom Nelligan photo)

One of the Interborough's original Composite cars, shown in later years when it was working on the Third Avenue el. Center door and fish-belly sill were innovations in the original design. (Phil Bonnet)

# 6 The Dual Subway System

THE DUAL CONTRACTS OF 1913 were agreements between the city and the two traction companies stipulating that the BRT and the Interborough would help in the financing of construction in return for attractive lease agreements. The Elsberg Law had, by this time, been superseded by new legislation suggested during the Dual Contracts talks. The agreement worked as follows: The city's debt ceiling was raised by passage of a state constitutional amendment allowing municipal bonds to be sold to finance most of, but not all, the construction costs. The BRT and the Interborough both had to put up some of their own funds for construction, and also were required to provide equipment for the new lines. In return they were given 49-year leases to operate the lines, leases to begin on January 1, 1917, the deadline for actual completion of the Dual System. Furthermore, the Interborough's earlier leases were rewritten to be conterminal with the Dual Contracts. The Centre Street loop, the Fourth Avenue subway, and other elements of the now moribund Triborough System were also incorporated into the Dual Contracts arrangement.

Both the IRT, as Belmont's Interborough had come to be known, and the BRT were profitable on-going operations prior to the Dual Contracts. The original IRT subway realized an annual profit of more than 6 million dollars, and the BRT was clearing 9 million dollars a year on its elevated lines alone. The new agreement stipulated that each company combine revenue from its Dual Contracts operations with revenue from established operations. Thus the IRT would pool Dual Contracts money with its gross from the original subway—although, interestingly, not from the Manhattan elevated lines—whereas the BRT would pool its Dual Contracts funds with its el revenues—but not its surface line fares. Out of the resultant sum of money, each company's first obligation was to pay all operating expenses.

One feature of the Dual Contracts stirred up considerable disagreement and controversy: After paying operating expenses, each line was entitled to draw from gross revenues a sum of money *in lieu* of profits it had been making from its older operations, the precise amount being established by formula. The rationale for this clause was that the older operations were proven profit-makers for the traction companies, and that they should not be denied this compensation after entering the Dual System. But opponents claimed this "preferential system," so called, amounted to a guaranteed profit for private interests, at municipal expense. It became still another argument on behalf of total public operation of the subways.

Each line was then required to service its own Dual Contracts bonds, and next to be responsible for meeting payments on the interest and principal of the city's Dual Contracts bonds, thereby freeing the municipal government from any direct financial liability. The city was lending its credit to the enterprise, and would generate funds from the sale of bonds. But it would be the two transit companies that would pay off these bonds, out of subway-generated revenues. Finally, the city and the companies were ultimately to share equally any and all remaining profits.

The clause concerning operating expenses pointedly excluded any payment of rent to the city, only the *equivalent* of rent through meeting payments on the city's Dual Contracts bonds, and the city's share of the profits. But none of these monies need ever be paid out until the traction companies *first* received their *guaranteed* profit—and here was the nub of concern with the whole arrangement. This agreement was, assuredly, a distinct departure from the one signed originally between the Interborough and the city for the first subway. At that time, rental payment to the city for the use of its subway tunnels was required *before* the company could realize any profits.

Hindsight wisdom may be critical of the Dual Contracts, a pioneer effort toward incorporating private interests into a large scale public works project. But the fact is that the city was totally unable to undertake such a massive transit project on its own; it had to have the cooperation of private enterprise and private investment. Private firms, on the other hand, could not go into the 1913 money market for financing without the guarantees provided by the Dual Contracts profit provisions.

Whatever their faults, the Dual Contracts were a major development, an extraordinary benchmark in the history of New York transit. Perhaps the most remarkable aspect of the Dual Subway System, as it came to be called, was that it offered more than a patchwork or piecemeal solution to a pressing municipal need—as the Triborough System would have been. It was a solution, or, in retrospect, an attempt at a solution, that was total in its scope. Only a precious few municipal undertakings can be so characterized.

The original cost estimate for the entire project was 301 million dollars. By comparison, the Contract One subway segment cost 38 million dollars. The Pennsylvania Railroad's New York Tunnel Extension bore a 116 million dollar price tag when Penn Station opened in 1910, and even such a dramatic undertaking as Henry Flagler's Key West Extension of his Florida East Coast Railway (1912) was modest in comparison with the Dual Contracts. The island-hopping line out from the Florida mainland cost 31 million dollars. In the first quarter of the century only the Panama Canal exceeded the cost of the Dual Subway System with an expenditure of 352 million dollars.[1] But it took a national government to build the canal, whereas the Dual System was the work of a mere city!

The *Times* of London had sufficient perspective, perhaps, for a balanced view: "After a long struggle against unprincipled politicians, self-interested financiers, and inefficient service, New York seems to have evolved a system of locomotion of which its citizens may well feel proud."

Although the IRT supposedly emerged from the negotiations in defeat, its share of the 301 million dollars was a hefty 140 million, just a shade under half of the cost. The city put up 63 million dollars for Interborough construction and the IRT itself put up 56 million dollars for construction, plus 21 million dollars for equipment. The BRT was apportioned a slightly larger share, 161 million dollars, but this figure included city payment for older projects such as the lower Manhattan loop under Centre Street and the Fourth Avenue line.

On Tuesday, March 18, 1913, the city Board of Estimate gave its final approval of the Dual Contracts, thirteen to three, and also voted an appropriation of 88.2 million dollars for initial construction costs. The stage was thus set for the signing of the Dual Contracts, which took place next day, Wednesday, March 19, at the New York headquarters of the state Public Service Commission in the Tribune Building.

The contracts were designed for immortality! The city-BRT pact—known as Contract Number Four—was printed on finest parchment, ran to 226 pages, and was bound in a heavy red cover. The seal was attached with red ribbon. Edward E. McCall, who had succeeded Wilcox as head of the PSC just before the contracts were readied, signed the BRT agreement at nine minutes after noon. Then, in a gesture appreciated by all parties, he asked Wilcox to witness his signature. The former commissioner, who had just missed out on his dream of seeing the Dual Contracts through to the final stages, was then given the honor of signing the documents.

Along with the BRT contract, additional certificates were signed outlining improvements on certain BRT elevated lines which would feed traffic into the subway. Technically, the BRT was not a signatory of the Dual Contracts at all. The New York Municipal Railway, a wholly owned subsidiary which the BRT created in 1912, was the signatory agency that actually entered into the pact with the city.

Interborough officials signed a 253-page document—Contract Number Three—which was bound in blue and secured with a blue ribbon. After the subway document was official, certificates for improvement to Interborough-controlled els were also signed. Before the parties headed off to a luncheon celebration, PSC chief McCall characterized matters thusly: "New York has never met a problem too big for it. It never will."

### Cutting Up the Pie

The original S-shaped trunk line of the Interborough was to be split into two separate and parallel north-south routes, and the short stretch across

42nd Street was to become a shuttle between Times Square and Grand Central. The S became an H, so to speak. Coming south on Broadway from the Bronx a new line was to be built out of Times Square down Seventh Avenue to South Ferry. This line was to branch off below Chambers Street and tunnel to Brooklyn, there to join the IRT's existing Contract Two line. Beyond the original terminal at Flatbush and Atlantic avenues the Interborough would probe deeper into Brooklyn by running out Eastern Parkway to Brownsville with a spur under Nostrand Avenue to tap Flatbush. The long-discussed

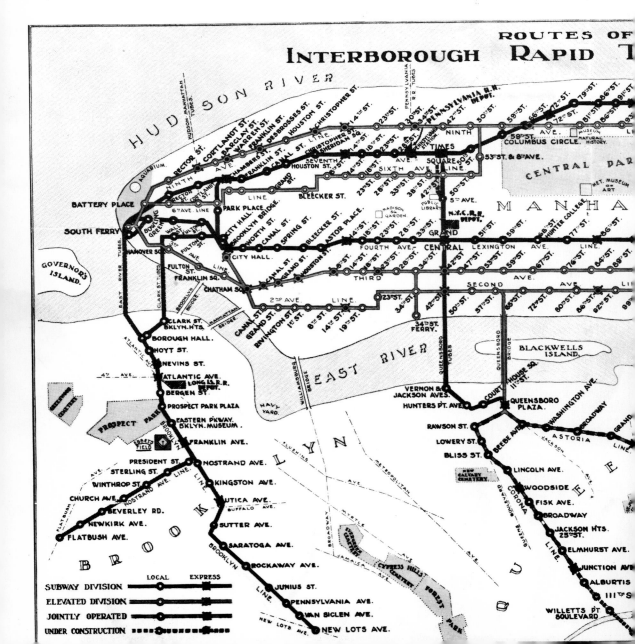

Lexington Avenue line was to tunnel up to the Bronx from Grand Central; the PSC had begun this line as part of the Triborough System even before the Dual Contracts were agreed upon, because such a line was a necessity in any event. Construction had begun in July, 1911. Triborough specifications were used on the project. Station platforms later had to be equipped with steel extension plates to accommodate narrower IRT rolling stock which would be used on the line.[2]

The Interborough made its biggest gains in the Bronx. A long three-track

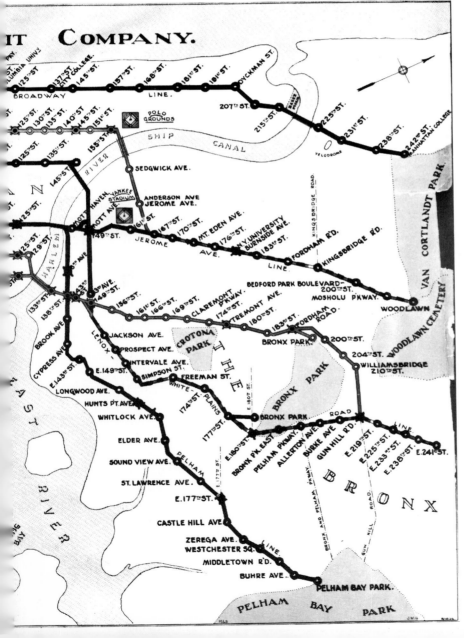

*Interborough Rapid Transit, 1924, shows interrelationship with el lines, and Dual Contracts segments still to be built. For five cents, one nickel—and a working knowledge of interchange points—one could ride all day on the subway. In fact, the subway was a night-time refuge for many a down-and-outer without the price of even the cheapest room. (Author's collection)*

*The cut-and-cover method of subway construction as used on the Dual System network called for building a temporary wooden "street" over the tunnel excavation, for minimum disruption of surface activity. Occasionally it didn't work quite that way! On September 22, 1915, at Seventh Avenue and 24th Street, the "street" collapsed. A streetcar and a brewery wagon fell into the pit; eight people were killed in the mishap. (Brown Bros.)*

elevated line up Jerome Avenue and another of equal size into the Pelham Bay section would feed the new Lexington Avenue subway; the original Contract One line to West Farms Square would extend to the Yonkers border at 241st Street and White Plains Road. In addition, the various el properties were to be improved and extended. In many cases the original two-track lines were increased to three to permit a measure of express service.

A third, or express, track was often easy to install on the elevated structures because many of the original two-track routes had room in the middle for a third track. In order to avoid costly re-construction, stations for the express trains were often built on a raised upper level, allowing the original tracks to retain their alignment below. This proved to be operationally sound as well, because the upgrade into the station and the downgrade out of it provided gravitational "pull" to the stopping and starting of trains.

BRT's big plum was, of course, the Broadway line up Manhattan and over to Queens. This line was to be fed by a pair of tracks on the Manhattan Bridge, and yet another pair in a tunnel under the East River from Montague Street in Brooklyn to Whitehall Street in Manhattan. In addition, a second pair of tracks on the Manhattan Bridge was to feed the Centre Street loop. The loop, then, would swing into the Montague-Whitehall tunnel to Brooklyn. Earlier plans to connect the loop with the Brooklyn Bridge el line were dropped.

All BRT's lines from Manhattan were to converge at an outsize junction in downtown Brooklyn at Flatbush Avenue Extension and DeKalb Avenue, and from there proceed into residential sections of Brooklyn by way of two principal trunk lines. The Fourth Avenue subway—the left-over of the Triborough System—was to feed Bay Ridge and divide into four separate branches. These were the Sea Beach, the West End, the Culver, and the Fourth Avenue line itself. The other line out of DeKalb Avenue was to connect with the BRT's existing Brighton Beach line at Malbone Street near the entrance to Prospect Park, and eventually connect again with the Sea Beach, West End and Culver at Coney Island. Prior to the Dual Contracts, the Brighton line ran to downtown Brooklyn over a connection with the Fulton Street el at Franklin Avenue. The Sea Beach, West End and Culver lines were former independent steam railroads that were electrified after they became part of the BRT complex. They connected with the elevated line that ran over Brooklyn's Fifth Avenue and into the Myrtle Avenue line at Hudson Street. Now they were to be upgraded to heavy-duty standards and become part of the subway system.

This group of lines was known, even in the days before the Dual Contracts, as the BRT's Southern Division. An Eastern Division, so called, embraced those lines which radiated out of the junction of the Broadway el and the Fulton Street el in East New York, a spot that was called Manhattan Junction before 1913 and Broadway Junction thereafter. Chiefly the Dual Contracts mandated the improvement and extension of older elevated lines on the Eastern Division. In later years the cry was raised, not without basis, that this area was seriously slighted in the Dual System. However one major new project was planned for the area—a line from East New York across the Bushwick section of Brooklyn, under the East River, and into Manhattan at 14th Street. It was to be called the 14th Street-Eastern line.

One additional Dual Contract provision stipulated that the paired East River tunnels completed in 1907 to bring trolley cars from Queens into Manhattan be absorbed into the city subway system. One of the backers of this early project was William Steinway, the Long Island City piano manufacturer, and the tunnels have since been known as the Steinway Tunnels. A group headed by Steinway purchased fifty trolley cars from the Brill Company to begin service but, after the first test run, a franchise dispute erupted. The tunnels sat empty until 1913, when they were made part of the Dual Contracts agreements, assigned to the IRT. Revenue subway service began in 1915.

The Steinway Tunnels extended from the Grand Central area in Manhattan to Long Island City. At Queensboro Plaza in Long Island City the IRT planned to link up with the BRT, whose Broadway line was to tunnel under the East River to Queens from 60th Street in Manhattan. Originally the BRT planned to cross the river at this point on the Queensboro Bridge. When concern developed over whether the bridge could bear up under the weight of all-steel subway trains, the decision was for a tunnel instead. The bridge was used, however, by a line which connected with the Second Avenue el, and ran only wooden el cars. The resulting junction, built on an elevated struc-

# B.M.T. Convention Subway Guide at 23rd St. and Broadway Station

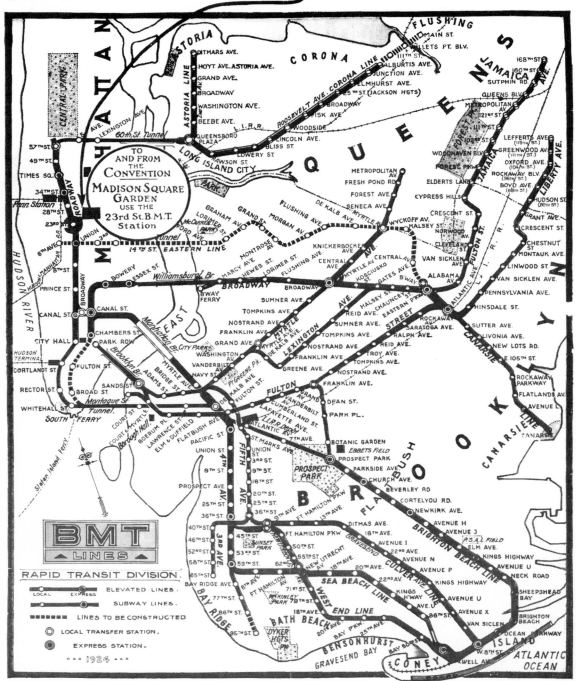

*The BMT system's historic "Convention Subway Guide" issued in 1924. This was the Democratic Party convention which, in sweltering summer heat – long before air-conditioning – was deadlocked for two weeks before nominating John W. Davis for the presidency on the 103rd ballot! But Cal Coolidge beat him in the November election that year. (Author's collection)*

ture at the approach to the Queensboro Bridge, was a complex assemblage of traction lines. The Queensboro Plaza station was a two-level, eight-track facility, and from it two elevated lines were to extend into the residential sections of Queens—one to Astoria and the other to Corona—which, according to the Dual Contracts, were to be joint BRT–IRT operations. Also, the BRT was toying the plans to extend a crosstown el from Franklin Avenue and Fulton Street in Brooklyn across Greenpoint to tie in at the huge Queens Plaza terminal. This projected line was never formally a part of the Dual System and, in fact, never materialized.

Soon after the contracts were signed, construction agreements were let out for bid. During the next decade, every borough except Staten Island was involved in developing the massive transit system. Besides the expected hassles over easements and other right-of-way problems, a rackety "flap" erupted when area businessmen learned that the BRT station at Times Square was to be—horrors!—a mere local stop. Merchant groups held meetings, and proclaimed that they had not been consulted. Only through the efforts and tact of both transit companies plus the City of New York was a plan worked out to the satisfaction of all: a *super* station at Times Square, a station that would include a large mezzanine area where passengers could transfer between the new IRT Seventh Avenue line, the BRT Broadway line, and the shuttle to Grand Central. The mistake of 1904 was not repeated; Times Square was made an express stop on all lines.

In 1913 the city felt it could not afford the disruptive traffic snarls caused by construction of the original subway. After an initial street excavation was made, it was roofed over by a temporary wooden "street" so that subway construction could continue while vehicles and pedestrians moved overhead. Although practical, temporary structures did not always prove to be safe. On the morning of September 22, 1915, eight New Yorkers were killed and more than 100 injured when a dynamite explosion blew out a large section of the planked "pavement" of Seventh Avenue between 24th and 25th streets. A streetcar and a large brewery wagon fell into the subway excavation. On September 25th of the same year, a similar accident at Broadway and 38th Street claimed one life. In July, 1916, a Nostrand Avenue trolley car in Brooklyn fell into the IRT subway between Beverly Road and Tilden Avenue, without casualties, fortunately.

Construction methods for the Dual System were similar to those of the Contract One and Two lines. Subway portions were built either by the cut-and-cover or deep tunneling methods. Five new twin-tube borings under the East River were put through, including the never-used Steinway Tunnels. Add on the rapid transit tracks already on the Brooklyn, Manhattan, Williamsburg and Queensboro bridges, plus the Interborough's original East River tunnel, and by 1920 ten rail connections linked Manhattan and Long Island.

Most underground routes of the Dual System were built as four-track lines, with all tracks on the same level. An exception was the upper Lexington Avenue route, where express tracks were put on a second level beneath the local tracks. A section of the IRT's Brooklyn line used a variation on this theme—two levels of track, but with local and express services in the same direction sharing the same level. Local stations on the new lines were built to accomodate trains as long as the expresses—a departure from the original subway, where it was presumed locals would or should be shorter than expresses—and tile work and design of the new stations was considerably less ornate than the "artistic" touches lavished on the Contract One route.[3]

More than half the mileage of the Dual Systems was not "subway" at all, but elevated structure, embankment or open cut. The most popular style of elevated structure was a three-track right of way, which allowed the operation of express service, but only in a single direction—inbound during the morning rush hour, outbound in the evening. (Some elevated lines were reconstructions of older pre-Dual Contracts els.) The three-track configuration became popular because four tracks were too wide for the average New York street. Columns of support girders were erected, often directly in the road or avenue over which the elevated line ran, providing a workable but far-from-ideal center corridor for various lanes of traffic. Streetcar lines regularly operated inside a kind of private reservation between elevated supports.

*Construction on the Sea Beach line in Brooklyn is proceeding in this 1914 photograph. (Robert L. Presbrey collection) Left: Many older elevated lines were built with room in the center for a third track, and the Dual Contracts called for expanding the el's capacity to take advantage of this feature. Stations on the new express track proved a problem, though, because engineers wanted to retain the alignment of the original route. The solution? Elevate the center track at stations, build platforms over the outside tracks. (NYCTA)*

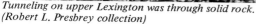

*Tunneling on upper Lexington was through solid rock. (Robert L. Presbrey collection)*

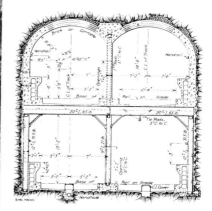

*Cross-section of double-deck Lexington Avenue subway built wholly in tunnel. (See also pages iv, v.) Drawing is from* Engineering News, *a contemporary issue.*

The Lexington Avenue line turned out to be a poser for IRT construction engineers. The older subway was under Fourth and Park avenues between 14th Street and Grand Central. Among many plans drawn up for linking this route into the new upper East Side trunk line, one proposed that the new route continue southward on Lexington to 14th Street, there to intercept the existing line. In the end, the connection was made at Grand Central—as envisioned when the Dual Contracts were signed—and the now famous 42nd Street Shuttle was put together out of the unneeded remains of the city's original subway. When the shuttle began its back-and-forth operations in September of 1918, the chairman of the PSC, Charles Buckley Hubbell, proposed that colored bands be painted on station ceilings to guide passengers through the labyrinth of passageways and stairways at both Times Square and Grand Central. Later supplemented with lights, the bands have led confused millions —perhaps even billions—to and from the shuttle trains over the years.

As might have been expected, delays pushed back the opening of the various portions of the Dual Contracts lines. (Rarely has a New York subway opened on schedule.) Finally on Tuesday, June 15, 1915, a two-car BRT train ran tests on the Fourth Avenue line and across the Manhattan Bridge to the station under the Municipal Building on the Centre Street loop. The bridge itself had opened for vehicular traffic on New Year's Eve in 1909, and the subway tracks on the lower level were installed either just before or just after that date, but they were not tied in with any tunnel routes, since none existed. In 1912 arrangements were made for trolley cars temporarily to use the idle subway tracks. Trolley service continued until 1915 when the streetcars were moved to the bridge's upper level roadways. There they served until late 1929.

On Saturday, June 19, 1915, an elaborate eight-car ceremonial train, with city, state and BRT officials aboard, ran from the Municipal Building in Manhattan to the West End Depot in Coney Island, over the Manhattan Bridge, and the Fourth Avenue and Sea Beach lines. Conspicuously absent was the city's mayor, John Purroy Mitchell. His Honor was upset because his invitation did not arrive until the night before. Thoroughly piqued, he passed up the BRT gala and went instead to the Brooklyn Navy Yard for the launching of the USS *Arizona,* a battleship fated to become a memorial to infamy at Pearl Harbor twenty-six years later.

The Fourth Avenue and Sea Beach lines, and the tracks over the Manhattan Bridge, opened to the public on Tuesday, June 22, 1915, the same day the Interborough opened the Steinway Tunnel for subway service. These lines were the first fruits of the Dual Contracts.

### SETTING A STANDARD IN ROLLING STOCK

By 1915 the BRT had rectified its lack of steel subway equipment, a deficiency which had caused the BRT such embarrassment when the Centre Street loop line began service in 1908. When the Fourth Avenue-Sea Beach segment opened, the BRT welcomed passengers aboard what has since proved to be as fine and durable a piece of railway rolling stock as this world has seen. Some 950 of these steel cars eventually took to the rails to form the backbone of the company fleet.

The cars were not put into service without some resistance. When BRT officials notified the state's Public Service Commission that they intended to design a new all-steel subway car, the state agency recommended that they instead modify the basic Interborough car to suit their needs—and pay the IRT a royalty for each unit. The BRT wanted none of this! In August 1913 the BRT sent plans to the PSC for a distinctive new car, strongly influenced by the imaginatively designed Boston Elevated Railway cars on the new Cambridge subway. The main difference from the older IRT model was that instead of having doors in the end vestibules, the new car had three sets of twin doors spaced along the side of the car, dispensing entirely with vestibules. The doors were opened and closed by an electro-pneumatic system operated by a conductor from the center of the car. Later, in January 1921, the BRT perfected a system that allowed a single conductor to operate all the doors on an eight-car train.

The new BRT car, without a real name but known throughout the years simply as the "Standard," was longer than IRT equipment, measuring sixty-

*A train of BMT Standards awaits call to service in the Fresh Pond yard in Queens. Letters "BX" on the end bulkhead of car No. 2473 signify that this is a semi-permanently coupled three-car unit, and the middle is a motorless trailer. The Standard fleet grew to 950 units in the decade after 1914; they would provide daily and dependable service to two generations of New Yorkers, especially Brooklynites. (NYCTA)*

*Interior view of a BMT Standard. The use of 3-2 seating is unusual in a city subway car. (NYCTA) At right: Conductors' door controls on the Standard were in the wide space between the two center doors. During crowded rush hours, it took some pushing for the operators to switch sides as required by either an outside or center-island station platform. (NYCTA)*

*A scene on the Brighton line in the mid-1950s, showing a train of Standards moving up out of the open cut onto the embankment right-of-way. (Author)*

seven feet as opposed to the IRT's fifty-one feet. The extra space allowed more seats per car. As a result, also, of the greater width in the Triborough Subway plans which the BRT inherited, the Standard was ten feet wide, whereas IRT cars were but eight feet, nine inches wide.[4]

To rally press and public support for its new design, the BRT unveiled a full-sized wooden mock-up of the car on September 24, 1913. The next day the PSC gave the O.K. to order the car in quantity.

When the first Standards arrived from American Car and Foundry in 1914, beautifully painted in dark brown with a black roof, they were tested along sections of the Sea Beach line. On March 31, 1915, two eight-car trains made demonstration runs for a group of special visitors—the president and the engineering staff of arch-rival Interborough. The cars were everything the BRT said they would be, and more. Lavishly praised in industry journals, they promptly settled down to the task for which they were built. When the Standards first went to work for the BRT, Woodrow Wilson was president of the United States. Standards would still be hauling passengers in New York when Richard Nixon entered the White House.

The new BRT steel cars first operated in revenue service in March 1915, when they replaced surface-type trolley cars that had been providing temporary shuttle service over the Sea Beach line between 86th Street and New Utrecht Avenue. More of the new equipment went to work on Sunday, May 23, 1915, a full month before the inaugural of the first Dual Contract lines, when the amusement areas at Coney Island opened for the season. BRT trolley cars from all over Brooklyn converged on 62nd Street and the Sea Beach line. From 62nd Street the Standards operated in nonstop express service directly to the old West End Depot in Coney Island.

The Standards should have been put to work on the Centre Street loop line as soon as they arrived on the property, but wooden cars continued to ply the Williamsburg Bridge until the Broadway el was upgraded to handle the heavier weight of all-steel equipment in 1916.

The Interborough's rolling stock design seemed to remain the same from 1903 through 1925. However, like European automobile ads that stress invisible and interior innovations despite external similarity year after year, the IRT made steady improvements on a basic design. One key distinction between cars built before 1915 and those built afterward was the designation of the earlier cars as "high voltage" and the later cars as "low voltage." All drew the same 600 volts of direct current from the third rail. The newer vehicles, however, employed a substantially lower current—32 volts—for the operation of the motor controller and the multiple-unit apparatus. Low voltage soon became a standard feature on all U.S. rapid transit equipment. It eliminated the danger of feeding a lethal charge of 600 volts through the motorman's control station, and allowed other technical improvements as

*Three days before Christmas 1915, and Times Square is alive with activity. Hobble-skirt streetcars were known as "Broadway battleships." Beneath all the surface traffic workmen are busy building the Dual Contracts subway lines. A steam crane under the Fatima cigarette sign chuffs away, and there is wooden planking on the streets. (Robert L. Presbrey collection)*

well. With a typical New York urge for brevity, high-voltage cars were called "Hi-V's" and low-voltage cars "Lo-V's." (The BRT Standard was a low voltage car, incidentally.)

The IRT was also instrumental in developing the "anti-climber," a device that prevents cars from telescoping into one another in a rear-end collision. A mishap on the Westchester Avenue viaduct on December 4, 1907, vividly demonstrated the value of the invention. Cars equipped with the knuckled, wrap-around apparatus merely butted against each other with minimal damage, whereas two cars without the anti-climber were seriously damaged by telescoping. In another improvement, the Interborough replaced the original Van Dorn couplers of its early cars with an advanced automatic model, a design the BRT adopted for its steel cars and which remained standard in New York until 1971.[5]

Through 1925 more than 2,500 descendants of the 1903 experimentals, *August Belmont* and *John B. McDonald,* had been delivered. The original Composites were retired from subway service in 1916. As early as 1906 a tunnel fire demonstrated that they were less flame resistant than originally claimed, and their inability to withstand even minor collisions made them far less desirable cars than their all-steel running mates. At the order of the PSC, they were exiled to the IRT's Bronx and Manhattan elevated lines to serve out their days, some remaining in passenger service until after World War II. They remained as good looking a car as they ever were, but their distinctive appearance was seriously altered when progress dictated that they, too, have automatic sliding doors cut into their sides. A fish-bellied side brace was installed to compensate for structural weakness because of the newly inserted door.

There are those subway enthusiasts who see Interborough equipment as a many-splendored thing, and look upon the slight differences between series of cars the way stamp collectors cherish watermark variations. A knowledgeable student of the IRT, for instance, usually could distinguish a train of 1905 model cars from the 1925 version merely by the sound of the motors running at speed. One of the most artful objects ever used in the subway was a large brass controller handle supplied as standard equipment on early Interborough rolling stock. To the dedicated connoisseur of subway accoutrements, this handsome object compares to the controllers on later cars as a Rembrandt painting to an amateur's daub.

The destiny that was in store for the Dual Contracts, however, was not decided in the conference rooms of the Public Service Commission or the executive offices of the two traction companies. It was shaped in Europe, where an Austrian archduke was assassinated by a Serbian terrorist, and in the sea lanes off Ireland where the Cunard Line's express mailboat RMS *Lusitania* was torpedoed on May 7, 1915. The *Lusitania* went down just six weeks before the BRT and IRT began service over the first Dual Contracts lines. On February 26, 1917, with work in progress all over New York on various segments of the Dual System, President Wilson asked Congress for authority to arm American merchant ships. On April 6 of the same year, the United States declared war on Germany. World War I would irreversibly alter the nation's economic posture, and produce conditions that were unforeseeable on March 18, 1913, when the Dual Contracts were signed.

*Notes to Chapter 6*

[1] Including money spent by earlier French efforts in Panama, the cost becomes 639 million dollars.

[2] This upper Lexington Avenue line was to have connected with a tunnel under Broadway, in lower Manhattan, also begun before the Dual Contracts were signed. In February 1912 construction workers building the Broadway line exhumed the remarkably well-preserved remains of Alfred Ely Beach's pneumatic subway. The Triborough's Broadway tunnel, of course, became part of the BRT system.

[3] Maximum express train length on the Interborough in 1904 was eight cars. In 1907 it was increased to ten. Local stations on the old system could handle five-car trains. The BRT's Dual Contracts lines planned for eight-car maximums; however, as the BRT will use a longer car than the Interborough (see below) its eight-car trains will be longer than ten-car trains on Belmont's system.

[4] Company men initially called the Standards "steel cars." In later years, when large numbers of single cars were permanently coupled into three-car sets, the resultant lash-up was called a B unit, while cars that remained single were know as A units. As a result, the fleet itself was sometimes called the "AB's." Of the company's roster of cars, 900 were motor cars: Nos. 2000 through 2899; and fifty were motorless trailers: Nos. 4000 through 4049. The motorless trailers were semi-permanently coupled between two motor units—this lash-up was called a BX unit.

[5] Many of these improvements were the work of Frank Hedley, hired by Belmont to be General Manager of the Interborough. Hedley came from a railroad family; his father was a railwayman in England and his brother worked for McAdoo's Hudson & Manhattan RR. Before joining Belmont's company, Hedley did a stint on the elevated lines of Chicago. Eventually he became president of the Interborough.

# 7 The Malbone Street Wreck

THE BRT'S BRIGHTON BEACH LINE was one of several older routes that came into downtown Brooklyn on the rails of the Fulton Street el. The line also cut across the center of residential Brooklyn, serving the growing communities of the Flatbush area, eventually reaching the Atlantic seashore resorts of Sheepshead Bay, Brighton Beach and Coney Island, its terminal at Culver Depot. Followers of electric traction regard this long-gone palace, where el trains and trolley cars congregated, with the kind of nostalgic affection burlesque enthusiasts have for the original Minsky's. On one end of the line, the Brighton was a typical city el; on the other end, like a good many other BRT lines that evolved from steam-powered railroads of the late 19th century, it was a country-style interurban. It ran at ground level through rural areas and to the beach front where wealthy New Yorkers of an older era indulged themselves at race tracks and exclusive seaside hotels. The beach front would entertain a later generation with the more egalitarian pleasures of a boardwalk, municipal bath houses, and amusement parks.

The Brighton line began life as the steam-powered Brooklyn and Brighton Beach Railroad, running to the shore from a terminal at Franklin and Atlantic avenues in Brooklyn. When the line became a BRT electric operation, it was extended two blocks to Franklin and Fulton to connect with the Fulton Street el. But the Dual Contracts brought about major alterations. The agreement of 1913 called for the Fulton Street el connection to be replaced by a subway tunnel down Flatbush Avenue to the Fourth Avenue line at DeKalb Avenue, giving Brighton passengers through service to both the Centre Street loop and the new line up Broadway.

In 1918 the American "AEF forces" were battling the Central Powers in Europe. Outside the BRT's Brooklyn headquarters on Clinton Street, a big, big flag waved, bearing a blue star for every company employee serving his country under arms. Women conductors were recruited to ease the manpower shortage. They were outfitted by the BRT in ankle-length skirts and standard railroad conductor hats, which looked strangely out of place atop 1918-style hairdos.

Also in 1918, the Brighton line was being upgraded for its important new role in the Dual Contracts scheme. Southward from a point near Prospect Park and Ebbets Field, where the new subway connection would join the el spur from Fulton Street, the line was a well-constructed four-track route to Coney Island. An earlier two-track surface line had been improved by the

Dual Contracts, and large segments had been upgraded by the BRT itself as early as 1907 under a grade-elimination project. Costs of this pre-Dual Contracts effort were shared by the company and the city. The BRT had pioneered a construction technique called "open cut" on the Brighton line, in which tracks are placed in an open-air, concrete-lined depression or trench fifteen to twenty feet deep. An open cut was far less costly than a subway, avoiding the unsightliness and noise of standard el construction, while keeping the trains as inconspicuous in the neighborhood as possible.

The Brighton line featured a variety of constructions styles. The open-cut extended from the subway-el junction at Malbone Street all the way to Foster Avenue. From there to Sheepshead Bay the line ran on a fifteen-foot high earthen embankment and, from Sheepshead Bay to Coney Island, on a standard steel elevated structure—one of the few instances in all of New York where such an installation boasted four tracks. With the exception of the large new Stillwell Avenue terminal in Coney Island, opened in May of 1919 as a replacement for both the Culver and West End depots, the southern portion of the Brighton line looks the same today as it did in 1918. It is easily the most distinctive rapid transit route in the whole city, and even the whole world, according to some partisans.

*A steam shovel takes big bites out of Flatbush real estate as the BRT upgrades the Brighton line to four-track alignment as part of the Dual Contracts network. (Robert L. Presbrey collection)*

*Heading for Astoria in the late 1950s, a Brighton express rolls through the open cut right-of-way in Flatbush. (Author photo)*

As an aside, the Brighton line then provided one of the city's most pleasant experiences on an otherwise unpleasant hot summer day. Imagine the sensation as a Coney Island-bound Brighton Local slows to take the curve into the Brighton Beach station and a fresh breeze off the ocean wafts in the windows and washes out the heat of the city with cool and salty air. Steel dust, traction motors, and uncomfortable passengers combine to underscore the oppressive heat of the day as the Brighton line approaches the ocean southbound at just the correct angle to capture any on-shore breeze. (Today, air conditioned trains have cancelled this bonus.)

The linkup between the upgraded old Brighton line and DeKalb Avenue was among the last Dual Contracts items to be built. In fact, the Fourth Avenue line was in service for more than a year before bids were finally advertised in September 1916. Therefore, in October 1918 most of the Brighton line south of Malbone Street had been brought up to Dual Contracts standards. However, because the subway link was unfinished, the line's only access to the business district of downtown Brooklyn and Manhattan remained the rickety structure of the Fulton Street el. The el was too lightly constructed for the new all-steel Standards, and Brighton service was provided with older wooden elevated equipment.

In that October, construction was well along on the subway connection, the junction already in place adjacent to the Malbone Street station where the subway line and the Fulton Street spur would join.

*November 1915, and the first Dual Contracts operations on the BRT have been in service less than a year. This is the old West End depot in Coney Island, the site-to-be of the existing Stillwell Avenue terminal. El trains, drawing current from trolley wires, are stored off to the left. On the right, new high-level platforms are in place to accommodate the new Standards, and third rail has been extended into the station. (Edward B. Watson collection)*

At 5:00 P.M., October 31, 1918—as the world took heart from rumors out of London that Kaiser Wilhelm had abdicated—the telephone rang in BRT's Brooklyn headquarters. On the other end of the line was a man the company had once fired, but now was the mayor of New York, John Francis Hylan— "Red Mike," as some called him (but never to his face!). In 1897, he had been an engineer on the BRT's Lexington Avenue el when the line operated steam engines. He was discharged unceremoniously by a company supervisor for, allegedly, operating his train in a reckless manner. Hylan's message on Halloween night of 1918 brought little joy to his former employers. He told company officials that motormen on all subway and elevated lines had voted to go out on strike at 5 A.M. next morning, November 1st.

In the days of private ownership, work stoppages were frequent. To keep trains rolling, dispatchers, supervisors, and other non-union personnel were hastily given rudimentary instruction in train operation. Thus, service of sorts was maintained. As much as seventy-five per cent of normal, according to some estimates.

A twenty-three year old BRT dispatcher, one Edward Luciano, put in a full day's work through midafternoon on November 1st, but instead of heading home as usual at the end of his shift, he reported to the Kings Highway station of the Brighton line and there was assigned as motorman on a five-car train to Park Row and back. Inbound his run was uneventful. The return trip left the vaulted trainshed near City Hall at the Manhattan end of the Brooklyn Bridge during the height of the evening rush hour. After passing through Sands Street on the Brooklyn side, the train took the cutoff near Tillary Street to the Fulton Street line, picking up additional homeward-bound passengers at various stations in the Borough Hall area. When the train reached the junction with the Brighton spur at Franklin Avenue and Fulton Street, the dispatcher-turned-motorman accepted an incorrectly set switch and signal, and proceeded out the Fulton Street line toward East New York before realizing his mistake. His error was understandable; with schedules thrown off by the strike, the towerman at Franklin Avenue could not always be sure which train was to go where, nor was the novice at the controls familiar with the Brighton route. The train returned to Franklin Avenue; after some switching it was rerouted over its proper course.

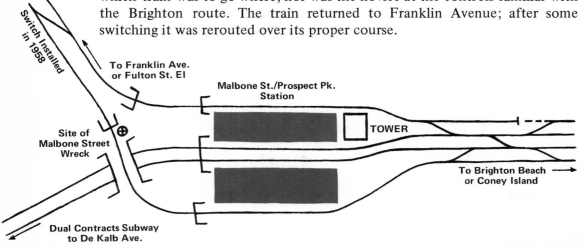

Switch Installed in 1958

To Franklin Ave. or Fulton St. El

Malbone St./Prospect Pk. Station

TOWER

Site of Malbone Street Wreck

To Brighton Beach or Coney Island

Dual Contracts Subway to De Kalb Ave.

Between Franklin-Fulton and Malbone Street, the run was downhill; Coney Island-bound trains had to negotiate a sharp S curve at the base of this grade, enter a short tunnel, and cross over the still incomplete subway that was later to run to DeKalb Avenue. The speed limit for this curve was six miles per hour.

Later, Luciano claimed that the air brakes failed on the downhill grade. Whatever the cause, the train gathered more and more speed as it approached Malbone Street and soon went out of control. The motorman later estimated his speed at 30 mph. A Naval officer traveling as a passenger claimed that 70 mph was more like it!

As the first of the five cars, open platform el car No. 725, swung into the curve, its rear truck derailed. The second car, motorless trailer No. 80, failed to follow the curve at all. It jumped the rails and slammed into a portion of the concrete wall separating north and southbound tracks, then jack-knifed at a right angle to the rest of the train. Instantly the third and fourth cars tore through the wooden vehicle. This was the worst disaster ever to befall the New York subways, or any U.S. transit line. The death toll was ninety-seven on the spot, not to mention the maimed and five later deaths from injuries.

Police and fire department rescue crews were forced to work at close quarters because the cars came to rest just inside the short tunnel under Malbone Street. As word spread through Brooklyn of the accident on the Brighton line, concerned families waited for news of their loved ones. Many waited in vain; few families in Flatbush were spared contact with the disaster —a cousin, a neighbor, an in-law, a friend.[1]

Charles Ebbets Jr., son of the owner of the Brooklyn Dodgers, feared at first that his father was aboard the train. After receiving news that he was not, Ebbets opened nearby Ebbets Field as an aid station for the least seriously injured victims. Most of the seriously injured passengers were taken to Kings County Hospital, about a mile away.

## PLAYING POLITICS

In the late evening hours on November 1, 1918, Mayor Hylan, then in the first of eight frantic years as New York's chief executive, arrived at the crash scene to begin the official investigation. Hylan, more than any previous mayor, vocally advocated full municipal ownership and operation of the subways. He thought the Dual Contracts were a terrible mistake, and never passed up an opportunity to mount an attack against what he called "the traction interests."

The mayor held that BRT management was criminally at fault in allowing untrained motormen to operate trains, and he instructed Kings County District Attorney Harry E. Lewis—who was inclined to place all the blame on

*Above: November 2, 1918 — the day after the fatal Malbone Street wreck. The curve off to the right is the one the train failed to negotiate; marks can be seen on the center wall where wooden el cars slammed into the concrete. (Robert L. Presbrey collection)*

*Right: Here are the remains of Car No. 100, just inside the tunnel at Malbone Street. The tragedy stands as by far the most dire accident ever to befall the New York subways. (Robert L. Presbrey collection)*

motorman Luciano—to proceed at once against the higher-ups. To insure the swift administration of justice, Hylan took advantage of a little-used clause in the City Charter. On the day after the accident, he assumed the role of "committing magistrate" and began to hear evidence on the case in the Flatbush Court on Snyder Avenue. The hanging judge had come to town!

Hylan's foes, and he had them in respectable numbers, cried that the mayor was using a municipal tragedy to further his own political ends. Nonetheless, indictments eventually were handed down against a roster of BRT officials from the top brass on down to the moonlighting motorman. Taken into custody from his Brooklyn home on the night of the accident, Luciano had no memory of how he had managed to get home after the crash.

Hylan's bias notwithstanding, no one was convicted in the Malbone Street case. The motorman was acquitted of a manslaughter charge. After a change of venue from Brooklyn to Mineola, the various BRT officials moved— successfully—for dismissal of all remaining indictments.

Less than two years after the wreck, on August 1, 1920, the tunnel connection to DeKalb Avenue opened for traffic, and steel cars began operating over the Brighton line. The spur to Fulton Street was turned into a shuttle operation at the same time, but using wooden el-type cars. In July of 1927, the wooden cars were replaced by steel cars. Signal techniques were also developed for electrically monitoring the speed of downhill trains. Should they exceed a prescribed limit, the brakes are applied automatically. Today, such a signal system protects every downgrade on the system.[2] In 1958 a new switch was installed, so that Franklin Avenue shuttle trains no longer had to negotiate the sharp S curve.

The accident of November 1, 1918, left such a strong impression that the name Malbone Street could not survive. Today the street is known as Empire Boulevard, and the Brighton station at the junction of the el spur and the subway connection is called Prospect Park.

## TROUBLE FOR BRT

For reasons that went far beyond the Malbone Street wreck, the BRT entered receivership on the last day of 1918. Judge Julius M. Mayer granted the petition of a creditor, the Westinghouse Electric Company, terminating BRT's private status. Lindley M. Garrison, a former U.S. Secretary of War, was appointed BRT receiver. Last minute efforts to save the company failed. And thus, in the year of the Malbone Street wreck, the end of the war in Europe, a worldwide epidemic of influenza, and the murder of Czar Nicholas and his family in Russia, came also the end of the Brooklyn Rapid Transit Company. Conjunctive with Garrison's appointment, BRT President Timothy S. Williams offered his resignation. Williams, who had presided over the company as chief officer since 1911, and in other executive positions before that, was the man principally responsible for preparing the once-disorganized transit property for entry into the Dual Contracts in 1913.

Receivership ended in 1923 when the BRT was renamed and reorganized as the Brooklyn-Manhattan Transit Corporation (the BMT). The BMT went on to fulfill the unfinished promise of the BRT. But the 1918 receivership brought into focus a drastic change in fiscal conditions over the preceding five years. In 1913, when the Dual Contracts were signed, subway profits were thought to be both lucrative and automatic. By 1918 municipal traction railway companies were in precarious financial straits, throughout the country as well as New York. Even the highly criticized system of preferentials in the Dual Contracts failed to keep the BRT from bankruptcy. To make bad times still worse for the New York companies, there was always the spectre of Red Mike—humorless, heavy-handed, and given to compulsive jousting with non-existent dragons—holding forth in City Hall, in no way sympathetic to any suffering by the "interests."

Two compelling factors contributed to the BRT's receivership in 1918, and to the IRT's narrow escape from a similar fate in 1921. First, the national economy was hurting from an inflationary turn brought on largely by the press of wartime spending. Second, the Dual Contracts specified that the subway fare remain at five cents for the life of the contracts—forty-nine years. At the time the contracts were signed, both the BRT and the IRT welcomed this provision, seeing it as protection against demands that the subway fare be *lowered*! In 1913, that seemed a more probable threat than inflation.

Inflation took its toll. In 1914 the BRT paid about $14,000 for its first Standard cars. By 1920, the same cars cost nearly $40,000 apiece. The war also caused extended delays in building the 1913 network of lines, and every delay meant steeper construction costs as inflation accelerated. January 1, 1917, was the target date specified in 1913 for the completion of all Dual Contracts lines. When that date arrived, only minor additions beyond the routes opened in June 1915 were ready for traffic. Often, a section of line was finished and apparently awaiting service. But it would not be tied in with the rest of the system. Interest payments had to be met on such a line's construction bonds, despite the fact the line was producing no income at all.

The companies lobbied for corrective legislation amending the Dual Contracts to raise the fare, but such proposals only gave Hylan the kind of ammunition he needed to go to war against private interests running subways in the first place. His major argument was that the preferential system was a raid on the public treasury. He was not moved by the fact the lines were losing money hand-over-fist despite the preferentials. In the face of such operating deficits, Hylan stood resolutely as the white knight defender of the nickel ride.

Subways were a major campaign theme in the 1921 mayoral and 1922 gubernatorial elections, in which Hylan was re-elected and Al Smith defeated the incumbent Republican, Nathan L. Miller. For Smith it was a return to the state's chief executive post; he had failed in a bid for re-election in 1920 when Miller rode into office on Warren Harding's coattails. But since the governor only served a two-year term, Smith was back in Albany in January 1923. He continued to serve for a total of four terms up through his unsuccessful run for the White House in 1928, and was as popular a governor as the state ever had.

In 1921, during his term in office, Miller had secured legislation creating an agency called the Transit Commission, another in a long and continuing series of state agencies that exercised broad control over city transit matters. This group, however, had a special mandate: to inquire into the possibility of some kind—any kind—of unification of the city's subways. Hylan, of course, had an easy answer for the commission. He advocated driving out the BMT and IRT and letting the city assume total control of the lines. In a speech from the steps of City Hall in 1921, when he accepted his party's nomination for a second mayoral term, he demanded that "the private operators turn the subways back to the city for municipal operation at a five-cent fare."

## HYLAN VS. TRANSIT COMMISSION

The Transit Commission, hardly ready to confiscate the subways as Hylan would have preferred, began to explore less severe alternatives, and the mayor began to view the new agency as his mortal foe. What is of overriding interest here, though, is that both Hylan and the Commission, despite their strong differences, were in agreement that the Dual Contracts were in need of radical repair.

In 1921, only seven years after the contracts were signed, and with most of the lines completed and in service, it became apparent that the two traction companies could not realize the more optimistic benefits of the pact. The city's population had grown to more than 5½ million by 1920. Thus even the extensive system of transit lines built under the Dual Contracts failed to meet the day-to-day requirements of the city's subway riders. More subway lines—or "transit relief" in the common phrase of the day—were clearly needed.

Hylan waged incessant political warfare against both the "interests" and Miller's Transit Commission. In 1925 he leveled a serious accusation against one of the commission's three members, Leroy T. Harkness, by insinuating that he was showing improper deference to his law partner, Judge Abel E. Blackman, a director of the Interborough. He accused the two members of the state bar of "actually fraternizing in private." To support this claim he presented the fact that Harkness' name appeared on their office door in smaller letters than Blackman's. Hylan's accusation overlooked a small item. By the mid-1920s the Transit Commission was entitled to name one director to the board of each company, the BMT and the IRT, and Blackman was the commission's man on the IRT. Hylan's scatter-gun demagoguery never concerned itself with such fine points.

On another occasion Hylan demanded that the commission declare the entire Interborough subway system forfeited to the city for supposedly failing to maintain requisite service standards. The commission, of course, refused to comply.

Al Smith made abolition of the Transit Commission a campaign pledge in 1922, and in 1923 a bill was filed to strip the agency of its authority over city transit matters. Smith and Hylan did not enjoy a cordial relationship; Hylan was a product of the Brooklyn Democratic organization of John H. McCooey, while Smith was a loyal son of Manhattan's Tammany Hall. In 1917, the two were contenders for the Democratic nomination for mayor. To avoid a primary fight, Tammany backed away from Smith and agreed to support Hylan. Love was not lost between those two men.

Despite such largely personal differences, any state Democrat in the 1920s could be expected to side with Hylan on transit matters, at least in broad substance. Abolition of the Transit Commission, which was staffed by Miller's Republican appointees, was considered part of the Democratic drive for increased "home rule" for the city. Furthermore, the upper crust of industry, including the transit industry, was not the constituency a Democratic lawmaker felt obliged to cultivate. It was Red Mike's ferocious style and flamboyant oratory, rather than his formal positions on issues, that put him in a class apart, even from his own party.

In 1923 Smith's measure to abolish the commission was soundly defeated. The Republican-dominated legislature was not about to turn control of the subways over to a bunch of city Democrats. But even as the proposal was going down in defeat, a new man was making his first appearance in the continuing drama of the New York subways. The bill was in the charge of the minority leader of the state senate, songwriter-turned-politician James J. Walker, the man who would succeed Hylan as mayor of New York.

---

*Notes to Chapter 7*

[1] The author's mother lost two cousins in the Malbone Street wreck. A third cousin barely missed the ill-fated train, and was thus spared.

[2] Despite all the precautions, the Malbone Street wreck "repeated itself" on December 1, 1974, fifty-six years and one month after the first crash. No lives were lost. The train of Budd-built R-32 units was traveling dead slow. But it derailed and hit the tunnel wall at the same spot the 1918 tragedy took place.

*This sequence of photographs was taken by the Interborough to illustrate the role of the motorman in operating a train.*

*Top left: With his "air handle" in his right hand, a motorman boards a Broadway-Seventh Avenue express. The operating station, or cab, is located on the end platform of the first car.*

*Top center: Ready to proceed. Motorman's left hand is placed on the controller, while his right hand holds the brake valve. The "wrench-like" device to the left of the controller is the reverse key.*

*Top right: Close-up of the controls in use. In the middle of the controller handle knob there is a button which functions as a dead man's control. Should the motorman relax his grip on this button while the train is under way, brakes would be thrown into emergency and the train would come to a sudden stop. Small box directly over the motorman's left wrist contains the starting light, an automatic signal which informs him when all the cars' doors are closed.*

*Above: Under way! Front-end position gives motorman clear view of the right-of-way and tracks. Car's bottom oil lamps are showing white, to indicate head end of train; roof-mounted lamps are showing color combination to identify train as a Broadway-Seventh Avenue express. Note overriding third-rail shoe protruding from truck, and multiple unit connection plugs directly under coupler; also, the small boxes mounted at the lower window frames on both sides of the car. Each is a control apparatus for the doors, and is used by a conductor stationed between two cars at some point back along the train. Ribbed bar across bottom end of car body is the "anti-climber" developed by the Interborough. See text, page 67. (All photos from NYCTA-Interborough collection)*

*Tom Nelligan photo*

## PLEASE FOLLOW THE BOOK OF RULES

Like most transit companies, the New York City Transit Authority publishes a book of rules. In addition to the version for employees, there is also a "book of rules" for passengers. Many of its dictates are ordinary enough, but consider some of the forms of prohibited on-board behavior: entertaining passengers by singing, dancing or playing a musical instrument; drinking, selling or giving away alcoholic beverages; conducting a religious service; and riding on the roof of a subway car.

# LOCATION OF STATIONS - INDEPENDENT CITY OWNED RAPID TRANSIT RAILROAD

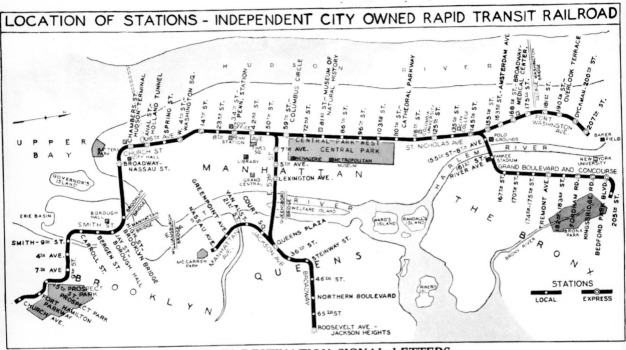

## TRAIN DESTINATION SIGNAL LETTERS

**Signal A** Washington Heights-Brooklyn-8th Avenue Express
**Signal C** Bronx Concourse-8th Avenue-Borough Hall, Brooklyn Express
**Signal CC** Bronx Concourse-8th Avenue Local
**Signal E** Queens-8th Avenue-All Local Stops
**Signal GG** Queens-Brooklyn Crosstown Line

Transfer to or from Washington Heights and Concourse trains in Manhattan; to or from Queens trains at 42nd Street, using underpass north end of southbound platform.

Transfer at Queens Plaza, Long Island City, to or from Brooklyn-Queens Crosstown trains stopping at Court Square, Van Alst, Greenpoint and Nassau Avenue Stations.

Queens trains operate between Roosevelt Avenue and Hudson Terminal, Manhattan, making all stops.

Queens-Brooklyn Crosstown trains operate between Queens Plaza and Nassau Avenue, Brooklyn.

Brooklyn passengers make *LOCAL* train transfers in Manhattan at Canal Street station.

BOARD OF TRANSPORTATION—CITY OF NEW YORK

JOHN H. DELANEY, Chairman.
FRANK X. SULLIVAN.
CHARLES V. HALLEY, Jr..
Commissioners.

May 1, 1934

## This Map is printed in the CLASSIFIED TELEPHONE DIRECTORIES (RED BOOKS) For New York City

*Where to go and what train to take to get there on the Independent or, simply, the "Eighth Avenue subway," as New Yorkers in the early 1930s were just as apt to call it. As of May 1934, this was the extent of the system. (Author's collection)*

# 8 The New Municipal Subway

ON A RAINY SUNDAY in August 1922, the year before Gov. Smith's bill to abolish the Transit Commission was defeated, Mayor Hylan had an announcement to make. He didn't make the announcement personally because he was on vacation at the racing meet in upstate Saratoga Springs. It was the mayor's secretary and son-in-law, John F. Sinnott, who called reporters to City Hall that afternoon of August 27th. On the same day, the rain washed out a St. Louis Browns baseball game with the Yankees[1] as well as a scheduled contest between Brooklyn and the Pittsburgh Pirates at Ebbets Field. The BRT, then in the depths of receivership and anxious to save a few dollars whenever it could, tried to take advantage of the poor weather and canceled the usual schedule of summer Sunday express trains to Coney Island. But rain or no rain, 100,000 people journeyed to the beach and amusement area. The impossible conditions on city-bound BRT trains that evening brought the company unfavorable front-page publicity in next morning's papers. The IRT also made Monday morning news when its uptown Manhattan service was disrupted for a spell on Sunday evening by a power failure.

The misfortunes of the traction companies were only a prelude to the big transit news for Monday, August 28, 1922. Reporters at City Hall for Sinnott's Sunday press conference had the real news: of a vast 600-million-dollar plan for a totally new transit system, a system that would tap areas in desperate need of transit relief. Until this time, transit investment in the original subway, plus the cost of the Dual Contracts lines, amounted to about 360 million dollars. This was just half the projected cost of Hylan's new super system, although this comparison fails to allow for inflated dollar values. Red Mike figured that a municipally run operation, even with the strictures imposed on city borrowing by the constitutional debt limit, could be completed in fifteen years.

Perhaps the most startling feature of the proposal was its plan to take away two of the private companies' most important lines: the BRT's Fourth Avenue route in Brooklyn and the IRT's West Side line in Manhattan. The technical term for this kind of seizure was "recapture," and, oddly, the Dual Contracts themselves made it all quite legal and proper and, what's more, possible. With or without the approval of the companies, the city had the right to buy back certain Dual System lines from the BRT and IRT at a nominal cost, amounting to little more than a repayment of the company's invested capital. Recapture also meant the private operators could no longer run trains over the lines in question. Without the important trunk lines coveted by Hylan, both transit systems would soon wither and die as private operations, unable to maintain ordinary service and hopelessly outclassed by the new municipal subway. George McAneny, the former Manhattan borough president and Dual Contracts negotiator, and then a member of the Transit Commission, labeled the mayor's plan a political ploy that was "ludicrous in the extreme."

The defeat of Smith's bill in 1923 dashed Hylan's chances of getting a fast start on his grandiose plan, but it gave him a priceless issue to take to the public. He assailed his opponents in speeches, letters to newspapers, and talks over the new municipal radio station, WNYC.

Hylan was able to bring greater pressure against the BMT since three important BMT Dual Contracts projects had yet to be built, and the company was starting to feel the pinch for lack of them. Hylan not only promised they would never be built, but that the city would never again put up money for construction of any privately run subway.

The three projects were the completion of the Centre Street loop from the station under the Municipal Building to a tie-in with the Montague Street tunnel, the construction of the final segment of the 14th Street-Eastern line, and the construction of modern subway repair shops at Coney Island. The first project was expected to ease the heavy traffic on all Southern Division BMT operations (since the lack of this connection forced the Manhattan Bridge routes to operate far below their designed capacity) and created a stringent bottleneck at the DeKalb Avenue-Gold Street interlocking plant in Brooklyn.

The two-track 14th Street line was especially urgent, for East New York had no direct service to midtown Manhattan. Passengers had to ride over the Williamsburg Bridge to Canal Street on the Centre Street loop, and there transfer to Broadway trains and backtrack uptown. Canal Street's narrow platforms were becoming so crowded that many BMT officials felt that a major disaster there could happen at any time.

The 14th Street line, Manhattan to the Montrose Avenue station in Brooklyn, did open in 1924, but the critical linkup with the rest of the Eastern Division at East New York was delayed by Hylan. The line was in partial operation only, separated from the rest of the BMT network. It carried only a handful of passengers, and offered no relief for the press of traffic at East New York. The BMT used an offbeat method to get subway cars into this isolated line. Twenty new Standard cars were hauled over the Long Island Rail Road to the LIRR Bushwick Yards, towed by truck along a temporary street track, and then eased down an inclined ramp into the subway.

One reason this vital linkup was delayed was that the 1913 contract called for it to be elevated between Montrose Avenue and East New York. Citizens of the Bushwick area objected and community pressures forced the city and the BRT to plan instead for a subway. It was this delay that allowed Hylan to get into the picture; the full line did not begin running until July of 1928, well into Walker's administration.

The BRT's main repair shops for elevated equipment were at 36th Street and Fifth Avenue in Brooklyn. The shop building, once the property of a BRT predecessor, the South Brooklyn Railroad and Terminal Company, serves to this day as a bus garage. The wooden mock-up of the Standard car was built at this shop in 1913, but it had insufficient facilities to maintain the company's steadily increasing fleet of steel subway cars. (Wooden mock-ups of the Standard, yes; real ones, no!) The original fleet swelled to a total of 950 cars by 1924, and the company needed a new maintenance and storage facility. Plans called for it to be built in Coney Island, but the Hylan administration refused to appropriate funds for the project, despite the fact that the Dual Contracts agreement legally bound the city to finance the project through completion. It, too, was finished only after Walker became mayor.

During the Hylan era the BMT and the IRT had more to cope with than their feud with Red Mike. Riding statistics continued to soar. In its first full year of service, the original Interborough subway carried 106 million passengers. In 1923, ridership was slightly less than 715 million passengers on the expanded lines of both companies. As an economic move, turnstiles were installed on a large scale in 1921.

In June 1922 color schemes were adopted by the Dual Contracts partners, to be used on signs, on entrance kiosks, and on illuminated globes atop the kiosks. The IRT used blue and white. The BRT, and later the BMT, used green and white, with a dash of red from time to time. The colors were not applied to rolling stock, however, which continued to be painted in muted earth tones—browns and blacks.

*Prior to 1921, passengers purchased tickets from what would now be a change booth, then deposited them in a chopping box operated by a uniformed guard. The turnstiles automated the "ticket choppers," as they were popularly called, out of business. Despite the use of slugs now and then by artful dodgers the turnstiles functioned smoothly and became standard equipment. Traffic through them was two-way, out as well as in. (NYCTA)*

On the afternoon of June 25, 1923, the newly reorganized BMT was hit with a tragic accident. A Fifth Avenue el train out of the 65th Street terminal in Bay Ridge derailed at the intersection of Fifth and Flatbush avenues in Brooklyn. Two cars—Nos. 913 and 919—left the track, fell off the elevated structure, and came to rest hanging between the tracks and the street. Eight passengers died; many were injured.

Oddly enough, BRT trains had had some bad luck at this location over the years, as on January 24, 1900, at 7:05 P.M. a five-car train from Bay Ridge caught fire just a few blocks from the 1923 crash scene. There were no injuries, but plenty of action that sounds, in retrospect, like the filming of a "Keystone Kops" comedy. Firemen began to direct hoses on the flaming lead car, No. 258, and were promptly sent sprawling when their streams hit the still-energized third rail. A substantial crowd attending a Knights of Columbus fair at the 13th Regiment Armory poured into the street to watch, and a *New York World* reporter noted that "the mid-air blaze gave to them and to many thousand others one of those delightful experiences that diversify life in Brooklyn Borough."

Following reorganization in 1923, the Brooklyn-Manhattan Transit Corporation[2] quickly became a strong and robust company. Hylan continued to claim that the reorganization failed to take proper regard of the city's interest in the bankrupt BRT, that a healthy BMT was secured only by double-dealing at municipal expense. One of the officers of the new corporation was Gerhard M. Dahl, an executive experienced in municipal transportation after serving as Street Railway Commissioner in Cleveland. He also had an extensive background in finance. To Hylan's bombast, Dahl replied with forceful and effective rhetoric; the BMT's case was also presented eloquently and well in a series of pamphlets, letters and position papers. As Hylan's second term drew to a close, the press began showing sympathy for the BMT's line of reasoning, and fell behind the company in its efforts to secure construction of the delayed links in the Dual Contracts network. Hylan, unable—or unwilling—to distinguish persuasive argument from unholy conspiracy, shouted all the louder. The Hearst papers remained on his side to the end.

### BMT Unveils a Novel Piece of Equipment

In November 1924, superintendent of equipment for the BMT, William Gove, whose name is linked with all the finely designed rolling stock produced by the line, unveiled plans for a most unusual piece of equipment, a "Triplex," consisting of three carbody sections permanently joined to form an articulated unit 137 feet long. (Articulation means that a single set of wheels does the work of two. Instead of each section riding on its own wheels, or trucks, the center section shares its trucks with the sections ahead and behind.) The pilot models arrived in 1925 from the Bessemer Works of the Pressed Steel

*An early and rare view of BMT's articulated triplex, or D units, shown on the express tracks of the Sea Beach line. When delivered from the builder, these first units did not feature illuminated side signs. The configuration of the car end would also, later, be reworked. Compare No. 6002 in this 1925 picture with views of the fleet in later years, on page 96 and in roster. (Author's collection)*

Car Company near Pittsburgh, and on August 31 the press took an inaugural ride from the BMT's City Hall station up to 57th Street and back. The Triplex was a comfortable, quiet and pleasant subway unit that did yeoman service on the BMT's Southern Division for forty years. Some devotees of the Triplex will claim in the face of all opposition that it is the finest piece of railway rolling stock *ever* produced.

The cars, also known as "D units," included such novel features as illuminated signs on either end of the train and illuminated line and destination signs inside the car. If the end sign was illuminated in white light, the train was operating via the Montague Street tunnel; if the end sign glowed green, the train was operating via the Manhattan Bridge. Some New Yorkers rode these cars to work for as long as thirty years without ever knowing the meaning of the BMT's carefully worked out symbols.

An order for sixty-seven additional Triplex units was placed after the pilots proved out, and all were in service by the end of 1927. Four Triplex units were the service equivalent of a train of eight Standard cars, and because of the economies of the articulation design, the BMT was able to buy a more

*Out of the 60th Street tunnel adjacent to Queensboro Bridge a train of BMT D units slowly maneuvers into the Queens Plaza station. (Author photo)*

modern car than the Standard for less money. The Triplex was heavy. An unloaded train of eight Standard cars grossed about 760,000 pounds, while four Triplex units tipped the scales at 832,000 pounds. Eventually, still more units were ordered. By the end of 1928 the fleet totaled 121 units carrying the numbers 6000 through 6120.

The BMT rebuilt some older el equipment in 1925. Under a Public Service

*Interior view of a BMT triplex equipped with illuminated side signs. The two slots under the word "VIA" indicated the train's route as either the Manhattan Bridge or the Montague Street tunnel. (NYCTA)*

Commission directive to replace some of its aging elevated cars—motorized leftovers from the steam era—the company instead rebuilt some eighty open platform el cars into closed platform vehicles, and permanently coupled them into three-car units for service on the Fulton Street line. These cars became known as the "C units." Although noisy and downright ugly, the C's were structurally and mechanically sound. They improved Fulton Street service markedly with minimum cash outlay.

New rolling stock was secondary, however, to the principal transit news of the second Hylan term; the mayor's plans for a new municipal subway. In 1924 Senator James Walker again co-sponsored legislation to abolish the Transit Commission and give Hylan a green light to proceed with his plans. A companion measure was also filed to alter the city's debt structure and permit additional subway borrowing. Both bills met with determined opposition, but a compromise was at least worked out which kept the Transit Commission in existence, with regulative powers over existing lines. A new Board of Transportation, appointed by the mayor, was then established to monitor Hylan's proposed municipal system.

The compromise passed the legislature in April 1924. The legislation included a passage stipulating that any new municipal subway would be held to a five-cent fare for its initial three years. After that time, the fare would have to be adjusted upward to cover operating expenses, and meet construction and equipment debts. Republicans were proud of themselves. They not only had saved the Transit Commission but had directly challenged Hylan to keep his many promises. Democrats, including the mayor, were disgruntled because the Transit Commission had not been abolished, and were disturbed even more over the legislature's refusal to take any action on raising the debt limit. Some felt they had received but "half a loaf"; Hylan cried aloud that it was more like "a few crumbs."

Essentially this legislation safeguarded the existing systems and kept them under the watchful eye of the Commission, but allowed Hylan to proceed with his own plans. The legislation pointedly excluded Hylan's 1923 goal of recapturing key BMT and IRT routes for inclusion in a municipal subway.

*BMT's first whack at rebuilding older open platform el cars into more modern units resulted in the C units, so called. Their venerable lineage easily discernible, they rocked and swayed along Brooklyn elevated trackage well into the 1950s. Scene is on the Fulton Avenue el. (NYCTA)*

Hylan could build his new city-run system, but it would have to co-exist with, not absorb, the private lines. There were very few legislators in Albany who did not realize that this 1924 compromise was a very temporary arrangement.

In its annual report issued early in 1923, the Transit Commission leveled serious charges at the Hylan administration for its failure to fulfill Dual Contracts obligations, and McAneny doggedly insisted that the city's credit could not support the borrowing required to build a totally new subway system.

Transit unification, an important topic in many influential quarters, was spurred on as Hylan's new municipal subway began to take shape. By 1924 the commission had formulated its own unification plans. They envisioned, roughly, a purchase by the city of both BMT and IRT interests. "Purchase" in this case did not mean a simple cash transaction, but a complex exchange of private and municipal bonds. The plans allowed the commission to show, on paper at least, that such a city takeover would free large blocks of frozen credits, allowing new subway lines to be built to tie in with the existing networks. According to the commission, a city takeover of the BMT and IRT—coupled with a major expansion program—would cost less than the construction of a third subway system.

The commission's unification plans remained a distant goal, however, as Hylan turned to the actual construction of his municipal subway. All city spending was held in check and rigid priorities were established so that as much credit as possible could be earmarked for subway bonds.[3]

## THE BOARD OF TRANSPORTATION

In July 1924, a new three-man Board of Transportation was sworn in. John E. Delaney, a former commissioner of the state PSC, served as its chief officer. Delaney immediately met with George McAneny to discuss the mutual jurisdiction of the two rival transit bodies. This must have been a delicate and touchy session, in view of the kind of open warfare that had prevailed between Hylan and the commission. McAneny's statement to the press afterward was measured: "In a case like this where authority and its commensurate responsibility are not always specifically defined in all their details, there is likely to be a 'twilight zone' of more or less doubt."

On December 9, 1924, the Board of Transportation adopted a basic route plan for the new system. It differed only slightly from the plan Hylan had announced in August of 1922, and included Manhattan trunk lines on both Sixth and Eighth avenues, a line to Washington Heights, a cross-Brooklyn line, and several other connections. One of the original Manhattan els, the Sixth Avenue line, would be replaced by the new subway, and soon removal of the els became a popular goal in New York, for by 1925 the Manhattan els had been running for half a century and their useful days were commonly felt to be just about over.

Two days before this plan was revealed, on December 7, 1924, Governor Al Smith named Justice John V. McAvoy to conduct a "summary investigation" of what the governor described as the "intolerable" conditions prevailing on the subways. Charges and countercharges flowed from Hylan, the Transit Commission, and the two companies. Now there was still another party to the disputes, the new Hylan-appointed Board of Transportation. While all these groups railed at each other, the full Dual Contracts system remained incomplete, needed new lines had yet to be constructed, and conditions on the subways themselves were crowded and congested. Major General John F. O'Ryan, a member of the Transit Commission, harked back to wartime for an appropriate comparison: "Had I treated German prisoners during the war as passengers on the transit lines are here being treated, I would have been court-martialed."

The McAvoy Commission heard testimony during December and January. Its findings, as reported to Governor Smith, were highly critical of Hylan, while generally praising the work of the Transit Commission. Former governor Miller's original appointees had by this time been replaced by Smith's own, and it is not unreasonable to see the McAvoy investigation as part of an effort to sandbag Hylan as the 1925 election drew near.

Although the Hearst papers continued to support the mayor, neither Smith nor the Tammany organization would accommodate Hylan for a third term. But because Red Mike was eager to stay in City Hall, a primary fight broke out for the Democratic nomination. In September 1925, Jimmy Walker, Tammany's man, dealt Hylan a crushing defeat. Walker carried all five boroughs including Hylan's own Brooklyn, where he outpolled the incumbent by 5,000 votes. It could easily be speculated that all 5,000 were BMT riders!

Hylan was at a disadvantage in his fight with Walker because his pet issue was effectively neutralized. He was unable to call Walker a tool of the hated interests. The senator's track record on transit was, if anything, better than Hylan's. Walker had always been a defender of the five-cent fare, and it was Walker who twice sponsored the legislation which allowed Hylan to begin work on the municipal subway. After polishing off Hylan, Walker then went on to defeat Republican Frank Waterman (of the fountain pen Watermans) in the November general election.

Not long before his defeat, Hylan enacted what may well have been his most triumphant performance. On Saturday, March 14, 1925, wielding a silver-plated shovel, he broke ground for his "baby," a municipal subway system, at the intersection of St. Nicholas Avenue and West 123rd Street. Orating to a crowd of some 2,000 onlookers at Hancock Square in Washington Heights, Hylan laced into the "railroad corporations," the Transit Commission and traction sympathizers generally. Vintage Hylan verbiage again excoriated the "million dollar traction conspiracy" perpetrated by his enemies. But this time the mayor was able to conclude on a victorious note. The ceremonial event of the day "means the beginning of the emancipation of the people of the City of New York from the serfdom inflicted upon them by the most powerful financial and traction dictatorship ever encountered."

On Thursday, April 3, 1925—Calvin Coolidge in the White House, Jack Dempsey the heavyweight champion of the world, and the Scopes trial about to become a nationwide sensation—the Rosoff Subway Construction Company put a steam shovel to work at St. Nicholas Avenue and West 128th Street.[4] The new municipal subway was underway.

Pressure to halt construction of the third system—and to expand instead the two earlier networks—intensified after Walker took office. The BMT had long been interested in the Washington Heights route, for instance. (There is still a short stretch of tunnel north of the BMT station at 57th Street and Seventh Avenue which was built in 1919 with such a link-up in mind.) But in early 1927, the Walker administration entered a contract for a tunnel under the East River at 53rd Street. Completion of this route made anything but a new independent system impractical.

The question of whether the new line should be built to the smaller IRT dimensions or the larger measurements the BMT inherited from the Triborough System was resolved in favor of BMT specifications. This decision was particularly significant, because in recent years the BMT and the Independent system have been fully merged and integrated, while the IRT remains unto itself.

Work on the new subway proceeded slowly. Before any city-operated train could run in the new system, additional lines had to be authorized and their contracts drafted. In Brooklyn it was proposed that the BMT's Culver line be recaptured so that the municipal subway might reach all the way from the Bronx to Coney Island. Also in Brooklyn, a new line out Fulton Street to East New York doomed the BMT's Fulton Street el. Even before the Dual Contracts were signed there were proposals to tear down the western end of this elevated line and replace it with a subway. After 1913 a more modest plan emerged to upgrade the Fulton Street el to handle steel subway equipment and connect the line with the BRT subway at DeKalb Avenue. Following the Dual Contracts, large segments of the el were actually upgraded and the many tunnels at DeKalb Avenue were designed to permit the construction of a ramp to the Fulton Street line. The plan, known as the Ashland Place connection, likely would have been completed had not a John Francis Hylan sat in City Hall for eight years. Now a new four-track municipal subway would replace the Fulton Street el, and even the rebuilt sections of the line would be torn down.

Regular operation on the first leg of the municipal subway began on Saturday, September 10, 1932, when the Eighth Avenue line opened from Washington Heights to Hudson Terminal in downtown Manhattan. The inaugural was unusual; there were no festivities, no speeches, no first train. Instead, at 12:01 A.M., all stations along the line opened simultaneously. Full schedules had actually been in effect since the previous Wednesday to get the line in shape for opening day. Not everyone was fully prepared to begin service, however. Many conductors put in several days work in uniform jackets with sleeves merely basted on, as the tailor was one contractor who failed to complete his task on time.

The lack of fanfare in 1932 contrasted sharply with the gala festivities that marked the beginning of Interborough service in 1904. Another difference between 1904 and 1932 is worthy of mention. When passengers first boarded the Independent Subway, as the new system was called,[5] there were no advertisements on the walls, owing to a delay in getting them installed. But soon enough the stations and cars were festooned with blurbs for chewing gum, soap powder, funeral parlors, and the latest movies, though not for beer or hard liquor—prohibition was in full swing. Ironically, passengers felt the line looked naked and incomplete without ads. In 1904 passengers had raised quite a hoot and a holler that the ads desecrated the subway.[6]

Twelve hours after the new subway opened for business the Italian liner *Conte Grande* backed slowly away from its pier at the foot of West 57th Street and steamed down the Hudson River and out to sea, bound for Gibraltar, Naples, and Genoa. Aboard was James Walker, now *ex*-mayor of New York. He had tendered his resignation to New York Governor Franklin D. Roosevelt several days earlier, after his administration's credibility and pub-

*Fresh from builder A. C. F., the first of the Independent's R-1 units are moved off a barge in the Harlem River into IND's 207th Street yards in upper Manhattan. Cars ran tests on the BMT before the Eighth Avenue line opened. (NYCTA)*

*Early days on the IND. Here the fabled "A Train" of Duke Ellington's theme song loads passengers into its original R-1 type cars. Note the absence of advertising in this station scene, and the IND's ties-in-concrete roadbed. Incidentally, the A train is still "the quickest way to get to Harlem." (NYCTA)*

lic confidence had been utterly destroyed through a series of dramatic public investigations. He was going to Europe to rest and regain his health. Walker returned to America in a few weeks, only to be hounded by creditors. Broken in spirit, he sailed once again on the *Conte Grande* in November, this time accompanied by Betty Compton, the girl he had courted for so long—a true voyage into exile from his beloved New York.

During Walker's six years as mayor, the bitterness and hostility of the Hylan era faded. Indeed, many feel that if New York has ever truly experienced that "one brief shining moment," it did so while the man who wrote "Will You Love Me in December?" was the mayor—a claim made in full cognizance of the tragic events which eventually doomed James Walker and destroyed his administration.

Times were changing on the transit scene as early as March 22, 1926, when the Walker administration celebrated the opening of its first new subway line. It was a minor addition to the city's network: the extension of the Interborough's Queens line a mere quarter-mile from Grand Central to a station adjacent to the Public Library on Fifth Avenue. But its inauguration was celebrated with gusto, and included movies at the nearby Hippodrome on into the night. The press saw the festivities as evidence that past transit difficulties had "seemingly ended with the advent of the new administration." Walker himself had sounded the same theme when he took the oath of office. "This administration will not seek to glorify itself at the expense of delay in this most essential necessity. More transit facilities must be provided without any kind of political or personal interference," he said.

(A few days before the opening of this new line in 1926, on March 16, the day before St. Patrick's Day, an event took place in New York that was not reported in the press, and which drew no reaction or response from the city's transit executives. On that day, twenty-one year old Mike Quill first set foot in America. He went to work at a pick and shovel job for one of the contractors building the municipal subway, and later that same year hired on with the IRT as a gateman.)

### TROUBLE, TROUBLE, AND THE FIVE-CENT FARE

Of course, the mere fact that the transit companies could expect civil behavior from the new mayor of the city was not enough to solve all their problems. While the BMT settled down to business, thankfully free of Red Mike, the Interborough was left to capture a few unpleasant headlines. It suffered a massive strike in July 1926, a near classic study out of the turbulent middle years of the American labor movement. The Interborough was unwilling to grant its workers the right to bargain through anything save an ineffectual company union, and management had the muscle to get its way. The IRT obtained an injunction in the state Supreme Court restraining the Consolidated Railroad Workers of Greater New York from "inducing" anyone to join its organization, and offered 100 dollars to any employee who supplied information leading to the arrest and conviction of anyone who violated the order. Six years later, when the new municipal subway was doing large-scale hiring, men who had been fired by the IRT for taking part in the 1926 strike were accorded preferential treatment. Rival BMT was no more progressive in labor relations than the Interborough. It, too, actively discouraged independent unions. For example, in 1920, each employee found in the November issue of the company magazine—then called the *BRT Monthly*—a pledge that the employee would not join a particular union trying to organize a membership drive at the time. All were expected to sign the pledge card and return it to the company. Elsewhere in the magazine, among the news items about picnics and the softball leagues, were pithy little quotations equating trade unionism with Bolshevism.

In addition to suffering from labor unrest, the IRT was feeling the pinch of the five-cent fare, and it began to push for a higher tariff. Unable to get relief through the legislative process, company attorneys were told to take the matter to court. Like many theological, political and matrimonial matters, the argument turned on a very tenuous distinction between two seemingly identical terms.

In 1907, the state Public Service Commission had been established with statutory power to set subway fares. IRT lawyers argued that this authority, later delegated to the 1922 Transit Commission, was itself sufficient to override the Dual Contracts' five-cent fare stipulation. But the PSC would only have authority to override the Dual Contracts fare requirement because these were signed *after* the PSC itself was established. Contract One, the original subway, and Contract Two, the Brooklyn extension of the Interborough, were signed in 1900 and in 1902, and their terms could not be put aside by PSC edict. Because these earlier contracts also specified a five-cent fare for the term of the contract, the IRT case centered on whether the Dual Contracts fare of five cents was a new and different obligation from the five-cent fare stipulation of Contracts One and Two.

The IRT won an initial victory before the United States Statutory Court in May 1928, and the Walker administration was faulted for not raising effective objection against even the assumption of Federal jurisdiction. Eighteen months after the court action, Walker was up for re-election. The IRT victory brought out the wolves calling for Walker's hide, and from the dark and depressing past came the thundering sound of John Francis Hylan, who finally was able to charge that Walker was "soft on the interests."

But Beau James was entitled to a miracle. He got it when the U.S. Supreme Court, in an unexpected opinion delivered by Associate Justice James Clark McReynolds, ruled that the Statutory Court order was "improvident and beyond the discretion of the court." The IRT lost its case, the five-cent fare remained in effect, and the thorny problem of whether five cents is really five cents remained unanswered. On the crest of this victory Walker rode into a second term as mayor.

The Interborough faced costs of more than a million dollars from its unsuccessful action. The line had been so confident of victory that it had even minted tokens, which would have been used when the fare was raised to either seven or eight cents.[7] But the taxpayers of the City of New York, in effect, wound up footing the bill, because the IRT charged up all the costs to operating expenses, the first category of cash outflow under the Dual Contracts.

The amount of subway fare had been a highly emotional issue from the beginning. Back in 1906, the BRT charged a double fare on el trains to and from Coney Island.[8] Justice (and later mayor) William J. Gaynor ruled in August that the company could not collect the double tariff, but the BRT would not be dissuaded. It hired a corps of 250 special policemen, or "heavyweight inspectors" in the words of the *Times*—and "goons" in anybody else's language—to enforce the company's double-fare policy. On Sunday, August 12th, disturbances broke out at the various points in Brooklyn where the extra fare was collected. More than 1,000 men, women and children were ejected from company trains and trolleys, including Brooklyn Borough President Bird S. Coler, a man who not unsurprisingly became a firm advocate of municipal operation of subways and els. An entire car full of passengers unwilling to pay the extra nickel was uncoupled from a Coney Island-bound train and left on an isolated siding. A young girl's body was found floating in Coney Island creek, and it was suggested her death was caused by the enthusiasm of the "heavyweight inspectors." In the middle of this overheated atmosphere, a BRT lawyer suggested that the line had the clear right to kill anyone who refused to pay the extra fare!

Even after winning the IRT case, Walker faced a potential time bomb on subway fares: the legal requirement that after three years of operation the Independent must charge a fare that would meet all expenses. To avoid the absurdity of the new municipal lines charging a higher fare than the BMT and the IRT, Walker pushed ahead with plans for full subway unification. Samuel Untermyer, who was retained by the Transit Commission as special counsel, worked out a plan for the city to assume complete title to the private lines for 400 million dollars. One of Walker's quiet aims in unification was the elimination of open trading in traction securities. For despite the annual operating deficits of the two companies, their complex schemes of financing and indebtedness made it possible for investors to earn dollars on BMT and IRT stocks and bonds.[9] Unification, as envisioned in the Untermyer plan, would end this speculation, Walker felt.

But unification proved to be an even more drawn out business than the negotiation of the Dual Contracts. If the formation of the Transit Commission in 1921 is considered the first step in the process, then unification took nineteen years to accomplish!

In 1932, the year the Independent opened, the Interborough entered receivership. Immediately speculation began as to whether receivership would aid or hinder unification. One possibility, strongly urged by Untermyer, was that the courts could move to dissolve the IRT's 999-year lease on the four elevated lines, the pact Belmont engineered in 1902. Although the IRT subways turned a small profit, the antiquated els more than ate up this net and prevented the company from achieving a sound fiscal position. In addition, the els had no long-range role to play in New York's transit picture. However, before the els could be eliminated, the claims of the original Manhattan Railway bond holders would have to be satisfied.

Thus, by the mid-1930's the Interborough was in dire straits, and the els were living on borrowed time. Meanwhile, the Independent subway was being

*Workhorses of the BMT's Southern Division over the years were the Standard and the Triplex. Here examples of both classes rest in the midday sun outside of Coney Island shops. (Author photo)*

opened piecemeal, unification was in the wind, and the BMT, although receptive to the general idea of unification, was enjoying, at least operationally, perhaps its finest hour.

*Notes to Chapter 8*

[1] Played at the Polo Grounds; Yankee Stadium didn't open until 1923.

[2] When the BMT was chartered in May 1923, "a great deal of thought," in the words of the *Times,* went into selecting a name for the new corporation. The word "Brooklyn" had to be included in the title, and "in a preferential position."

[3] Hylan deserves stout praise for this administrative *tour de force,* even with a 1920-size municipal government.

[4] The Rosoff company was headed by "Subway Sam" Rosoff, a high wheeler of extraordinary proportions who frequented race tracks and gambling casinos the world over.

[5] Also on nomenclature, the new Independent system, in whole or any part, was frequently called, simply, "The Eighth Avenue Subway." Including the line under Sixth Avenue.

[6] Subway advertising had become a major industry unto itself by 1932. Artemas Ward sold his franchise to a man named Barron G. Collier in 1925, and Collier's company continued to place ads in the subways until 1940. Among the young copywriters who at one time produced persuasive prose for Collier's advertisements were F. Scott Fitzgerald and Ogden Nash.

[7] Today prized collectors items.

[8] The double el fare to Coney Island was dropped with the advent of the Dual Contracts. Oddly enough, it continued on certain BMT-controlled streetcar lines to Coney Island until after World War II.

[9] At the turn of the century, traction companies in the City of Brotherly Love were put together with such complex financial arrangements that nobody knew who owned what. Transit attorneys responsible for such work have achieved immortality as "Philadelphia lawyers."

# 9 The Road Toward Unification

IN 1934 FIORELLO LA GUARDIA walked into City Hall as the standard bearer of a "fusion" administration. The former Republican congressman was not a representative of a conventional political party, but a crusader for reform that transcended traditional party lines and drew support from both Republicans and Democrats. After several years of investigations into the doings of the Walker administration, New York was ready for new solutions to its problems.

Despite the oppressive Great Depression, New Yorkers, during the decade before World War II, indulged in a variety of pursuits. The 102-story Empire State Building was completed in May 1931; price, 41 million dollars. The skyscraper was built by a syndicate headed by former governor Al Smith, and instantly became a source of considerable civic pride, its observation tower a potent tourist attraction, though not foreseen as the site of "King Kong's last stand." There was the trans-Atlantic speed competition being waged season after season by two fine ocean liners, French Line's *Normandie* and Cunard's *Queen Mary,* to beguile New Yorkers after 1935. The vessels would tie up at the city's new deep-water piers on the Hudson River north of West 43rd Street, each arrival dutifully covered by photographers from New York's two popular tabloids, the *Daily News* and the *Mirror.* In June 1937, a major American legend had its beginnings when Joe Louis, a young boxer from Detroit, knocked out James J. Braddock to become heavyweight champion of the world. Adjacent to the 161st Street station of the IRT's Lexington-Jerome line, other sporting legends flourished throughout the 1930s. There in Yankee Stadium teams led by Babe Ruth and Lou Gherig rewrote the American League record book.[1] It was a time for debates on isolationism and rearmament; it was a time when the zeppelin seemed the harbinger of things to come; it was a time when everyone had his own theory on the mysterious disappearance of Judge Joseph F. Crater in New York on the sixth day of August in 1930; and it was a time when the best-known telephone number in town was "PEnnsylvania 6-5000," the title of a popular Glen Miller tune.

Through the La Guardia years, the Independent continued to expand. The last major link to be placed in service was the Sixth Avenue route* in Manhattan, on which the first revenue train ran on December 15, 1940. But certain segments of the new system were delayed until after World War II.

Originally the Sixth Avenue subway was planned to take over the existing Hudson and Manhattan subway tunnel under Sixth Avenue south of West

*See page 107*

*Forty years after the Independent first opened, a yard full of R-4 units awaits the call to rush hour service on the CC line. Addition of sealed beam headlamps is the only noticeable external change in the cars over all the years. (Tom Nelligan photo)*

33rd Street for local service; a new two-track tunnel was to be constructed for express service. This plan was later abandoned because the H&M was built to IRT-size clearances, and the cost of refitting the tunnels to handle ten-foot wide cars would have been prohibitive. So the H&M was not ousted from its tunnel; indeed, it was given a completely new terminal at 33rd Street and Sixth, and the Independent built a right-of-way for itself around and under the old tunnel. Only a two-track line opened in 1940, however; proposed express tracks were not constructed for another quarter century.

### FEATURES OF THE INDEPENDENT

Compared to both the BMT and IRT the new municipal subway was an engineering marvel. Its stations were built to generous dimensions with color-coded tile on station walls to help passengers identify their stops with ease. The spacing of stations was worked out by precise formula.

From time immemorial, New Yorkers have had a positive addiction for riding express trains, much to the chagrin of transit planners. Local trains regularly carry large numbers of passengers only as far as the next express stop, where everyone gets off to catch the express. Independent engineers attempted to induce local riders to stay aboard their trains right through to final destinations. To this end the number of local-only stations in the central business district of Manhattan, the area below 57th Street, was held to a bare minimum—three out of twenty. The major express line down from the Bronx under Eighth Avenue and Central Park West had no express stops at all between 125th Street and Columbus Circle. The reason: Local passengers boarding trains below 125th Street would see no advantage in changing to an express. There isn't, and they haven't.

Sharp curves force subway trains to operate at inefficiently slow speeds, so the new municipal lines were built with wide, high-speed curves. Costly "flying junctions" were constructed so trains could proceed on diverging routes with minimum delay. In general, the physical plant of the new system was a glistening and shiny showpiece of a subway—a far cry from the older systems which were starting to show not only their age, but the incremental character of their construction.

Thanks to its well-built roadbed and efficient signal system, the Independent subway featured a passenger capacity of 90,160 per hour per track. The comparable BMT statistic was 73,680, while the IRT rate was 59,400.[2]

Several other features of the Independent are of interest. The older lines generally operated on conventional railroad-style roadbeds—rails spiked to crossties sitting in stone ballast. The new system largely adopted a technique which had previously been used only in stations. Ties were not imbedded in ballast but in indentations in the concrete flooring. Full-length ties were not used, but rather "half ties" were placed under each rail, with a drainage ditch between them. This arrangement has more than once saved a life because a person falling in front of an approaching train has sufficient room in the ditch to lie flat and allow the train to pass over. The technical rationale for the ties-set-in-concrete method was that it resulted in a more secure roadbed, free from the frequent distortions of ordinary ballast and ties.

At two spots, one in Astoria and the other in Flatbush, the Independent tried something different. Express tracks at these points diverged from the right-of-way used by locals, took a short cut along the "third leg" of an imaginary triangle, and arrived at a common terminal over a shorter route. The Independent also pushed three more two-track tunnels under the East River, raising the number of transit river crossings to thirteen.

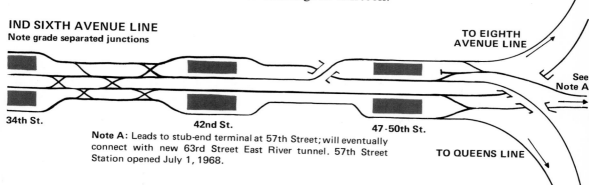

**IND SIXTH AVENUE LINE**
Note grade separated junctions

TO EIGHTH
AVENUE LINE

See
Note A

34th St.     42nd St.     47-50th St.

TO QUEENS LINE

Note A: Leads to stub-end terminal at 57th Street; will eventually connect with new 63rd Street East River tunnel. 57th Street Station opened July 1, 1968.

Rolling stock for the new subway was nice, but utilitarian, equipment. The cars measured sixty feet six inches long, ten feet wide, and a shade over twelve feet high. They could accomodate 282 passengers per car, though only sixty could be seated. Each weighed 80,000 pounds and cost the city $38,000 each. Among other innovations they featured left-handed screw threads in the emergency lighting system to thwart bulb snatchers. The regular light bulbs, officials presumed, would always be burning and their heat alone would be ample defense against larceny. But the emergency system, which is battery powered and designed to take over during power outages, needed added protection because its bulbs were always cool. The new cars borrowed an idea from the BMT Triplex: end signs to identify both the route of the train and its destination. But whereas the BMT used numbers to designate its various lines, the Independent adopted a letter code.

The first cars were ordered under contract R-1, and the cars have since been known by this contract number. In fact the R Series has been continued into modern times on the New York subways; the most recent subway cars, for instance, are R-46 units.

The cars ordered for the Independent subway in the 1930s—1703 of them, designated R-1 through R-9—offered swift acceleration and generous speed capabilities, but they were not as comfortable or as quiet as the BMT Standard, nor were they any match for the Triplex. Comparisons may be unfair, however, because few who made them were without bias, including BMT men who had a chance to operate some of the new units. They were put in service on the Sea Beach line in July 1931 for tests. (Independent cars could run on BMT rails, of course, because both the BMT and the municipal lines were built to the same specifications—in effect, the old Triborough measurements.) The "city cars," as they were called on the BMT, continued to run on the Sea Beach until November, when they were returned to the Independent, which was still ten months away from inaugurating service.

## Meanwhile, Back on the BMT

During the 1930s the BMT completed its long-delayed Dual Contracts links. The Nassau Street line in Manhattan was opened with fitting ceremony on May 29, 1931, when Mayor Walker rode into the new Broad Street station aboard a freshly scrubbed Triplex. The line was the last of the network of transit lines mandated by the Dual Contracts of 1913.

The Nassau Street line linked the station under the Municipal Building—by then known as the Chambers Street station—and the Montague Street tunnel. It had been difficult and expensive to build because it had to thread its way through a highly congested district under a narrow street, dodging three older subway lines in the process. The present BMT station at Fulton and Nassau streets, with its puzzling complex of passageways, is testimony to why this

*The new Municipal Subway was opening piece by piece when the photographer posed this train in the Jay Street station, Brooklyn, during the last day in January 1933. (NYCTA)*

*A train of veteran R units at Columbus Circle in the spring of 1972, by which time headlights and a stirrup had been added to this generation of cars. (Tom Nelligan photo)*

*IND R units kept passengers informed with dual destination signs – lighted in the operating direction – and a large line sign displaying the letter code of the route. (Author)*

line, which is less than a mile long, carried a price tag of 10 million dollars. Once the Nassau Street line opened for traffic, the Centre Street loop subway was finally complete. Ironically, the first venture in underground transit for the BRT was in 1908 when the company began to run el trains over the Williamsburg Bridge and into the north end of the Centre Street loop.[3] Since 1931 the loop has generally been known as the Nassau Street loop. The two

*A Brighton local rolls along the double-deck approach to Stillwell Avenue terminal on 4th July 1954. Structure just ahead of the train's first car is the "parachute jump," a 250-foot-high amusement device that simulated a real parachute descent. It was moved to Coney Island after serving as a 1939-40 World's Fair attraction. (Author)*

Left: Called the Green Hornet, this was the Pullman-built experimental the BMT put in service in 1934. Today both the train and the elevated line — the Fulton Street el in downtown Brooklyn — are but memories. (Edward B. Watson collection)

Below: The other 1934 experimental, in gleaming stainless steel, was turned out by Budd. It had a longer service life than its Pullman running mate, operating until 1955. (Author's collection)

Passengers hurry aboard St. Louis-built multi-section unit No. 7004, the first production-model vehicle of a design pioneered by the two 1934 experimentals. The year is 1936 and the location is the BMT's Rockaway Parkway station in Canarsie. (NYCTA)

stations that were opened in 1931 were finished off in the same style of color-coded tile work that was used on the Independent.

The BMT opened its maintenance facility in Coney Island during Walker's administration, thereby cementing a long relationship between the Brooklyn traction company and the seaside resort. Before the turn of the century Brooklyn transit lines had converged on Coney Island. By building the principal repair facilities of the system within a mile of the ocean, the company retained its historic identity with the area.

The BMT's Stillwell Avenue terminal, which replaced the older Culver Depot and the West End Depot in 1919, and which is served by four different subway lines, stands but a stone's throw from the ocean in the middle of the Coney Island amusement area. The eight-track Stillwell Avenue facility— replete with popcorn and saltwater taffy stands—is today perhaps the busiest rail passenger terminal in the country, with almost a thousand departures and arrivals daily.[4]

In the 1930s, the BMT again earned high marks for equipment development. In 1934 the company took delivery of two radical pieces of rolling stock. One was built by Pullman-Standard and equipped with Westinghouse electrical components; the other was turned out by the Budd Company of Philadelphia, with electrical gear by General Electric. Both the Budd train and its Pullman running mate were five-unit articulateds designed to be sufficiently light in weight to operate on elevated lines where standard steel subway cars were prohibited. The Budd unit met this challenge by using stainless steel for its body shell, while the Pullman product was built of aluminum. The Budd train was unofficially called *Zephyr* because it resembled the Budd-built *Zephyr* streamliners of the Chicago, Burlington & Quincy Railroad, while the Pullman train, with its two-tone green color scheme, was dubbed the *Green Hornet,* after a popular radio character of the day. Both units measured 170 feet in overall length, roughly the equivalent of two-and-a-half Standard cars. Their newly designed mechanical and electrical gear gave them swift acceleration rates.

These experimentals were put through a series of convincing demonstrations on the Fulton Street el. They featured modern and comfortable appointments which the riding public found quite pleasant. Both were equipped with indirect lighting, quite the vogue at the time, and the *Green Hornet* had a system of chimes that sounded when the doors were operated. The Budd train had a relatively long service life, running chiefly on the Franklin Avenue shuttle when its demonstration days were over. It was not scrapped until 1959, and ran as late as 1954. But the *Green Hornet's* aluminum body was just what the scrap drive needed, and in 1942 it "went to war." The government's requisition of the train was done with such secrecy that many BMT workers had no idea what happened to the unit. Only a postwar announcement by Mayor La Guardia's office dispelled some imaginative rumors. One romantic tale had the train running through a secretly built tunnel under the English Channel ferrying counterspies into France and bringing rescued bomber crews back to England!

The major innovation pioneered by the two new trains was operational. Their metal construction fitted them to run in the subway; their light weight allowed them to run on els. Previously only lightweight wooden cars could navigate the older els. Steel subway equipment was too heavy for such lines, and the law prohibited wooden equipment from carrying passengers underground.

All of this raises an interesting point—more semantics than engineering—the difference between a genuine el and a rapid transit line that happens to be built on an elevated structure. In the late 1960s, for instance, the Myrtle Avenue el was referred to as the city's "last el." Yet a score or more of avenues all over town had—and still have—extensive overhead transit lines, operating on what certainly *look* like els.

In New York a bona fide el is best described as an elevated line dating back to pre-subway days that is not operated as an extension of the underground system. The distinction quickly looses clarity, though, because New Yorkers tend to call any elevated line an el, even those that were built as subway extensions during the Dual Contracts program. Then too, many of

*Running on the 14th Street-Canarsie line, a train of two five-section articulated units drifts into Broadway Junction in the East New York section of Brooklyn. The geometry of a complex elevated network is quite apparent in this photo. (NYCTA)*

these Dual Contracts elevated lines were rebuilt from older, genuine els. To confuse matters more, on some of these rebuilt elevated lines wooden el trains and steel subway trains operated in joint service.

Despite the eminent demise of the downtown segments of the Fifth Avenue complex and the Fulton Street line—routes no longer needed with the opening of the municipal subway—the BMT felt there was ample call for equipment such as the Budd train and the *Green Hornet.* The Myrtle Avenue el, for example, seemed to have a definite future, and the Transit Commission, which had a hand in the experiments, was anxious to work up a design for lightweight equipment on the off chance that the Manhattan els might somehow be given a reprieve and thus need new rolling stock.

The BMT soon ordered a fleet of production-model units with specifications similar to the two experimentals. Twenty-five of the five-section articulateds, called multi-section cars, were delivered in 1936. They provided base service on the 14th Street line for a number of years, and capitalized on their light-weight design by operating out to Richmond Hill over a section of the Fulton Street el where orthodox steel subway cars could never run. The "multis" became a non-standard item on the subway roster once the elevated lines were phased out after World War II. They were scrapped in 1960.

### Good-by, Sixth Avenue El; Hello, World's Fair

The IRT was not in sound health through the 1930s. It performed its daily tasks; nevertheless, the line could not shake off receivership. It was definitely a poor sister of BMT and the spanking-new Independent. In anticipation of the forthcoming municipal subway for the same route, IRT's Sixth Avenue el departed the New York scene on December 4, 1938. Through a deal which was heavily criticized later, its steel work was sold as scrap to interests in Japan. The IRT did manage to design and order a new subway car

*Only once did the Interborough order rolling stock that differed essentially from the car body design the company adopted in 1902. That was a 50-car order for service to the 1939-40 World's Fair. Here five of the units are shown at the plant of St. Louis Car Company prior to shipment east. (GSI-St. Louis)*

for service on the Flushing line out to the 1939–40 World's Fair, the line's first new equipment since 1925. Although it was the first IRT car without end vestibules, it was not an outstanding vehicle because it was designed to mate with some of the line's oldest equipment. The "World's Fair cars" followed the Interborough tradition of old-fashioned metal plates for car interior route and destination signs, years after cloth roller signs had become standard practice in the traction industry. They did have illuminated roll signs on the car ends, however.

Although built to the IRT's narrower specifications, both Flushing and Astoria lines were operated jointly by the BMT and IRT as specified in the Dual Contracts. The BMT could not, of course, use its ten-foot wide steel subway cars on these lines. It instead maintained its half of the service with open-platform elevated type cars, built in 1907, which were compatible with IRT standards. As the World's Fair approached, the BMT was in a quandry about equipment. It could not justify the expense of newly designing a car which could only be used on the Flushing and Astoria routes. Yet it was not content to use outdated el equipment in blue-ribbon World's Fair service. The dilemma was solved by rebuilding older open-platform el cars—at the Coney Island shops—into closed vehicles that became known as the "Q units." (The Q stood for Queens.) These typically sound BMT products were designed under the supervision of William Gove, a man whose name deserves to be enshrined in the very highest ranks of a railroad hall of fame, were one to be established. Painted in World's Fair colors of blue and orange, the cars were as snappy looking a fleet of transit vehicles as ever hauled passengers in New York. The Q units would also go on to chalk up many additional distinctions over their remaining thirty years of service.

Like the private companies, the new Independent also operated to the 1939–1940 World's Fair. Trains from the Queens line ran through the Kew Gardens storage yards, then into the fair grounds over a specially built line that was torn up after the fair closed. Today this right-of-way forms part of the Van Wyck Expressway.

*Notes to Chapter 9*

[1] Until it was rebuilt in the 1970's, one could manage a fleeting glimpse of the action at Yankee Stadium from passing IRT trains. Also, the 161st Street station was one of the last sites on the entire system where pre-turnstile ticket choppers were employed. As late as 1948 arriving fans were encouraged by megaphone to purchase a ticket for the trip home. Use of the long outmoded system eased congestion at game's end, although regular turnstiles handled day-to-day traffic.

[2] These figures were valid when the Independent was new. New signals and new rolling stock have improved BMT and IRT performance.

[3] Purists could fault this statement, since the actual terminal used in 1908 later became a trolley car facility, and the route of the Centre Street subway line was laid out to the north of the original underground station.

[4] Although it may be the busiest *terminal* in the country, it is not the busiest *station* in New York. That honor belongs to the West 4th Street subway station in Manhattan, where more than a thousand movements pass (but do not terminate) every twenty-four hours.

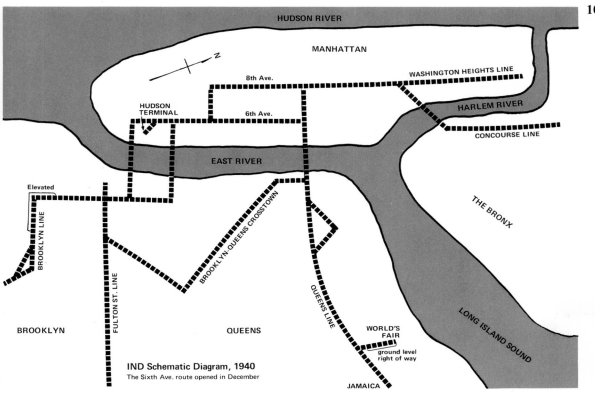

HUDSON RIVER

MANHATTAN

8th Ave.

WASHINGTON HEIGHTS LINE

HUDSON TERMINAL

6th Ave.

HARLEM RIVER

CONCOURSE LINE

EAST RIVER

THE BRONX

Elevated

BROOKLYN LINE

FULTON ST. LINE

BROOKLYN-QUEENS CROSSTOWN

QUEENS LINE

LONG ISLAND SOUND

WORLD'S FAIR

ground level right of way

BROOKLYN

QUEENS

**IND Schematic Diagram, 1940**
The Sixth Ave. route opened in December

JAMAICA

*A four-car train of R units heads for Manhattan on a special right-of-way that was constructed to serve the 1939-40 World's Fair. (NYCTA)*

# 10 Unification: the Board of Transportation

THERE IS A RECURRING PATTERN in the story of the New York subways; each decade appears to have been dominated by a single theme. In the century's first decade, the prime item was the building of the city's first subway. From 1910 through 1920 the Dual Contracts provided the focus of interest. In the 1920s it was Hylan's drive for a municipal subway. During the 'thirties, the theme was "unification."

The fiscal picture in the 1930s was especially cloudy. Thus money problems served as the principal spur toward unification. From the time the Dual Contracts lines were in full operation—officially 1919 for the IRT, 1920 for the BRT, even though several links in both systems were incomplete—through the La Guardia years, the city only collected 19 million dollars from the IRT to service its Dual Contracts debt. No money was ever received from the BRT or the BMT. To avoid default on its Dual Contracts bonds, the city had been forced to divert 183 million dollars from general revenues over this period. Theoretically, turnstile receipts were to have been the source of this money and the city should have been free from any liability. Because of a general deterioration of the Dual Contracts vision money had to be raised from other sources, since the notes were backed by the city's credit.

As each of the two subway operators slid into receivership during this period, some degree of unification appeared to be highly desirable. Moreover, while the city juggled its accounts to raise 183 million unanticipated dollars, the two traction firms were able to post profits, in varying years, amounting to some 91 million dollars. Such revelations, naturally, provided fuel for arguments on behalf of total public operation of the subways.

Although early talk of unification did not necessarily envision complete public operation of the subway system, gradually it became obvious that such was the only plausible alternative. Substitution of low interest, tax exempt, municipal bonds for the outstanding BMT and IRT private notes, coupled with the replacement of three operating agencies by one, were felt to be the central features of any workable unification plan.

Another item bearing on unification and subway finances was that after reaching slightly over 2 billion annual riders in 1930, the number of passengers using the subway began to fall off in 1931—a full year before the Independent Subway opened for business.

Samuel Untermyer's final unification plan never cleared the Board of Estimate; therefore La Guardia felt a fresh start was needed. The mayor appointed

Adolph Berle and Judge Samuel Seabury[1] to deal with the transit companies. In 1935 both the BMT and IRT signed "memoranda of understanding" for transit unification under municipal ownership according to what became known as the Seabury-Berle plan.

After protracted deliberations the Transit Commission rejected the plan in the Spring of 1937.[2] Many suspected the Democratic members of the commission were anxious to embarrass the La Guardia administration. Whatever the reason, the commission's action served to cool enthusiasm for transit unification on all fronts for more than a year. But in May 1938, transit conditions were still critical and La Guardia and the Transit Commission decided to ignore past differences and work together for unification. An amendment passed by the legislature was ratified by the state's voters in November 1938. This exempted 315 million dollars from the city's debt ceiling. With funds thus earmarked for buying out BMT and IRT, negotiators were able to approach their task with enthusiasm.

### The Old Order Passeth

Full and final unification was eventually achieved in 1940. On Saturday, June 1st, with the British Expeditionary Force being hastily evacuated from Dunkerque, a ceremony was held at City Hall. Some 175 million dollars in three per cent municipal bonds was given to the BMT in exchange for the company's tangible assets. The previous evening, as part of a separate but concurrent deal, service was terminated on the downtown portion of the BMT Fulton Street el and on the entire Fifth Avenue line. These structures were then purchased by the city for removal. Money to buy the el lines— a transaction apart from the 175 million dollars—was principally raised by assessing property owners along the el routes for the betterment that their removal would bring about.

The final Fulton Street el train left Park Row for the trip over the Brooklyn Bridge shortly after 11 P.M. on Friday, May 31st, with Mayor La Guardia aboard. As it pulled out of each stop in Brooklyn for the last time, the station lights were extinguished in a moving gesture to dramatize the passing of an old order. The outer leg of the Fulton Street line, from East New York to Richmond Hill, yet remained in service, as did the tracks on the Brooklyn Bridge, which were used by the BMT's Myrtle Avenue el.

The next night another ceremony was held. Seventy-one year old Joseph McCann, who was retiring as a BMT motorman, commanded a train of BMT Standards from the 57th Street Manhattan terminal to the Times Square station. When he arrived, both McCann and the BMT had made their last run. The platform was awash with dignitaries and reporters, because at exactly 12:01 A.M. on Sunday, June 2, 1940, the Brooklyn-Manhattan Transit Corporation formally, officially and irrevocably surrendered its properties to the city as specified in the terms of the agreement signed at City Hall several hours before. BMT president William S. Menden spoke first and presented La Guardia with the keys, as it were, to the system. It was fitting that Menden be the corporate officer who presided at the line's obsequies. Years earlier as a young and promising engineer heading up the BRT's design section, it was Menden who helped perfect plans for the Standard subway car. If anything typified the BRT and the BMT it was this fine piece of equipment.

La Guardia turned to John Delaney, whose Board of Transportation now controlled the BMT, and said, "I hereby entrust these properties and the safety of millions of passengers to you. I know you will do a good job."

Delaney then appointed La Guardia a motorman—with badge No. 1—and ordered His Honor to take out the train McCann had just brought in from 57th Street. As flashbulbs exploded, the mayor donned a motorman's jacket and hat, took hold of a special set of chrome-plated control handles, and posed for a picture in the cab of a freshly painted train. When it came time actually to run the first city-operated subway train on what had just become the BMT Division of the city's Board of Transportation, La Guardia deferred to a regular motorman.

A week and a half later, on Wednesday, June 12, 1940, ceremonies were again held at City Hall. Backed by an issue of 151 million dollars in municipal obligations, the properties of the IRT were purchased by the city. Thomas E. Murray, the Interborough's receiver, gave the mayor the company's copy of Contract Number Three, the IRT's Dual System Pact, a contract that would soon cease to be the operating mandate for the system. At 12:01 A.M. next morning—June 13th, the day Nazi troops would march into Paris—the Interborough Rapid Transit Company, after thirty-eight years, unceremoniously became the IRT Division of the Board of Transportation. As in the sale of the BMT, most of the Second Avenue el and all of the Ninth were abandoned, and their structures deeded over to the city for dismantling. Of the original four elevated lines, only the Third Avenue line remained in full operation. It survived for another fifteen years. Its abandonment was not sought in 1940 on the theory that the el would be needed until a proposed Second Avenue subway was completed.

Labor difficulties almost derailed the whole unification process. By 1940 Mike Quill had emerged as the prime spokesman for the transit workers; his Transport Workers Union (TWU) enjoyed union shop status with both the BMT and the IRT. Quill himself had become a colorful and controversial character on the New York scene in the late 1930s, and his distinctive Irish brogue was often heard on the air waves. He was called "Red Mike"—again the nickname appears in the subway saga!—but not because of the color of his hair. Quill was a vocal apologist for all manner of left-wing political causes, regularly espoused pro-Soviet sentiments, and carried a Communist

Party card.[3] His appearance before Congressman Martin Dies' House Committee on un-American Activities in May 1940, for example, was a tumultuous scene that resulted in his ejection from the hearing room. Quill also had a magnificent forum at his disposal—he called it his "soapbox"—for, until the 1939 election put him out of office, Michael J. Quill was a bona fide member of the potent New York City Council.

Although La Guardia had been an early ally of Quill, he saw subway unification as a means of breaking Mike's hold on BMT and IRT. Consequently the mayor suggested that after unification the 13,000 BMT and 15,000 IRT employees who would be absorbed into the civil service system thenceforth work under an open shop policy.

Quill would have none of this. "We won our freedom through the closed shop," he maintained, "and we aren't going to give it up." With an ominous strike threatened, John L. Lewis, then president of TWU's parent organization, the CIO, was engaged to mediate the dispute between Mike and the mayor. "Mediate" he did. The closed shop was retained, and shortly after unification, the TWU expanded into the ranks of the independent.

### REPRIEVE FOR THE NICKEL RIDE

Unification brought few immediate or visible results. The Independent System became known as the IND Division of the larger complex. Another experimental train which the BMT had ordered from the Clark Railway Equipment Corporation was delivered to the Board of Transportation in late 1940.[4] However, the three divisions in general retained their pre-unification character and identity until well into the postwar period. The war itself brought a swinging increase in riders, taxing the system to its utmost, reversing the downward trend in patronage that had begun during the Depression. And for the first time since World War I the five-cent fare was not in danger.

One capital improvement was the purchase of a four-mile segment of a former electrified railway in the Bronx, the New York, Westchester & Boston. This was a suburban line which ran from the east bank of the Harlem River to Port Chester and White Plains. Despite its name, the line never came within 150 miles of Boston. In December 1937 the entire line was abandoned, a victim of the Depression, increased automobile travel, and its own lack of a mid-Manhattan terminal. (In postwar years, when Westchester County became a genuine boom territory, NY, W&B was sorely missed.)

On May 1, 1940, the city assumed title to the old right-of-way that was located within city limits. Shuttle service was instituted on May 15, 1941, using refurbished open-gate el cars. In the mid-1950s the line was tied into the IRT subway network, and is now known as the Dyre Avenue line. Something of an oddity is that when the service was initially taken over by the

*A Lexington Avenue express heads for Dyre Avenue along a right-of-way that once belonged to the ill-fated New York, Westchester & Boston Railway. (Tom Nelligan photo)*

city in 1941, although it *looked* like a component of the IRT Division, it was administered as part of the IND and operated by IND personnel.

But it was the war that affected other desirable developments. Even minor construction projects, such as the completion of a few IND routes that were only months away from being finished, had to sit idle until after VJ Day. What did happen during the war, though, were a couple of interesting abandonments. The final leg of the Second Avenue el, which ran from South Ferry to East 59th Street and then over the Queensboro Bridge to Queens Plaza, was phased out in 1941. The BMT's Myrtle Avenue el, damaged by

*The distinctive outline of a BMT Triplex is visible despite the snow that's swirling across the "subway" in this scene on an open-air portion of the Brighton line. (Author photo)*

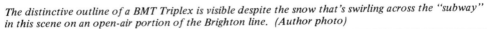

fire, was cut back from Park Row in Manhattan to Jay Street and Myrtle Avenue in Brooklyn. These are the only times rapid transit crossings of the East River were ever eliminated. Removal of IRT tracks from the Queensboro Bridge served to isolate the Flushing and Astoria lines from the rest of the IRT; the BMT's Coney Island Shops then became the major site for repairing the equipment of these two IRT lines.

Brooklyn Bridge el service had been the city's very first electrified rapid transit, dating back to 1896 when the original cable cars were supplemented by electric equipment. With the cutback to Jay Street, the famous old Sands Street station at the Brooklyn end of the bridge passed from the scene. In the days before the Brooklyn els were electrified, Sands Street served as a union depot for steam powered trains of several companies from all over the western end of Long Island.[5]

Transit unification was established as war broke out over Europe. Two companies, long on heritage if short in years, had participated as best they could through forty years of unbelievable growth and development in New York City. Although unification under municipal aegis eventually became an economic necessity, the very construction and operation of subway lines in New York in the first quarter of the 20th century would not have been possible without the Dual Contracts partners. Their status as profit-seeking corporations was a liability in 1940; it had been salvation in 1913!

*Here, in 1972, we see four R-12 units approaching Gun Hill Road in the Bronx over the then sole surviving section of the venerable Third Avenue el, the rest of which had been taken down some seventeen years earlier. (Tom Nelligan photo)*

*Notes to Chapter 10*

[1] Seabury was the man who conducted the hearings that brought on Walker's downfall.

[2] Thundered La Guardia: "The Transit Commission has been stalling on this problem for sixteen years at a cost to the public of 16 million dollars in salaries."

[3] A story still told among TWU old-timers claims that Quill joined the Communist Party not because of any strong ideological conviction, but rather because the Communists were willing to rent his fledgling union a meeting room from time to time.

[4] A novel, three-section articulated design based on the then new PCC streetcar, and many of the innovations it pioneered.

[5] To this day, railway buffs will stoutly argue as to whether Sands Street, Park Row, or possibly South Ferry was *the* place to watch el trains in action in New York. See illustration, page 46.

*Above left: From the time the first trains rolled, track walkers have patrolled the subway right-of-way, inspecting rails, signals and other vital components of the plant. Here a man gives a rail joint a close look before continuing his trek. Right: After the commuters have gone home, TA crews get to work cleaning the city's vast transit network. Here a mechanized vacuum device sucks up trash at the 145th Street station, where IRT's first opening-day train terminated back in 1904. (Both photos, NYCTA)*

## CURB YOUR OCELOT

Every so often, newspapers carry an off-beat story about some strange animal that has been collared while running through a subway tunnel. Dogs and cats rarely rate a mention anymore; it has to be something exotic like an ocelot, or an orangutan, or a dozen rare finches. Where they come from often remains a mystery, since ownership of certain species is prohibited by law and reclaiming one's pet could result in a brush with the authorities. When an explanation is provided, it is usually reasonable enough—a snake being taken to the veterinarian manages to slither out of its carrier, for example. Rumors persist, although the TA regularly denies them, that all the lost animals have not been recaptured and strange beasts survive in the tunnels and adjoining caverns. The stories go on to recount mutations that have taken place over the years as the animals adapt to their new environment.

One animal does genuinely thrive in the subway—the rat. Even here fact and fancy are difficult to separate. Stories are told of rodents the size of cocker spaniels whose ferocity is enough to terrorize the most fearless trackwalker. The trackwalkers, reportedly, had grave misgivings about resuming their duties after a two-week strike in 1966.

Several years ago an off-duty policeman, en route home on the Culver route in Brooklyn, was attacked by a real, live penguin. The officer gathered his wits and subdued his assailant, and the wayward bird was eventually returned to its home in the Coney Island Aquarium, but not before five police cars came racing up to the 18th Avenue station, sirens screaming, in response to an "officer in distress" call.

# 11 Enter the TA

THE END OF THE WAR brought back many chronic transit maladies that had been obscured by the extraordinary press of wartime traffic. Inflationary pressures at last doomed the nickel ride. On July 1, 1947, the Board of Transportation raised the tariff to ten cents. With the 100 per cent rise in fare, many additional free transfer points were established between the three divisions. Wherever practical, barriers were torn down so that passengers could pass unhindered between BMT, IRT and IND. "IRT sheep mingled today with BMT goats," quipped the *Daily News*.

Equipment was in very short supply all over the sprawling system at war's end. The first postwar cars specifically designed for service over either BMT or IND were ordered in 1946. Designated the R-10 units, 400 of them were turned out by American Car and Foundry in 1948 and 1949. These vehicles were built to the same external dimension as the prewar IND cars, but featured improved interiors and more modern electrical equipment developed during experiments on a standard R-9 at the IND's 207th Street shops.[1]

The R-10 cost more than $77,000 per car, a barometer of the way rapid transit expenses were reflecting post-war economic conditions. The newcomers were assigned to service on the IND "A" line, where they remained for years. Their arrival allowed the transfer of some older R-1 cars to help ease the situation on the BMT. Their usual assignment was the Fourth Avenue local route.

Scaled down versions of the R-10—the R-12 and the R-14—were ordered at the same time for the narrower confines of the IRT and placed in service on the Flushing line, easing a critical shortage of equipment on the city's oldest division. A different looking car, the R-15, appeared in Flushing service in 1950. This unit had a rounded "turtle back" roof, a new ventilation system, and other features that would become standard on all new subway cars in New York over the next two decades.

The new IRT cars were assigned solely to the Flushing line, and not to the basic Manhattan routes of the old Interborough, because the upper Broadway line and the lower Lexington Avenue line (the original Contract One route) were oriented on the vestibuled body style of August Belmont's basic car. New equipment, with a different door arrangement, could not travel these older routes unless considerable re-engineering work was done. The platform gap-fillers, for instance, installed at several stations built on curves, would not function at all with cars of a different design.

A dramatic service improvement took place in Fall 1949 when the Dual Contracts arrangement of joint BMT-IRT service on the Flushing and Astoria lines was eliminated. The Flushing line with its new cars became the exclusive responsibility of the IRT, while the Astoria route had its platforms shaved back to take care of operation as an extension of the BMT's regular subway service. Routes through the eight-track Queens Plaza station were consolidated, and half the sprawling structure was afterward torn down.

The Q units, designed for BMT service to the 1939–40 World's Fair, became surplus property. Because they had been rebuilt in 1938, they were too valuable to scrap at a time when equipment was at a premium. They were transferred to the Third Avenue el. However, they proved to be too heavy for service there. Although the Qs were originally el cars themselves, rebuilding had upped their gross tonnage to more than the spindly el could handle. The solution? Discard the Q's BMT trucks and remount their bodies on lighter running gear made available when the old IRT Composites were retired. Thus equipped, the final series of cars designed for BMT began running on the last Manhattan Railway elevated line. One observation must be added: Even with lighter trucks, the Q's were still heavyweight units authorized to carry passengers only while running on the center, or express, track of the three-track Third Avenue el. They had to deadhead in one direction, and operated only during rush hour. Base service on the Third Avenue line was provided by a fleet of so-called multiple-unit door control (M.U.D.C.) cars—standard el cars whose open platforms had been hastily enclosed and equipped with remote controlled sliding doors. During the Hylan era bitter court battles had been waged between the Interborough and the city as each side tried to get the other party to foot the million-dollar bill for improvements.

*At the site of what is today Lincoln Center, trains on the Sixth and Ninth Avenue els promenade for the camera. The station is one of the upper level express stops added to former two-track lines as part of the Dual Contracts. Topmost train consists of open-platform el cars, while the local down below is made up of M.U.D.C. cars which were once open-platform vehicles themselves. (NYCTA)*

The Third Avenue el was gradually reduced in size during post-war years.
Finally, on May 12, 1955, the line ran its very last train, and the colorful
history of the Manhattan els came to an end.

Of course, a few qualifications are necessary in any absolute statement
about New York transit matters! A six-mile leg of the Third Avenue el of
the Bronx survived until 1973, and a miniscule segment of the Ninth Avenue
el actually survived longer than the Manhattan portion of the Third Avenue
el. When the Ninth Avenue el was abandoned in 1940 a section less than a
mile long, from 155th Street and the Harlem River to a junction with the
Jerome Avenue line in the Bronx, remained in service. This shuttle served the
Polo Grounds and the New York Central's Putnam Division terminal at
Sedgewick Avenue. After the New York Giants moved to San Francisco
following the 1957 season and the railroad gave up passenger service on the
"Put" in 1958, the shuttle was phased out. It was not around, unfortunately,
when the New York Mets came into existence in 1962 and made the Polo
Grounds their home for two baseball seasons.[2]

## Post-war Subway Ailments

Returning to the immediate postwar years, the Board of Transportation
was simply not working out as the instrument of subway governance. Master
plans were forever, it seemed, being issued; construction of new high-speed
lines was always in the news. Somehow a daily straphanger could not appre-
ciate reading about a glorious subway future when he was stalled in a cold
and dirty train and delayed by some unexplained mechanical failure. Even
the more modest goals envisioned by proponents of subway unification in
1940 were largely unachieved by 1950, and the Board of Transportation was
overseeing three subway divisions that were unified more in name than in actuality. Meanwhile increasing numbers of riders took advantage of the high-
ways built after the war for travel to and from work in private automobiles.
As a result, subway service and conditions began to deteriorate in the late
1940s. Labor relations went from bad to worse; the annual operating deficit
of the system continued to soar (despite the 1947 fare increase); lack of
money resulted in a backlog of deferred maintenance. With only insufficient
and undependable equipment available, service became deplorable.

The attempted solution to the city's postwar transit ills was a new operating agency, the New York City Transit Authority. Created by state legislation, the TA assumed jurisdiction on June 15, 1953, and remained in sole
charge of things until March 1, 1968, when it was absorbed into the larger
and more comprehensive Metropolitan Transportation Authority, the MTA.

Essentially the TA was responsible only for the operation of the still city-
owned transit plant. Income and outgo of cash had to be balanced, although
the new agency was not responsible for securing funds for capital improve-

ments such as new line construction and the purchase of subway cars. Such improvements were to be financed by other monies, chiefly municipal bonds which were exempt from the city's constitutional borrowing limit. (An important although unspectacular piece of legislation was passed in 1962, an amendment to the State Public Authorities Act, which permitted the TA to sell its own revenue bonds, up to 92 million dollars worth, for the purchase of new rolling stock.)

At the heart of the power structure of the Transit Authority was an unsalaried five-man board. Two members were appointed by the governor, and two were appointed by the mayor. Together these four members chose the fifth. The entire board then selected its own chairman. In 1955 a three-man salaried panel replaced the original five-man board.

When the TA assumed control, political hay was pitched in every possible direction as spokesmen for the downtrodden arose to defend the ten-cent fare—for an agency bound by law to avoid deficit operations would inevitably have to raise the fare to at least fifteen cents. On July 25, 1953, that is precisely what happened and a small brass turnstile token became the new medium of exchange. A problem arose after the token fare was instituted: A German coin, worth but a few pennies, as well as several kinds of play money available in any dime store, could actuate the turnstiles. After the TA increased the sensitivity of its mechanical coin collectors—at least, it *claimed* to have done so—the problem subsided. One man profited from the new fare, Manhattan Borough President Robert F. Wagner Jr. Entering the 1953 Democratic primary race for mayor, Wagner adopted the slogan "New York deserves more than a token mayor." On January 1, 1954, he was sworn in as the city's chief executive.

Much of the TA's early success—and there was quite a bit of it—must be attributed to things begun by the old Board of Transportation. At noontime on a rainy Saturday, October 30, 1954, a train of IND prewar R units operating on the D train out of the Bronx emerged from a tunnel portal in the middle of Brooklyn's McDonald Avenue. It ran all the way to Stillwell Avenue Terminal over tracks that up until that morning were the BMT's Culver line. Thus, sixteen months into the TA era, John Hylan's goal of through service from the Bronx to Coney Island was fulfilled, although unification made recapture of the BMT by the IND unnecessary. The BMT Division simply ceased operations on the Culver between Coney Island and Ditmas Avenue. BMT trains continued to operate on a small elevated remnant of the Culver between Ditmas and a connection with the West End at Ninth Avenue. In 1975, even this 1.1-mile leg was abandoned outright.

IND cars used on the Culver line had been confined to underground tunnel routes for their entire previous service life, except for a short viaduct over Brooklyn's Gowanus Canal and two summers of service to the 1939–40

*When the Independent was extended to Coney Island over the former BMT Culver line, Stillwell Avenue terminal saw some strange bedfellows. Above, a BMT Standard on the Brighton local stands next to an arriving train of R units on IND's D train. (Author photo)*

World's Fair. When faced with the outdoor adversities of rain and snow on the Culver's elevated structure, they had to be equipped with a device never before needed—windshield wipers on the motorman's cab.

Thirteen months later, on December 1, 1955, a connecting tunnel was opened in Long Island City connecting the BMT's 60th Street tube under the East River and the IND Queens Plaza station, permitting BMT trains to operate over the IND to Forest Hills. For the first time, the compatible rolling stock of the two divisions shared common trackage. Trains of BMT Standards began running on John Hylan's municipal subway, intermixed with trains of IND R units.

### THE CITY BUYS PART OF A RAIL ROAD

A major transit extension was mapped out by the TA in the late 1950s when the city acquired title to the Long Island Rail Road's Rockaway line. A long trestle over Jamaica Bay on this route often caught fire. After an especially destructive blaze on May 8, 1950, the hard-pressed and bankrupt commuter railroad was thankful to negotiate the line's sale. On June 11, 1953, for 8.5 million dollars, the City of New York bought itself a railroad. Extensive rebuilding included sand fills in lieu of the fire-prone trestles. On June 28, 1956, subway service was extended to the Rockaways. The new line stretched more than eleven miles, making it one of the longest chunks of new subway ever to open for service at one time. The line's price tag—purchase price plus rebuilding—was 56 million dollars. Perhaps the most startling feature of the Rockaway line was that it opened for business precisely on its target date, a first for a New York transit line.[3]

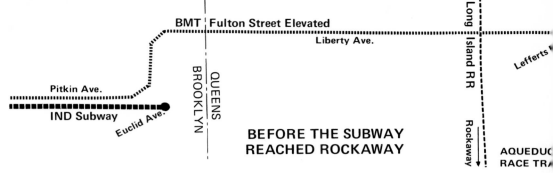

**BEFORE THE SUBWAY
REACHED ROCKAWAY**

The double fare charged on the Rockaway line was a departure from long standing practice. Not since the days prior to the Dual Contracts, when BRT trains to Coney Island required a double fare, had more than a single payment been necessary on the subway. The double fare lasted from 1956 until 1975 when it was lifted with the introduction of the fifty-cent subway fare. (But a "premium fare" was instituted on the Rockaway line in 1978.)

Before IND trains could begin service across Jamaica Bay, several other improvements and adjustments were necessary. The Fulton Street IND line was opened from East New York to Euclid Avenue in November 1948. (This link in the municipal subway was almost complete before the war, but not quite.) Early in 1956, the IND was again extended—this time from the Euclid Avenue terminal out over the elevated structure on the eastern end of the BMT's Fulton Street el, the second invasion of BMT territory by the Independent. The eastern end of the el had been rebuilt to heavy-duty standards at the time of the Dual Contracts in anticipation of construction of an Ashland Place connection, which never happened. Prior to 1956 this rebuilt section of el could only be reached over an older and lightly constructed segment of the Fulton Street el. Consequently it was served by BMT C-type el cars, and the 1936 BMT multi-section articulated units. The extension over the Fulton Street el by the IND gave it access to the LIRR's Rockaway line.

After a connecting ramp was built at Liberty Avenue near Woodhaven Boulevard, subway trains began operating to stations with such breezy names as Wavecrest, Seaside and Rockaway Park. Yet the historian must clear his throat—ahem!—when boldly claiming "novelty" for the Rockaway line. From July 1898 until 1917—fifty-eight years before the IND arrived—BRT el trains were operating to the Rockaways over the same trestle that the TA rebuilt in 1956, and through trains ran from Manhattan to the seashore under a joint BRT–LIRR arrangement. One connection between the two lines was at Chestnut Street on the Broadway-Brooklyn el, and the other was at Flatbush and Atlantic avenues. At both locations, structural evidence of the connections can still be seen.[4]

The Rockaway line enabled the TA to provide direct subway service to one of New York's race tracks, Aqueduct Park, the first station on the new line. Extra-fare premiere service is provided, in season, for improvers of the breed. An oddity of the Rockaway line is that it appeared, in 1956, to be an expansion and extension of the IND Division. In actuality it was supervised and operated as the TA's *fourth* subway division. Through trains from Manhattan to Rockaway, for example, changed crews at Euclid Avenue in a manner not unlike a railroad division point in the middle of Kansas or Nebraska.

What surely must be considered the TA's most important expansion was completed on November 26, 1967, when the Chrystie Street connection opened.[5] This project affected service on nearly every BMT and IND line in the city. Indeed following the service changes brought about by Chrystie Street, the separate identities of the BMT and IND divisions—and the Rockaway Division—vanished.

The connection itself is but a short tunnel in downtown Manhattan, but it allows BMT trains off the Manhattan Bridge to operate into the IND's Sixth Avenue trunk line, a route that was upgraded from two to four track capacity as part of the same project. BMT trains from the Williamsburg Bridge were also given access to the Sixth Avenue line, and a rebuilding of the BMT's complex DeKalb Avenue-Gold Street interlocking plant in 1958 greatly increased the capacity of the Manhattan Bridge and improved operational flexibility.[6]

The first twenty-four hours of business on the Chrystie Street link were chaotic. With the new line came new schedules and operating practices, and it often seemed that no two TA employees were following the same timetable. Every trip that day was an adventure into the unknown. Not even the motormen knew for sure where any train would wind up. The newspapers were filled with stories of misplaced persons who found themselves on the Grand Concourse when they were trying to get to Kew Gardens, and in Coney Island when they were headed for Harlem.

In essence, the Chrystie Street connection completed the unification process that was begun in 1940. Following November 1967, the TA even tried

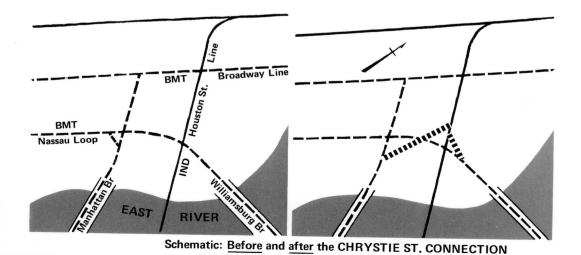

Schematic: <u>Before</u> and <u>after</u> the CHRYSTIE ST. CONNECTION

to discourage public reference to the BMT, IRT and IND. The former IRT lines were to be called the A Division, and the joint BMT-IND routes constituted the B Division. Happily the effort was a failure, and the more traditional nomenclature has been allowed to resurface.

Trains on the combined BMT-IND network are now identified by letter code, essentially an expansion of the original IND notation, while the IRT uses a number system. In more recent years a color code has been developed to work in conjunction with the letters and numbers to identify the various routes and lines. The newest BMT-IND subway cars have abandoned destination signs on the head end. In their place is a huge letter code, brightly illuminated in the color of the route on which the train is operating.

This new system of subway identification took a heavy toll from the BMT's colorful and historic names and destinations. Many claim the integration effectively absorbed the BMT into the IND. Such old titles as Sea Beach Express and West End Local are no longer in official use, and trains that once bore the name Brighton Express now read "D–Avenue of the Americas Express" on their roll signs. But just as New Yorkers stubbornly resist calling Sixth Avenue by the name it has officially borne since the La Guardia years, people in Brooklyn still use the old BMT titles.

### The "TA Look" Under the Sidewalks of New York

By the late 1960s the TA had moved forward and turned what had been three separate subway systems into a smoothly functioning unit. Nowhere was the TA's work more evident than in the cars that run in the subway. Prior to the TA takeover, there was no long range car replacement policy. Many IRT units had been in daily service for fifty years, and in 1955 the oldest of the BMT Standards celebrated their fortieth anniversary.

*A train of new R-16 units made the first trip over the Rockaway line on June 28, 1956. Here a ribbon cutting ceremony makes it all official. (NYCTA)*

*Spanking new (A.C.F. 1948-49) R-10 interior. Note the small roll signs and ceiling fans; air-conditioning is an idea whose time has not yet come, for the subway, that is. (NYCTA)*

In 1953 the TA ordered its first rolling stock—200 BMT-IND cars designated the R-16 units. They were assigned to the BMT's Broadway-Brooklyn line, freeing other rolling stock for the opening of the Rockaway line, as well as several routes operating without enough equipment. Prior to 1954 the BMT was forced to rely on units such as old el cars to serve outlying stations on the Culver and West End lines during rush hour, because of the shortage of steel subway cars. Trains from Manhattan terminated at places such as Bay Parkway and Kings Highway, and older wooden cars ran in shuttle service beyond-to Coney Island, a picturesque though inefficient arrangement.

The first R-16, painted in a glossy coat of olive green paint and bearing the number 6400, arrived from the American Car and Foundry Company on October 21, 1954, just in time to participate in a low-key ceremony marking the fiftieth anniversary of the New York subways. The newcomer was displayed on the lower level of the City Hall BMT station together with an IRT car that had been in operation for half a century, No. 3453, one of the first all-steel Gibbs cars.

As an indication of how costs were soaring, the R-16 units cost the TA $121,441.11 each. Basic R-1 exterior dimensions again were followed. However, the total weight of each car was 85,000 pounds, two and one-half tons heavier than the prewar R units. The R-16s returned to large and legible roll signs on the sides of the cars. The immediate postwar cars featured small roll signs positioned at the roof lines of the cars, an arrangement that drew a good deal of criticism.

Because the TA couldn't order new equipment fast enough, it also purchased thirty cars from the Staten Island Rapid Transit in 1954, after SIRT had abandoned a portion of its passenger service. The units were reasonably similar in looks to the BMT standard—except for end vestibules, IRT style—and they are the only secondhand cars ever to run in the New York subway.

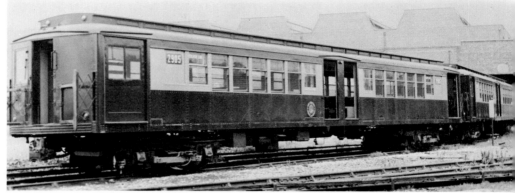

*After being renovated at Coney Island shops, two ex-Staten Island cars are ready for service on the BMT Culver line. Note similarities between this design and the BMT Standard. (Author photo)*

Twenty-five were motor cars that ran for several years; the other five were trailers that never saw passenger service for the TA.

It is ironic that a small independent railway on Staten Island would ever own a fleet of cars similar to the Standard. The BRT had long thought about a tunnel under the Narrows from Bay Ridge to the island. South of the subway station at Fourth Avenue and 59th Street, for instance, construction can still be seen that would have become a junction to such a tunnel. In the mid-1920s the Baltimore and Ohio Railroad, which owned the SIRT, electrified the lines and ordered multiple-unit cars that would be compatible with BRT subway equipment. For a variety of reasons the tunnel was never built. The SIRT cars got to Brooklyn only by barge, when the TA bought them.

When the ex-SIRT vehicles arrived on TA property, lo and behold they would not m.u. with BMT Standards, although such was expected. Consequently they ran only in trains made up exclusively of Staten Island veterans and were generally assigned to the Culver line.[7]

In 1954 the Transit Authority began to turn its attention to the IRT. The old line had not been so thoroughly attended to since the days of August Belmont and Frank Hedley! Between 1954 and 1962, 2,510 cars were ordered. Together with the 350 units purchased in 1946 and 1947, these cars replaced the entire Interborough fleet. Cars that had been ordered over a period of twenty-five years, 1903 to 1925, were replaced in eight. In addition to acquiring new rolling stock, the TA devoted considerable energy—and cash—to upgrading and replacing the IRT's aging signal system, extending the length of local platforms on the original 1904 route, and improving the electrical power distribution system that feeds current to the third rail. The whole IRT improvement program cost over 500 million dollars, considerably more than the cost of constructing the IRT in the first place.

The IRT's replacement cars were ordered under eight different contract numbers between R-17 and R-36. They were look-alike units with the exception of the R-36 cars, ordered in a blue and white color scheme for service to the 1964–65 World's Fair at Flushing Meadow—the same site as the 1939–40 fair. In 1958, the R-26 units introduced a feature which would become standard on new car orders for a dozen years. Every two cars were semi-permanently coupled into a two-car set, an arrangement generally known in the transit industry as a "married pair." Because the two cars share a common motor-generator set and compressor unit, cost and weight reductions are significant. The R-26 and R-28 units are coupled into married pairs using a conventional TA-style automatic coupler, while R-29 and later married pair units are more permanently joined with a non-automatic drawbar. One slight deviation from the married pair concept was that forty of the R-33 units came as single cars. They were painted in the same livery as the World's Fair R-36 fleet, and made possible the operation of eleven-car trains on the Flushing line–the only service on the entire TA system ever to exceed ten-car train lengths. (A train of ten sixty-foot cars on the BMT or IND was, nonetheless, longer than an eleven car train of IRT fifty-one footers.)

Before this new rolling stock could be phased into regular IRT service,[8] certain station platforms had to be altered. At such locations as Union Square and South Ferry, mechanical gap fillers that moved out to meet the open doors of stopped trains were positioned according to the door locations

*IRT's Flushing line runs eleven-car trains on barely believable 90-second headways during rush hours. This view at Grand Central station, however, was taken at midday, as the uncrowded platform attests. Train will proceed under the East River via Steinway tunnel. (NYCTA)*

of a standard pre-World War I Interborough car. They were modified—part of the 500 million dollar project—to mate with the new R units. At some stations, the entire platform was simply moved to eliminate the very need for the gap fillers. Prior to 1953, a hapless Board of Transportation spokesman ventured the opinion that because of these platform irregularities the IRT would "never be able to operate new cars."

A noble experiment—air conditioning—was tried in 1956 on a train of new R-17 units. It failed. As a result the TA began to feel air conditioning was an impossible dream for subway trains. This view, however, overlooked the fact that the Hudson Tubes had an entire fleet of cars proving just the opposite.

### FAREWELL TO THE STANDARDS

Then in the 1960s, before anyone could really get used to the idea, the final BMT Standards came due for retirement. The TA had more than 200 Standards rebuilt in the late 1950s, but even the rebuilds failed to see the dawn of the 1970s. In late summer of 1969 the lines of the former Brooklyn Rapid Transit Company were moving their usual numbers of people, but the famous and durable subway car that had so long been identified with the BRT and the BMT was no longer in on the action. The newer Triplex units had been retired even earlier, the last of these heavyweights having been withdrawn in 1965 before the opening of the Chrystie Street connection. Suddenly many people realized how the years were passing as still another link with the days of their youth vanished from the scene.

"It was bad enough when the Dodgers moved to Los Angeles," one Flatbush native remarked, "but Brooklyn isn't Brooklyn without the old BMT cars."

*Curtain call for a fine old trouper! In the spring of 1969 the final Standards of the system were performing on the 14th Street-Canarsie line. But here we see the future—an R-42 unit freshly built by GSI-St. Louis which has just been assigned to the line. The Standards were all gone by year's end. (Author)*

*BMT-IND R-32 type cars on their inaugural run from Mott Haven yard on the New York Central into Grand Central Terminal on September 9, 1964. (NYCTA)*

Between 1953 and 1968 the Transit Authority signed orders for 1,950 subway cars for the IND and BMT. Together with the new IRT cars, the TA had thus equipped the entire Dual Contracts network of subway lines with second-generation equipment. When R-42 units began to arrive in 1969, the TA started to phase out the R-1 cars that had opened service on the Independent subway in 1932.

In 1963 the TA contracted with the Budd Company for 600 BMT-IND cars. It was the largest single order ever placed for passenger equipment with a U.S. car builder to that time. Budd proposed to finish off the R-32 units in stainless steel. (Prior to 1963, standard TA rolling stock was sheathed in a low-alloy, high-tensile steel exterior.) The Budd "Brightliners," as they were called when new, were not only more pleasant to look at, but they also impressed TA engineers with the weight reductions of stainless steel. In subsequent invitations for bids, the Authority formulated a cost-reduction factor that potential builders could subtract from their quoted price to make allowance for the reduced power costs of a lighter-weight car. Budd, however, won the R-32 contract without such a factor.

The Budd Company was back after several years' absence from the New York subway scene. Budd's first subway train had been the prewar BMT experimental. Then a postwar ten-car experimental—the R-11 units—had been ordered by the Board of Transportation, but a further order for production model cars never materialized.

The arrival of the new R-32's was celebrated in unusual fashion. On Wednesday, September 9, 1964, a first run was staged for the press, TA brass,

*Left and above: Putting R-32 cars together at the Red Lion plant of the Budd company. We see side panels being hoisted and guided into position and the man-handling of a roll destination sign into its aperture. At right (opposite page) a train of the newly finished cars poses in a tunnel location for the company photographer shortly after delivery. (All photos from NYCTA)*

and officials of the carbuilder. But the route was not along TA trackage. Instead, the special ran out of New York Central RR's Mott Haven Yard, down the Park Avenue tunnel, and into Grand Central Terminal, where the train was met by a twenty-piece band, on Track 37. The standard TA overriding third-rail shoes were adapted so the train could draw current from GCT's co-developed underriding type of third rail (called the Wilgus-Sprague system, as it was developed by the man who invented m.u. control). An NYC engineman and a TA motorman rode in the cab.

The R-32 units, as well as subsequent stainless steel equipment, are indeed bright and shiny compared with older subway cars, and have retained much of their sparkle. The gritty exterior of the typical non-stainless steel vehicle has long defied color classification. A British journalist commented in the 1920s that the subway "carriages," as he called them, "seem to have adopted the protective colouration of all ground-burrowing animals." New TA cars through the late 1950s arrived on the property freshly enameled in green, red or deep maroon. However, after only a few weeks service in the hostile environment of the underground tunnels, the difference between a red car and a green one could not be detected by the naked eye. If dust and dirt are sufficient to discolor totally the body of a car, they must be taking a heavy toll on the mechanical and electrical systems of the vehicle, not to mention the pulmonary apparatus of passengers.

In the 1960s the TA began to install mechanical carwashing units at principal repair shops,[9] and experiments were conducted with soaps and detergents. As the prewar IND R units inched through the newly installed car washers, gold lettering reading "City of New York" that had been applied to

their sides in the 1930s once again became visible after years of being covered over by dirt.

As luck would have it, no sooner had the TA moved its car washing program into high gear than the scourge of spray-painted graffiti arrived. The investment in fancy mechanical car washers was largely obliterated by slobs apparently under compulsion to paint six-foot high messages in vivid colors on TA rolling stock.

Beginning with the R-40 order, built by St. Louis Car Company in 1968, New York finally adopted air conditioning as standard equipment on its new subway cars, the TA's previous dogma notwithstanding! The R-40 also featured major design variations from the general car profile pioneered by the R-15 units in 1947. In place of a vertical bulkhead with line and destination signs over the end door, the R-40 had an angular shovel nose on a fifteen-degree slant, and a large illuminated letter code next to the end door, a design developed for the TA by Loewy/Snaith. The shovel nose feature was not especially well received. It used up valuable interior car space, as capital a transit crime as there is. The final cars in the order came with a new bulbous nose developed by the Sundberg-Ferar firm—*the* design for the foreseeable future.

The R-40s, however, did revive a design long out of favor on the subways: car sides that taper slightly toward the roof. The BMT's *Green Hornet* and the original Interborough Composites were the only prior cars with such a feature.

The TA's rolling stock policy places firm trust in comparatively heavy-weight equipment. The use of stainless steel in the R-32 reduced weight per car to 70,000 pounds, compared with 80,000 pounds for a similar but non-stainless steel car. By comparison, Boston's M.B.T.A. operates a subway car four feet longer than the R-32's but similar in width and height. Yet the Boston car weighs only 63,000 pounds. Boston also has a subway-el line that uses a car similar to IRT units in width, but four feet longer, with a gross weight of 58,000 pounds, versus 69,500 for a typical IRT unit. Much, if not all, of the extra weight on TA rolling stock is accounted for by the trucks. Indeed, half the weight of a TA car is in its running gear! The standard product is a cast-steel equalized truck with outboard journal boxes and roller bearings. When Budd was negotiating the R-32 contract, Red Lion engineers tried to convince the Authority of the merits of a more lightweight truck, and recommended their own inboard Pioneer III design. A handful of cars actually came equipped with Pioneer III trucks for tests. But TA officials still believe heavyweight hardware means a more trouble-free car. Conventional trucks have since replaced the Pioneer IIIs, which are sitting unused in Coney Island shops.

Thus the New York City Transit Authority passed the interval from 1953 to 1968. It obeyed its legislative mandate of meeting operating expenses out of revenues, and it also convinced city authorities of the urgent need to make large-scale capital investments in the existing transit plant.[10] In fact, one of the most controversial fiscal policies of the 1952-1968 TA was its diversion of the revenue raised in a 500-million-dollar 1951 bond issue to such improvement projects. When voters approved this expenditure they presumed—and were told—that they were earmarking funds for totally new transit lines such as the long-discussed Second Avenue subway in Manhattan.

A realtor in Flatbush once sold a house to a young couple with a promise that the IRT subway would soon be extended out along Nostrand Avenue. That was in 1937. After the 1951 bond issue was approved in a referendum, the new subway was thought to be just months away. The young marrieds have meanwhile grown up and retired to Florida. The subway has yet to be built.

### Quill's Last Hurrah

John Vliet Lindsay was the mayor of New York for two hectic terms, from 1966 through 1973. Of the approximately 3,000 days he served as the city's chief executive, none matched the first thirteen!

Lindsay took over as mayor at 12:01 A.M. on January 1, 1966, and during his very first *hour* of incumbency he had to sit by helplessly as officials of the Transport Workers Union stormed angrily out of a bargaining session with the Transit Authority at the Hotel Americana. A paralyzing subway and bus line strike was underway, pending agreement on a new labor contract.

Local 100 of the TWU was under the command of Michael Joseph Quill, its president, by now a peppery sixty-one years old.

THE R-40 DESIGN AS ORIGINALLY DEVELOPED. As the model above shows, it was a radical departure from previous subway vehicle design.

Above: THE R-40 CARS AS DELIVERED. All sleek and shiny, but the "shovel nose" unfortunately, posed some problems! Below: THE R-40 CARS AS REWORKED – by the grafting on of utilitarian, but scarcely sightly, hardware. Back to the drawing board! Last batch of cars delivered had a redesigned end adopted also for the R-42 cars to come. See illustrations, pages 126 and 141. (Tom Nelligan photo; top two from NYCTA)

*Author photo*

## THE MOVING FINGER WRITES

From its very beginning the subway has been plagued by the problem of graffiti, but in the early 1970s the matter escalated to previously unimagined heights.

"My administration will not rest until this epidemic is wiped out," said then-mayor John Lindsay, but the mayor's resolve was not enough. The epidemic was running strong long after Lindsay left office.

The IRT Division suffered the early ravages of garish spray paint. After the TA managed to secure the storage yards where the deeds were being nightly performed, other lines and divisions began to sprout the unofficial decoration. Graffiti in the 1970s does not mean a neat and tidy Kilroy-like inscription. The style can often involve lettering in three colors four or more feet high, as on the IND–BMT R-27 unit pictured above.

Contemporary graffiti tends away from obscenity, political slogans and social protest. Rather the popular message is simply someone's first name, often together with a street number, such as "Rollo 126" or "Enzo 208." Academic types around town regularly break into print with terribly serious interpretations of the graffiti phenomenon, and the Museum of Modern Art featured showings by some of the more famous "underground artists." Framed canvases executed in subway-style graffiti command high prices in chic circles. The sad fact, however, was that by 1973 virtually every piece of subway rolling stock was adorned from end to end with the new art form.

Most observers feel that it was the onset of the new administration that doomed the collective bargaining effort. Under the former mayor, Robert F. Wagner, accomodations were always reached—always at the last minute, it seemed, and always with a strike just hours away, but reached in any event.

It's interesting to note that while the contract talks were nominally between the TWU and the Transit Authority, the municipal administration always played a key role. Under New York State law, the TA had to have a balanced budget. Since subway fare increases are never popular, it would only be the mayor—with access to the full city fiscal apparatus—who could "find" some last minute cash to reach an accomodation with the union. And Wagner was extremely resourceful in this regard. On one occasion he might agree to have the city absorb the cost of the TA's police force; at another time, he could arrange to have additional monies turned over to the TA in exchange for the cut-rate fares that are charged for students riding the subway to school.

Lindsay, who joined the negotiations in late December, spoke of lofty principles of collective bargaining and lectured Quill on his civic and moral responsibility. The strike became inevitable.

Quill and the union leadership were hauled off to jail, and when a settlement was finally reached after thirteen awful days in New York, most people felt that it was the union which emerged victorious. Furthermore it was also generally felt that Lindsay, had he used different tactics, could have reached such an agreement with Quill and company without the city having to endure a thirteen-day strike.

While in jail, Quill suffered a heart attack and was rushed to Bellevue Hospital. He recovered, was released from custody after the strike, and seemed ready to resume command of his union. Indeed he even appeared willing to patch up his differences with John Lindsay, a man who he had deliberately referred to as "Mister Lind-sley" in the heated and angry days before the strike. But such was not to be. On January 28th, 1966, Mike Quill passed away, and four days later 3,000 transport workers filed silently into St.

*Prewar IND R units were subjected to rigorous cleaning after the MTA was created, and the gold lettering originally applied to the cars in the 1930s could again be seen, after years of obliteration by accumulated dirt and grime. At right, swabs and rollers in the car washing machine mop the drip off cars passing through. (MTA, NYCTA photos)*

Patrick's Cathedral to pay last respects to their leader. The flag of the Irish Republican Army draped his casket, and with the kind of touch Mike would have appreciated, his funeral took place while the city's hearse drivers were out on strike. The Teamsters authorized a union driver anyway for Quill's last ride.

Mike Quill was one of the most colorful characters in the entire seventy-five-year saga of the New York subways. To his credit, he was also a man who played the game fair and square. "If Mike gave you his word on something," a TA official later said, "you better believe he'd deliver."

Still Quill will best be remembered as the shrill-voiced Irishman who, though he probably never heard of Marshall McLuhan, knew how to use the communications media like few men before or since. Just before his arrest at the start of the 1966 strike he was asked if he would obey a court order directing his men to return to work. His reply was classic Mike Quill: "The judge can drop dead in his black robes, and we would not call off the strike."

---

*Notes to Chapter 11*

[1] This R-9 unit, No. 1575, served for many years. Because the four-motor R-10's never ran in multiple with the older two-motor Rs, many traction buffs were surprised to find what *looked* like an R-10 in a train of pre-war cars.

[2] The Mets' new ball park—Shea Stadium—is directly served by the IRT Flushing line. Bill Shea, after whom the stadium is named and who was instrumental in returning National League baseball to New York, served for a time as a board member of the Metropolitan Transportation Authority.

[3] Although the Rockaway line *opened* in June 1956, it was really not *finished*. Electrical sub-stations were incomplete and full power was not available. For several months the line operated under these restrictions: reduced speed, short trains, and a complete ban on the IND's four-motor R-10 units. Only two-motor prewar R units could travel the Rockaway line.

[4] Flatbush and Atlantic avenues were also the site of a track connection between the Long Island Rail Road and the Interborough. LIRR–IRT connecting service was never implemented, however, despite the fact that August Belmont served on the Long Island's board of directors.

[5] Mayor Robert Wagner presided at the ground breaking for the Chrystie Street project on August 25, 1957. There were young rail buffs aboard the inaugural runs ten years later who *weren't born* when the project was begun.

[6] Since 1915, two tracks on the south side of the Manhattan Bridge fed the Centre Street loop, while two tracks on the north side fed the Broadway line. The latter now feed into the Sixth Avenue line, and the former connect with the Broadway line. It is no longer possible to go from the Manhattan Bridge to the Centre, or Nassau, loop.

[7] Rather than install expensive new roll signs, the TA rigged the SIRT cars with metal plate destination signs rescued from scrapped elevated equipment.

[8] Rapid arrival of new IRT cars allowed for some novel car assignments in the late 1950s. A group of IRT Lo-Vs were fitted with extension plates at the door sills and operated on various BMT shuttle lines until that division received new rolling stock.

[9] The subway's very first mechanical car washing unit was installed in the 207th Street Yards in June 1960. How the New York subways managed to do without such a device for fifty-six years must remain one of the city's better unanswerable questions.

[10] One long-neglected area upgraded by the TA in a somewhat different manner was the system's electrical generating stations. It sold the old power houses—two IRT installations and one for the BMT—to the city's commercial power company, Con Edison, and then bought electricity from the utility. (The IND always relied on purchased power.) When word went out that the power houses were "for sale," O. Roy Chalk, the often irrepressible owner of Washington's DC Transit, offered to buy the *entire* Transit Authority—for 61.5 million dollars! In recent years the MTA has purchased most of its electricity from the State Power Authority.

*Not many standees in this R-32 interior scene under the sidewalks of New York. But the doors on the left are open; an influx of passengers could happen any second. Picture shows the F train. (NYCTA)*

## LOST AND FOUND

No writer of fiction could possibly do justice to the melange of trivial and terrifying articles that enter the portals of the TA's lost and found department: live bombs left by absentminded terrorists while en route to chosen targets; an original Salvador Dali; enough eyeglasses over a year's time to outfit all near- and far-sighted people in Wilkes-Barre, Pa., with new spectacles; sufficient firearms to mount a respectable revolution; paper bags full of one-hundred dollar bills; artificial limbs; plus the more prosaic items such as umbrellas, briefcases and topcoats.

## SUBWAY RIDERS OF THE WORLD, UNITE! ...

There are few social issues in the world at large that do not crop up in microcosm in the subway. In the late 1960s disgruntled passengers borrowed a page or two from the revolutionary manuals. Homeward-bound commuters on the IND Washington Heights line refused to get off a B Train at 168th Street, because the following A Train to 207th Street would inevitably be too crowded and the going-out-of-service B Train had to deadhead to 207th Street anyway. After a hurried call to the dispatcher by the train's conductor, the "activists" won their point. Next morning there was all manner of handwringing by citizens who view such tactics as evidence the Republic is about to founder.

Flash back to the supposedly tranquil days of 1924. On the Interborough's Broadway line passengers on a train which the IRT attempted to terminate at 103rd Street refused to get off and transfer to the next train to continue their journey to 242nd Street. A firm appeal to the dispatcher—and these forerunners of today's activists won their point, too.

New York City rapid transit, 1979. The only borough without a subway link to the system is Richmond, Staten Island. To get there, however, you have your choice of the Verrazano Bridge and — just as in 1904, when the Interborough opened — the Staten Island ferry. Dotted line on map is the route of the partially completed Second Avenue subway. (MTA)

# 12 From TA to M to Infinity

IN A MIDTOWN MANHATTAN OFFICE in 1956, the chairman of the New York State Temporary Commission on Constitutional Reform had a long talk over coffee and doughnuts with the first deputy city administrator of Mayor Robert Wagner's administration. Thus did Nelson Rockefeller, then two years away from his first term as governor, meet Buffalo-born William J. Ronan, an academician with a doctorate from New York University in international law and diplomacy, and a man destined to inherit the mantle of August Belmont a dozen years later. "I've been a Rockefeller Republican ever since," Ronan mused when recalling the meeting.

When Rockefeller went to Albany as the state's chief executive in 1958, he took Ronan along as his private secretary. In 1965 the state completed a deal to buy out the troubled Long Island Rail Road, and Ronan was placed in charge of the Metropolitan Commuter Transportation Authority (MCTA), the public agency that was formed to run the line.

But the MCTA was a short-lived enterprise. In November 1967 Rockefeller and Ronan were successful in securing voter approval of a 2.5-billion-dollar bond issue. As a result of accompanying legislation, the MCTA was transformed into the MTA, Metropolitan Transportation Authority, an agency of much greater scope and responsibility.

The MTA assumed control over a variety of existing public transport agencies on March 1, 1968, and was given a mandate to bring privately-run commuter rail lines under its wing as well. Part of the 2.5 billion dollars was to be used to buy railroad coaches and locomotives for the Penn Central, for instance. The new authority's twelve-county transportation district covers some 4,000 square miles and includes 12 million residents. Its principal responsibility, however, was and is the properties, routes, equipment and good name of the New York City Transit Authority.[1]

The MTA—or just plain M, as its image makers would have us say—coordinates metropolitan transportation matters from its mid-Manhattan headquarters, and achieves unity amid diversity by a statutory requirement that makes the MTA chairman and ten other board members the chief officers of the component agencies as well. In addition to managing the TA, Ronan and his colleagues became the executives of record for the Triborough Bridge and Tunnel Authority, the state-owned Long Island Rail Road, and the TA's awkwardly named subsidiary, the Manhattan and Bronx Surface Transit Operating Authority (MaBSTOA, an acronym which New Yorkers actually *pro-*

*nounce*). Over the years since its founding, additional agencies—such as the Staten Island Rapid Transit—have become part of the MTA complex.

On February 28, 1968, two days before the MTA assumed power, the first phase of its long range plan for New York-area transit improvements was unveiled. The initial program was scheduled to be completed within ten years (it wasn't!) and called for an expenditure of 2.5 billion dollars. A portion of that amount would come from funds approved in the 1967 bond issue. The rest would be met with local and Federal assistance. Of prime note was the fact that beginning in 1964, Washington had begun to make dollars available to urban areas for capital investment in mass transit facilities.

Many of the new transit lines envisioned by the MTA were routes that have been long discussed in New York, such as the Second Avenue subway, once a far-off gleam in the eye of Red Mike Hylan. Other plans, proposed in the light of shifting patterns in residential development, included a line into the Rosedale section of Queens to connect with both the BMT Jamaica Avenue line and the IND Queens Boulevard subway. In any event, the MTA set its sights on what certainly appeared to be New York's most ambitious scheme for transit expansion since the Independent was begun.

With the creation of the MTA, the New York subways were provided with a management structure of contemporary design. Yet in the final years of the 1960s and early years of the 1970s it was the personality of square-jawed, six-foot-two William Ronan—articulate, flamboyant, and frequently abrasive —that became the main issue on the subway scene. The eleven-member MTA board, for instance, supposedly was pieced together with many checks and balances. Yet few would deny that Ronan was in complete charge. A frequently heard cliché was that the MTA was a "wholly Ronan empire."[2]

Ronan's early problems developed when the LIRR's highly vocal riders focused on him as the source of their discontent. Until new MTA-designed cars were in service and de-bugged, the Long Island managed to grab the adverse headlines and keep late-night television comedians well supplied with one-liners for their monologues. But as conditions gradually improved on the former suburban railroad, the TA became a disaster area in its own right, and Ronan was again on center stage. "Ronan stinks" was the complete and entire text of a letter to the editor of the *Daily News* during one of numerous crises. A series of accidents, breakdowns, fires and derailments, including a serious sideswipe crash on the IND Queens line in May 1970 which claimed two lives and injured seventy, effectively dramatized that the subway was not well. A newspaper account in late 1969 summarized matters: "The Transit Authority's performance record has plunged recently to its lowest level in decades."

The breakdown of subway performance during the early years of the MTA era can be, in part, attributed to the after effects of a benefit the TWU won for its members in the 1968 contract, a pact negotiated before the MTA takeover. Essentially it allowed a transit worker to retire under favorable terms after twenty years of service, a policy long in force for city police and fire department employees. The resultant loss of skilled workers was heavier than anticipated. In one key 4,000-man maintenance section, 1,400 trained workers retired during the first year of the contract, and new workers could not be trained quickly enough to take their place. Many observers regard the new retirement program as the leading cause of the deterioration in subway service since 1968.

A more speculative reason can be found in the always murky area of preserving the transit fare. In January 1970 subway patrons began coughing up thirty cents per ride. A new and larger token was distributed—26 million of them—and the system's 3,047 turnstiles were adjusted to accept the new coin. Pressure to hold the line on fares was so strong that there was speculation in many city rooms that Ronan had ordered a cutback in routine maintenance in an effort to avoid the increase. Ronan, as a matter of fact, was willing to admit that the system suffered from deferred maintenance. But he insisted this was a condition the MTA inherited, not one it created.

### "THINKING BIG" FOR THE FUTURE

Even if day-to-day operations during the early MTA years left something to be desired, the new agency initiated capital development programs with verve and enthusiasm. By the mid-1970s, sad to relate, the city's general financial problems had stalled a good many MTA projects, and its initial ten-year program was largely unfinished when the agency celebrated its tenth anniversary. But an excellent start was made in spite of all the handicaps.

Curiously, in the 1970s, the need for new transit lines—or "transit relief" to borrow a phrase from an older era—is not due to constantly increasing ridership levels, as it was in the days of the Dual Contracts. Annual subway patronage, reflecting national transit trends, has been in steady decline since World War II. Indeed, aside from the abnormal days of wartime gasoline rationing, the New York subway carried its record number of passengers in the pre-IND year of 1930, when slightly more than two billion passengers rode the BMT and IRT. Performance is now down to almost half that figure, although the TA has been somewhat successful of late in stabilizing subway patronage and even racking up short-term increases now and again. For purposes of comparison, though, the 1976 rider count was 1,027,084,901.

New transit facilities, and new transit routes, are needed today because of a larger social issue which the bold patronage figures can not indicate. For unless New Yorkers begin to leave their automobiles at home and use public transportation in greater numbers, the economic and environmental future of the city will not be as promising as it might be. Therefore subway service must be extended into newly developed residential areas, better midtown distribution patterns must be developed, and key bottlenecks in the existing transit system overcome. Ironically, back in the early days of the century, the Hearst papers and others strongly argued that municipal operation of the then privately operated subway was the only means that would permit construction of new routes in advance of actual need, thus expediting orderly and planned growth for the city. Even without municipal operation, the Dual Contracts did just that, extending transit lines into urban "wildernesses" that quickly became choice real estate. Today, with full public sector operation of the subways, such talk sounds downright Utopian; transit service is long overdue in many areas that are already built up.

The MTA master plan is an attempt to correct these shortcomings. A four-track, two-level river tunnel was begun in the early 1970s from the foot of East 63rd Street in Manhattan to Long Island City. A station is to be located midway through the tube where it passes under Roosevelt Island. The bottom tracks of this tunnel will be used by Long Island RR trains enroute to a new Manhattan terminal,[3] and the upper level is to be used by TA subway trains from Queens. These subway operations from the new tunnel will funnel into the IND Sixth Avenue line, the BMT Broadway line, and the new Second Avenue subway.

Ground was broken for the long-planned, long-discussed, and even longer postponed Second Avenue subway on October 27, 1972, sixty-eight years to the day after the opening of the city's first subway. After three years of work, the effort had to be halted, a victim of the city's monumental fiscal problems of the mid-1970s. Thus the Second Avenue line seems destined to take after elements of the Dual Subway System—sections completed, but not tied into the larger system, and therefore quite useless.

Another by-product of the city's monetary problems was yet another subway fare increase on September 1, 1975. At that time the tariff rose to fifty cents. To forestall the hoarding of tokens, the TA announced that a new and different size token would be issued for the new fare. Then at the last minute, it was revealed that, no, there would not be a new token, merely an increase in price of existing tokens on the effective date.[4]

Although TA and LIRR operations will be more closely coordinated in the years ahead because of common MTA guardianship, there is no current plan to merge the services in any real sense. Overlapping union jurisdictions are cited as one formidable bar to this unification, as well as the fact that a merged LIRR and NYCTA could well be subject to the gamut of Federal railroad regulation, and this could be costly. Thus, although the Long Island is losing much of its old-time railroad look and emerging as more of a rapid transit operation, it will retain a certain autonomy for the foreseeable future.

However, both LIRR and TA rolling stock now sport what MTA wags call

*An eight-car train of R-44 units runs tests on the Long Island Rail Road shortly after delivery from GSI-St. Louis. The 75-foot cars clocked a top speed of 83 mph during these trials. (Tom Nelligan photo)*

"family resemblances." The TA's R-42, R-44 and R-46 units are outwardly similar to the LIRR's new Budd-built "Metropolitan" cars, and are finished in the same stainless steel with blue trim. Even older equipment on both railroad and subway now sport similar hues of blue and grey—assuming one can detect the TA's color scheme under all the graffiti. New commuter equipment on Conrail's ex-New York Central and ex-New Haven routes is also similar to the LIRR fleet, enlarging the family to a genuine clan.

In July 1969 the MTA made official something that had been in the wind for months. Ironically, the announcement that Brooklyn's old Myrtle Avenue El was to be closed down was reported in the newspapers on Sunday, the 29th, the day men first set foot on the surface of the moon. The Myrtle

*St. Louis-built R-42 units. (NYCTA)*

*A mere shadow of their former selves, three cars of BMT's stable of Q units serve out their days on the Myrtle Avenue line. Rebuilt from old open-platform el cars at the time of the 1939-40 World's Fair, these units had the strangest career of any New York transit equipment. (Roger J. Cudahy)*

Avenue El was the city's last full-blooded, bona fide el. Originally a steam-powered BRT operation, it had been the last transit line in North America to operate wooden equipment. Actually, for more than half its length, the Myrtle Avenue El had shared trackage with an elevated subway line. This portion of the trackage was built to heavy duty standards at the time of the Dual Contracts and remains in service. But west of the intersection of Broadway and Myrtle Avenue, the line remained an unreconstructed elevated route, little changed from the days when steam engines hauled open-platform cars and passengers wore starched collars and derby hats.

Formal service on the thirty-five block, eight station stretch of line ended at 12:01 A.M. on Saturday, October 4, 1969. Later that same day, several chartered train loads of railway buffs toured the route and paid their last respects to the old el. The equipment the line operated during its final years were BMT's Q cars, rebuilt for the 1939–40 World's Fair, transferred to the IRT's Third Avenue El after the war, and finally sent back to the BMT in the late 1950s. With the passing of the Qs, the last BMT-designed rolling stock departed from active service. Thus the small fleet of rebuilt el cars outlived the Standards and the Triplex units.

But the MTA is more interested in the future than the past. In 1970 the Authority made a bold decision concerning new subway rolling stock. On the unified BMT-IND routes, the basic dimensions of the prewar R units continued to govern car specifications through the 400-unit R-42 order in 1968. But when the original 1930-era IND cars came due for large scale replacement, the R-44 design was developed—"the most revolutionary subway car in fifty years," said the press release issued by the MTA. The rhetoric was correct.

The R-44 measures seventy-five feet in length, the longest subway cars ever built for New York service. The extra length means that eight cars will do the work of ten sixty-footers, which translates into significant savings in both capital investment and long-term maintenance. Instead of married pairs of cars permanently coupled, the R-44's feature two different body styles that are not permanently, or even semi-permanently, coupled. One has a full width motorman's cab across a single end of the car, and the other has no cabs at all. In other words, one car is a single-ended control motor, and the other is a motorized trailer. In general practice the cars are run in four-unit combinations—cab, trailer, trailer, cab.

The MTA ordered 300 R-44's from the St. Louis Car Division of General Steel Industries for TA service, plus an additional fifty-two to re-equip the Staten Island Rapid Transit, which became an MTA, but not a TA, responsibility in July 1971.

The first four R-44's arrived on TA property in the Fall of 1971. They made their debut for the press on October 5, smack in the middle of a heated, but unsuccessful, campaign to win electoral approval for yet another transportation bond issue—a 2.5 billion package to continue financing the MTA master plan.

The R-44's are not compatible with earlier TA equipment—they have a different kind of coupler, for instance, the first change in design since the Interborough replaced its original Van Dorn couplers in the century's first decade—and the new cars are capable of speeds up to 80 mph. The MTA intends to limit their actual speed to 70 mph, but even this performance will not be achieved until such new lines as the Second Avenue subway are ready for service. On existing lines, the R-44s will be limited to 50 mph, the speed of conventional subway trains.

St. Louis had only begun to deliver the R-44 order when the MTA announced that a 745-car fleet of similar equipment—the R-46s—had been ordered from Pullman-Standard. This 214-million-dollar purchase—two-thirds of which was paid for by the Federal government's Urban Mass Transporta-

*Unit No. 564 takes a ride on the transfer table at the Pullman plant in South Chicago as she and a sister R-46 near completion in 1975. (Author photo)*

tion Administration (UMTA)—replaced all of the remaining original R units from the IND, and gave the subway an entire fleet of postwar cars. The final revenue trip using the old R units took place on March 31, 1977, and the order for the R-46s was the largest ever written for any kind of rail passenger cars in the United States. When the MTA agreed to alter its payment schedule to the manufacturer, the order was increased from 745 to 754 cars at no increase in cost.

New York had not ordered equipment from Pullman-Standard since 1940, when some R-9 units were purchased by the IND. However, Pullman-Standard's relationship with the MTA's predecessors dates back to the early 1880s when the firm turned out trailer coaches to be hauled behind steam engines on the Brooklyn els.[5]

In keeping with the novelty of the R-46, Pullman-Standard developed a unique way of delivering the cars from its South Chicago plant to New York. Previously, subway cars had been hauled in freight trains on their own wheels. The R-46s were lifted aboard flat cars at the factory, and unloaded by crane when they reached Jersey City. Subway cars traveling as "passengers" on flatcars are not subject to the special handling restrictions—and costs —incurred when the cars are coupled into a freight train as part of its consist. What's more, railroad clearances require that subway cars running on their own wheels must have their third-rail shoe beams[6] removed en route, to be reinstalled after delivery by TA crews. The R-46s arrived with all hardware in place.

The R-46 employs a new truck design. Built by Rockwell-International, it retains New York's long-standing preference for relatively heavy, outboard-frame running gear, but incorporates an air suspension system, a "first" for New York. The R-46s can m.u. with the R-44s, and they are outfitted with a number of what the space program people like to call "redundant systems" to guard against in-service failures. Each motorman's cab, for instance, includes a back-up set of operating controls in case the regular apparatus malfunctions.

### Endless Cycles

If anything has emerged as a timeless and universal characterization of the New York subway, it is the endless search for some future salvation, some not-yet-realized resolution of its difficulties and cure for its ills. Plans are made, programs developed, goals established. But somehow they never quite live up to their initial expectations, and a new cycle must begin.

The other constant in the subway story has been the series of Runyon-esque characters who have emerged from obscurity to steal all the thunder. William Ronan's background may not have prepared him to share the stage with Mike Quill and John Hylan, but share it he did, and with a style and vigor that was remarkable. This classic and probably apocryphal quote is attributed to an unnamed Rockefeller aide: "If what's-his-name (*sic*) hadn't said, 'Let 'em eat cake,' Ronan would have."

Ronan resigned his MTA post in the Spring of 1974, but the color and tempo of the Ronan era will remain alive for some time. He possessed an invaluable characteristic for a New York subway chieftain: He enjoyed the limelight! His face was forever staring up at morning commuters from their newspapers, he was instinctively able to talk in short "20-second takes" for the benefit of television news, and a reporter in need of a fresh angle for a story could usually count on Ronan for a quotable comment or two. One event at which he presided was clearly a subway "first": On October 6, 1970, Ronan and his entourage traveled south to Port Deposit, Maryland, for the launching of the first piece of New York subway right-of-way to be built in a shipyard. A 375-foot-long concrete tube slid into the Susquehanna River and was later towed up to New York to form part of the 63rd Street tunnel. Another novelty of the Ronan regime took place on June 20, 1971, when R-42 units Nos. 4753 and 4765 were dispatched on a most untypical journey. Their destination was not Washington Heights or Coney Island; it was the U.S. Department of Transportation's new rail test facility in the desert outside Pueblo, Colorado. The pair became the first transit vehicles to perform at the facility, a research center that will be instrumental in creating designs

*Above, at Port Deposit, Maryland, the first section of the MTA's new East River tunnel slides down the ways and, at right, sails away to its destined resting place at the foot of East 63rd Street, Manhattan. (MTA photos)*

*A long way from Times Square! Two New York subway cars sit in the sun at DOT's Pueblo test track, with Pike's Peak looming in the background. The pair are serving as a test bed for developing instruments which will become part of a rail diagnostic system. (Author photo)*

*A long way from Pike's Peak! A duo of State of the Art Cars testing on the Brighton line, 1974. (Boeing Vertol)*

*Action in the desert! In a scene reminiscent of period photographs of the* Rocky Mountain Rocket, *R-42 units from the New York subway roll along the test track at Pueblo, Colorado. Until commercial power could be fed into the remote desert site, DOT's U-boat No. 001 supplied third-rail current for the transit cars. (Boeing Vertol)*

for tomorrow's subway and transit cars.

The second transit cars to operate at Pueblo—joining the R-42s—were called SOAC, or *State Of the Art Cars*. Built under the management of the Boeing Vertol Company, this Federally-funded experiment was an effort to produce a transit vehicle that exemplified the optimum of hardware, components and design. After undergoing preliminary tests at Pueblo, the two cars then barnstormed the country and ran revenue tests on transit systems from Boston to the midwest. Their first port of call was New York.

No sooner had the SOACs left town than the New York subways collided full tilt with the cloak and dagger world of the Central Intelligence Agency. CIA agents, unbeknown to subway authorities, had used the IRT's Seventh Avenue subway to test the dispersal properties of certain gases. The experiments were conducted with benign samples in aerosol spray cans, and the agency was interested in learning how poison gas would behave in a subway. The columnists, predictably, had a field day with this one. A topper among many comments was the observation that lethal toxins are simply no match for the normal vapors found in New York subway tunnels.

Getting back to Ronan, he began his career as MTA chairman with an extraordinary liability: His $70,000 annual salary made him the state's highest paid public official. Another problem was his highly visible Lincoln Continental limousine. Pundits, friendly and otherwise, were forever pointing out that if the chairman would only leave his chauffeur-driven car at home and take the subway, he would have a better idea of what things were "really like" in his troubled domain. Ronan would stoutly reply that he did ride the subways, "frequently," and the non-debate went on.[7]

Instead of vilifying Ronan for his fancy automobile, New Yorkers should have harkened back to the heady days of James J. Walker. Walker, who knew the value of a headline with unerring instinct, was anxious to dramatize his concern for the plight of transit riders during an especially nasty outbreak of citizen dissatisfaction with subway service.

One fine sunny day, Walker got into his car at City Hall and was driven over to Brooklyn. In an act of sheer *noblesse oblige*, he actually descended the staircase into the Interborough's Atlantic Avenue station, where he was photographed shaking hands with the change agent. Only the Hearst papers even hinted that His Honor's actions were less than substantive. The general reaction was one of genuine appreciation that the mayor had the public's interest uppermost in his mind. Ronan, perhaps, was just born out of his time.

Ronan was succeeded in 1974 by department store executive David Yunich, and he in turn was replaced by Harold Fisher, a Brooklyn attorney who had served on the MTA board of directors under both Ronan and Yunich. In 1977, former U.S. Congressman Edward Koch was elected mayor. Thus, when the year of the Interborough's "Diamond Jubilee"[8] began, it was Koch and Fisher who were on center stage. Two facets of information about these gentlemen may augur well for the New York subways as the system enters upon its second seventy-five years: Koch hasn't owned an automobile since 1965, and Fisher doesn't even have a driver's license!

---

*Notes to Chapter 12*

[1] It remains both common and correct in New York to refer to the subway and bus network as the Transit Authority despite the existence of MTA and the presence of its logo on stations and cars.

[2] The original MTA board had eight members and a chairman. In 1970 it was increased to its current size.

[3] Original plans called for a brand new LIRR terminal on Manhattan's East Side. This was later changed in the face of community opposition, and LIRR trains will now run into Grand Central.

[4] Despite the increase in fare, extensive subsidies are today necessary to meet ordinary subway operating expenses. The true cost of each subway ride is well over a dollar.

[5] After completing the R-46 order Pullman withdrew from the passenger-car business, ironically enough.

[6] The insulated material to which the third rail shoes are attached.

[7] Ronan's automobile was no match for the private subway car *Mineola* in which August Belmont was wont to travel. Carried on the Interborough roster as No. 3344, its inlaid wood interior was the rival in oppulence of any railroad president's car. Sold by the Board of Transportation in 1947, *Mineola* was recently discovered on a farm in New Jersey. It was trucked to the Branford Trolley Museum in East Haven, Conn., soon to be restored to its former splendor.

[8] MTA wags insisted on using this regal-sounding nomenclature.

*Sprawling Coney Island yards. Shops in background are always busy keeping subway equipment in repair. (NYCTA)*

*Below: The TA-owned South Brooklyn Railway is a freight hauling line that today is completely dieselized. But as late as the mid-1950s steeple-cab electric locos were hauling box cars along private right-of-way and down the middle of Brooklyn's McDonald Avenue. The line's principal customer? The TA's own Coney Island shops! (NYCTA)*

# EPILOGUE:
# A Ride on "the Sea Beach"

THE CREW ROOM AT CONEY ISLAND differs little from similar facilities at subway and railroad terminals the world over. There are lockers, pool tables, bulletin boards, a short-order food counter, some chairs and benches. It is a very busy place because Stillwell Avenue is a terminal for no fewer than four important subway routes. As I sat with a Transit Authority public relations man waiting for the motorman in whose cab I was to ride on a sunny but cold December afternoon, nursing a cup of coffee and nibbling on a piece of packaged crumb cake, the sights and sounds of the place were irresistibly distracting. The terminal has eight tracks built on a poured concrete elevated structure, with four 600-foot platforms between each pair. The crew room is located on an overpass that provides access from platform to platform. In other words, I was several stories high and had a bird's-eye view of trains coming and going in what is surely the nation's busiest railway passenger terminal.

The view does not end with the trains; beyond them one sees a mixture of Coney Island's past in the form of roller coasters and boarded-up concession stands, and its present and future in the many red brick high-rise apartments that have been built on the sites of such long-gone amusement parks as Dreamland and Luna Park. From the crew room one can also see a sweeping panorama of the Atlantic Ocean and the approach from the sea to New York Harbor. On this crisp and clear winter day, a glistening white cruise ship headed toward the far horizon, mid-way between Coney Island and the beaches of Sandy Hook.

"Too bad you weren't here earlier. We could've gone to Nathan's for a hot dog," said the motorman who would be my host for the next several hours when he arrived in the crew room. One of the incidental advantages of working out of Stillwell Avenue is the proximity of the terminal to Nathan's, surely the most famous frankfurter emporium in the free world. The TA public relations man took his leave after the introductions; a subway cab is hardly big enough for two people, much less three. Indeed, my presence meant that the motorman's cab seat had to be folded down. Both of us, therefore, spent the entire ride standing up. When I later apologized for this I was told that standing is the preferred position anyway.

I chatted about my purposes with the motorman, a heavy-set man we'll call Frank Ruffino, who joined the ranks as a conductor in 1959 and advanced to motorman seven years later. He was married and the father of two teen-age daughters. I estimated his age at just shy of forty. Although many of the motormen in the crew room wore traditional garb of striped denim coveralls and black peaked cap, Frank was hatless and clothed in slacks, a turtleneck shirt and a blue quilted skiing jacket. Attached to the collar was a green and yellow TWU button.

Idle conversation ended when the clock signaled that our 4:05 P.M. departure was drawing near. The Stillwell Avenue terminal was alive with preparation for the impending rush hour.

My trip was to be aboard a train that carries the designation "N–Broadway Express," but no veteran of the BMT ever uses this newfangled jargon. To us the train is the "Sea Beach Express," and I selected this route for my cab trip principally because it largely retraces the BRT's first Dual Contracts operation of 1915. We were to leave Coney Island and head over the open cut of the Sea Beach, into the Fourth Avenue subway at 59th Street, through the De Kalb Avenue interlocking plant, across the Manhattan Bridge, and then up to 57th Street on the Broadway line. The timetable gave us forty-seven minutes to make the 15.36-mile run. We will stop at sixteen stations, bypass twelve others, and average, if we keep to the advertised, 19.61 mph enroute to our mid-Manhattan destination. Such a mark is not impressive compared to the performance, say, of Amtrak's *Metroliner*. But it is typical for a New York subway service. The highest terminal-to-terminal average speed on the entire system is 22.80 mph, on the Rockaway line where stations are widely spaced. The next best mark is the 22.63 mph which the IRT's Flushing Express manages.

Frank and I left the crew room and headed downstairs to the platform between Tracks 1 and 2, the area where Sea Beach trains terminate at Coney Island. A train was leaving for 57th Street from Track 1. As soon as it had cleared the platform and gone beyond the throat north of the station I could see an inbound train making its way up the short incline that leads to the elevated terminal.

"That's us," Frank said, as he pointed to the train of R-32 units pulling into the recently evacuated Track 1. With a gush of escaping air the inbound motorman brought his charge to a halt and disconnected his brake handle. The doors opened, but no passengers stepped off because the train was being put in service for the rush hour out of lay-up status in nearby Coney Island Yard. Sea Beach trains are serviced and stored only at this end of the line; other TA operations can take advantage of lay-up and/or repair facilities at each end of the line.

Frank checked in at the small dispatcher's office on the platform, a business-like shed that handles the "N" line. Here he was issued a bulky two-way radio that would keep him in contact with supervisory personnel throughout our trip. As we walked to the head end of the platform, a train

*Above: Four major transit lines terminate at Coney Island. Here are an IND D train and a train of BMT Standards on the scene as it was in 1954. (Author photo)*

*Below: Same place twenty-odd years later, looking toward the terminal throat. A train of R-32 units rolls up the incline and into the station. Just under a thousand departures and arrivals are carded at this terminal each weekday. (Tom Nelligan photo)*

of R-42 units departed for 57th Street from Track 2. We would leave in five minutes.

As we entered the first car, No. 3721, Frank was giving off a distinctive "jingle," typical of motormen on the New York subway. This jingle is caused by the assortment of hardware each motorman must carry in addition to the radio. A motorman has his own "air handle" to actuate the brakes, an assortment of keys, and the all-important reverse lever—essentially an open-end wrench. All of this combines to create a sound as distinctive to the subway as the roar of an express train or the clank of a turnstile.

Ruffino unlocked the cab door and, once inside, dropped the radio into a bracket under the window. He engaged the air handle on its socket and pumped up the train line with a quick flick of his wrist. Outside the cab he checked the head-end sign; an orange and white "N" was correctly displayed. He also turned on the proper marker lights—red and white—and checked a switch that illuminated a small red sign reading "EXP." This ritual was formerly more complex, and will soon be even simpler. Subway cars earlier than the R-40's of 1968 included both line and destination signs on the head end, and Ruffino's predecessors had to be certain their trains were showing a numeral "4" in the line slot and "57th Street Manh't'n" on the destination roller curtain. As soon as the R-40 had ushered in the simplified color-coded graphics, older units such as our R-32 were converted to the new system. R-40 and newer cars are not equipped with marker lights, either. [1]

We both squeezed into the cab. Frank did not close the door, but rather peered out onto the platform, which was on the opposite side of the car from the cab, and watched for the starting lights. His wrist watch showed a few seconds before 4:05, and he was hoping we would get an "early light." The light is a platform mounted amber signal that authorizes the conductor of an out-bound train to close the doors and proceed.

"There it is," said Frank as the three-cluster signal began to glow. He slammed the windowless door shut, and turned to face his control station.

### Off and Running

"Watch the doors, please," echoed over the train's public address system; with a swish they slid shut, and two loud buzzes echoed harshly through the steel cab. Subway trains are equipped with automatic indicator lights, so Frank did not require a signal from the conductor to know the doors were closed and that we were ready to go. Also, the doors interlock with the master controller, and power cannot be fed to the motors with the doors open. Despite this, the TA's book-of-rules states that a two-buzz highball must be given before any train departs a terminal point. A highball from the conductor is not necessary at intermediate stations, unless cars are added or dropped en route or a train makes an emergency stop.

The actual operation of a subway train is relatively simple, as compared to such things as steam locomotives, nuclear submarines and multi-engine airplanes. Only two operational controls are required for routine service. The first is the controller, located to the motorman's left, which has three notches and operates through a ninety-degree arc. Without pressure from the motorman's hand, the controller juts up at an angle. Depression of the controller is necessary to operate the train; should the motorman relax his grip while under way, the controller will resume its angular jut, thereby applying the "deadman's brake" and bringing the train to an emergency halt.

The second major control apparatus is the air handle, located to the motorman's right, and it operates the brakes. Over the years, almost all New York subway trains have had a similar arrangement. A significant exception was the BMT, which preferred to install the controller on the right and the brake on the left. BMT cabs also had little glass windows, permitting passengers to monitor the motorman's activities.[2]

After receiving his highball from the train's single conductor in the fourth car, Frank depressed the controller with his left hand, pushed the reverse key ahead into the forward position with his right hand, and then moved the brake valve into running position, also with his right hand. The releasing brakes gave off a soft sigh, Frank swung the controller into the third notch, and we were off for 57th Street.

Although they have three-notch controllers, subway trains normally run in either third notch or they coast. No sooner had we moved away from the

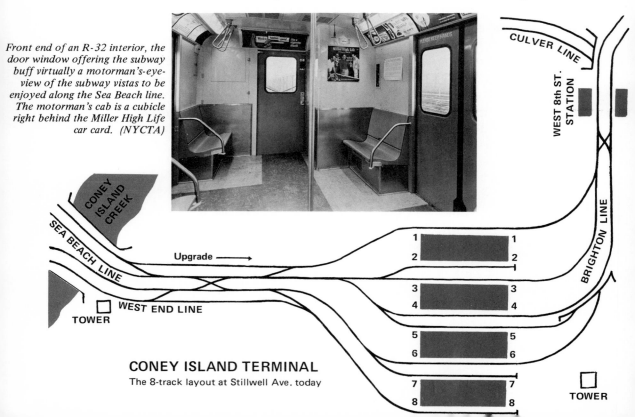

*Front end of an R-32 interior, the door window offering the subway buff virtually a motorman's-eye-view of the subway vistas to be enjoyed along the Sea Beach line. The motorman's cab is a cubicle right behind the Miller High Life car card. (NYCTA)*

CULVER LINE

WEST 8th ST. STATION

BRIGHTON LINE

CONEY ISLAND CREEK

SEA BEACH LINE

Upgrade →

1 1
2 2
3 3
4 4
5 5
6 6
7 7
8 8

WEST END LINE

TOWER

TOWER

**CONEY ISLAND TERMINAL**
The 8-track layout at Stillwell Ave. today

platform than Frank shut off the throttle and began to manipulate the air handle as we drifted through the complex terminal lead, seeking the rails of the Sea Beach line that would lead us across Brooklyn to Manhattan. Less than a train length from the end of the platform tracks descend from the elevated structure to ground level. The West End line takes an easy swing to the left and then reascends an elevated structure for its journey across Brooklyn. The Sea Beach, on the other hand, continues at ground level for about half a mile on a section of route that remains remarkably unchanged from the days before the Dual Contracts, when open-platform el cars operated out of the old West End depot, drawing electric current from overhead trolley wires. Some of the old trolley line poles carry feeder cables for today's operation.

Off to our right was the vast expanse of the BMT's Coney Island Yards, a teeming congregation of traction equipment, including some newly arrived R-46 units waiting to undergo acceptance trials, and some ex-IRT equipment, circa 1920, consigned to work train service and painted in such unlikely colors as red and yellow.

"You're lucky; we got a good fast train today," Frank remarked as we moved along the surface right-of-way toward the Sea Beach's open cut. I nodded approval as we rumbled over a series of switches that give the Sea Beach entry to Coney Island Yards, turned slightly to the left, and entered the 86th Street station. Frank moved the air handle to service position, made several swift applications, and brought the train to a smooth halt adjacent to a small porcelain plate displaying the numeral "8." Meaning? Spot the cab of a train of eight cars at the marker.

The Sea Beach line is distinctive; for 4½ miles, from 86th Street to the subway portal near Fourth Avenue, it is four tracks wide, built inside a poured concrete open cut. Tracks are below ground level; except for the lack of a roof, it's much the same as a subway.[3] Interestingly, regular service operates only on the outside pair of tracks. In bygone years there was an operation that used the center, or express, tracks. It ran from the Chambers Street station on the Centre Street loop, over the Manhattan Bridge, out the Fourth Avenue line, and then non-stop from 59th Street to Coney Island over the express tracks on the Sea Beach. From Coney Island, trains continued onto the Brighton line (four routes lead to Stillwell Avenue, two from each direction) and finally terminated at Franklin Avenue, the tail end of the shuttle line that once connected the Brighton with the Fulton Street el. But this was not a regular operation. It ran on "sunny, summer Sundays" only, as the schedules used to say, and has not operated since 1954. The center Sea Beach tracks more than earn their keep now by serving as test tracks for various TA experiments, including acceptance tests for new rolling stock.

Platforms at the nine stations along the Sea Beach's open cut route were

*On early maps of the BMT system the open-cut portions of the Brighton and Sea Beach lines were designated as "subway." Above, a train of Budd-built R-32 units rumbles past some Brooklyn back yards; only the cars' roof tops are visible to residents sunning themselves therein. (Author's collection)*

not crowded. Trains were running at very close headways to meet the requirements of homeward-bound workers, and consequently passengers along the Sea Beach did not have to wait long for a train. At 20th Avenue Ruffino cracked open the cab door; no more than half the seats in the car were filled. Leaving the station at Eighth Avenue the center express tracks merge with the outside tracks, then dip downgrade and enter the subway tunnel. The gray shadows of the December afternoon had deepened into dusk as our train left the out-of-doors and headed for its natural habitat. As we approached the tunnel portal, a trackless right-of-way ramped upward between the two outside tracks. This right-of-way once connected with a BRT el along Third Avenue, and provided the pre-Dual Contracts Sea Beach line with access to Manhattan via the company's elevated network and the Brooklyn Bridge.

Once inside the tunnel, we veered sharply to the right, the train's sealed beam headlights cutting through the darkness. Though headlights seem obviously natural for a subway train, it was not until the mid-1950's that the TA was won over to the idea of trains with headlamps.

Frank muttered as we entered the station at 59th Street. A series of amber lights were glowing along the express tracks, lights not unlike the starting signal at Coney Island. At mid-line points these lights serve as "hold" signals

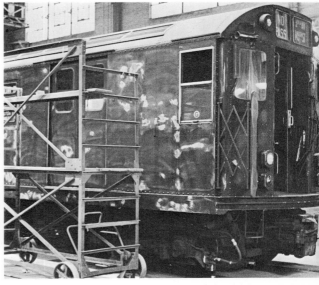

*Above: A late model IRT car gets scrubbed down in preparation for a complete repainting.*

*Maintenance of subway cars is a not often seen but vital component of TA operations. These are R-16 and R-27 units under repair at the huge Coney Island shops. (Both photos, Tom Nelligan)*

—just the opposite from their function at terminals. A conductor cannot depart until they are extinguished. The reason for the hold was that we were now on the express tracks of the four-track Fourth Avenue subway, and had to wait for a local from 95th Street to arrive, so that its passengers could go through the time honored ritual of changing to an express.

"They shouldn't hold us at this time of day," Frank complained. "There's plenty of trains running, and we've got a rush hour to worry about. This is all right at two in the morning, but not now."

The hold lasted less than sixty seconds as a train of R-27 units on the Fourth Avenue Local pulled in next to us. Then it was out of 59th Street and we began the exhilarating experience of roaring past local stations on the center express tracks, the same kind of operation that thrilled one George B. McClellan on the afternoon of October 27, 1904, and has lost none of its excitement since. New York subways do not operate at fast speeds, all things considered. Post-war cars have a "balancing speed" of 50 mph, but in the close confines of a tunnel, the impression of far greater speed is easily generated. (A 50 mph ride in a subway train clearly *seems* to be faster than a 55 mph drive along an Interstate highway!) The noise level inside the car was considerably higher in the subway tunnel than it was on the open air portions of the Sea Beach. Even the dispatcher's crisp jargon which continually spilled out of the two-way radio seemed louder in the tunnel. Incidentally, the channel arrangement of the radio system is such that all trains in a given sector hear all the dispatcher's messages, but only the dispatcher can hear transmissions from the motormen. Frank didn't have to make use of the radio during our entire round trip; some of the old-time motormen have had difficulty adjusting to the very idea of two-way communication, I was told.

At 36th Street, the next express stop, the West End line joins the Fourth Avenue subway. We were delayed briefly as a West End train was sent along ahead of us, but by the time we had made our stop at 36th Street, the West End train had moved far enough ahead for us to run at full speed. The next station was Pacific Street and we were nearing more heavily trafficked territory. The level of conversation in the cab subsided. Leaving Pacific Street we held the express track and bypassed DeKalb Avenue. The DeKalb station, once known as "the heart of the BMT," has six tracks, four for trains stopping at DeKalb, and two for non-stop trains heading for the Manhattan Bridge.

We then began the most dramatic portion of our trip. Beyond DeKalb Avenue, the line runs steadily uphill, eventually debouching onto the lower deck of the Manhattan Bridge for passage over the East River. Except for a few seconds at a sharp switch beyond the old Myrtle Avenue station—a stop that was eliminated during the 1958 DeKalb reconstruction—Frank kept the train in the third notch. Even with full power our speed was only 25 mph while climbing the stiff grade. All thirty-two traction motors drew maximum amperes from the third rail as we headed up the south side bridge tracks, the same rails over which the BRT's first Dual Contracts service had operated over sixty years earlier. Coming toward us was an endless procession of Brooklyn-bound trains, R-32 units on the N line, R-27s on the QB Broadway-Brighton service. On parallel tracks on the north side of the bridge across the three-lane roadway, D and B trains from Chrystie Street added to the scene.

Just before midpoint of the bridge high above the East River Frank cut power, setting off a vivid blue, crackling electric arc. He then started to work the air handle for the long descent to the Manhattan side. Signals ahead glowed red; these were "time signals," so called, adjusted to keep our downgrade speed within safe limits. Each winked to yellow, and then green, as we approached.[4]

## The Epitome

Beyond the bridge right-of-way darkness had enveloped New York, although there was still a slight reddish-purple tint in the western sky beyond the Battery out over Jersey. In the foreground, downtown Manhattan stood in incredible splendor. Lights glowed from the windows of skyscrapers, turning the financial center of the nation into an enchanted crystal wonderland, and below, on the black surface of the river, I could see white puffs of vapor as a tugboat headed toward Governor's Island. Now I've sampled a good many notable train rides in my day—across the night plains of Nebraska in a dome car on the Union Pacific, up to Gallitzin in a roomette on *The Broadway Limited*, out of Toronto late one memorable Spring evening in the cab of a Canadian National 4–8–4 with eighty-three cars in tow. But none of these compares with a ride across the Manhattan Bridge on the BMT. This is the epitome; everything else can compete only for second place.

After crossing the bridge, we dipped back underground through a slow twisting tunnel and drew up to the narrow platform at Canal Street. Frank pulled the reverse key into neutral, let his hand off the controller, and opened the cab window. Suspended from the ceiling was a small box containing a series of buttons; Frank pushed one, thus confirming our train's identity to an operator sequestered in a distant tower. This was a ritual Frank performed several times during our round trip.

Leaving Canal Street, we saw evidence of the way the Dual Contracts of 1913 superseded the earlier Triborough Subway plan. Ahead of the Canal Street station is a straight tunnel, one that has never been used! Our train, instead, took a sharp 90-degree turn to the right, climbed a short grade, and emerged on the center tracks of the four-track Broadway line. This routing —which trains have been following since 1915—was clearly an afterthought. The four-track Broadway subway, as planned in Triborough days, was not to have connected with the Manhattan Bridge line; it was only during the course of negotiations for the Dual Contracts that the BRT was awarded rights to the Broadway line, and plans were altered during the then abuilding project to allow trains from the Manhattan Bridge to reach midtown Manhattan . . . as we were now effortlessly doing.

We moved up the Broadway line quickly, pausing briefly at the 14th and 34th Street express stations. At both there were platform-filling crowds on the downtown side, with many shopping bags filled with holiday gifts in evidence. Few people were waiting for our train, since all Broadway express service terminates at 57th Street. But local service continues beyond 57th Street, under the East River to residential sections of Queens, so that the uptown local station platforms were jammed.

The station at 34th Street seems ordinary enough—it is a conventional four-track express stop. But it is part of what well may be the most complicated concentration of subway tunnels in the world.[5] Under Greeley Square,* where Sixth Avenue, Broadway, and West 32nd Street intersect, are the following: our four-track BMT Broadway line; the four-track IND Sixth Avenue line; a three-track stub-end terminal of PATH, the Port Authority's Trans-Hudson operation, better known as the Hudson Tubes; and beneath all this, four more tracks take Amtrak, Conrail and Long Island RR trains to their East River tunnel crossing—fifteen electrified tracks in all, carrying

*See illustration, page 21*

equipment ranging from our R-32 units to double-bedroom sleepers. Yet a pedestrian strolling along Broadway can not get so much as a glimpse of the action!

We made another stop at 42nd Street, once the terminal point for BMT express trains, and on past the 49th Street local station. Signals ahead of the entrance to 57th Street glowed red, and Frank reduced speed; but before we had to come to a halt, an interlocking signal changed to green over yellow and we drifted through a crossover into the 57th Street station. Before we stopped, Frank let out three blasts on the air horn, taking me by surprise. It was a call for help from a road-car inspector. As Ruffino was setting the marker lights to all red, a troubleshooter arrived.

"Didn't get a light at 14th Street," Frank explained. What happened back at 14th Street was that the conductor had had to open and close the doors several times before the signal light came on in the cab. Afterward, Frank told me his decision to inform the inspector of this minor problem was some- what motivated by self interest.

"If I didn't report that and the train later goes cripple at Canal Street and ties up the bridge, I'd be called down to Jay Street," which is to say: the TA's head office in Brooklyn, at 370 Jay Street. I've heard it called "the Kremlin," and other things too. . . .

Although their equipment consists of but a few hand tools, road-car in- spectors often work miracles in keeping TA trains in service. Our train departed on schedule and, I later learned, performed flawlessly. Frank and I were not aboard. His schedule gives him a fourteen-minute layover at 57th Street.

*With its doors open to receive transferring passengers, an end car of a Sea Beach train rests in a tunnel station along the N line. (NYCTA)*

The terminal at 57th Street is not elaborate. Trains are turned around on either of the two center tracks. North of the station two tracks take a sharp right turn and head for the 60th Street tunnel to Queens. Another short stretch of tunnel points north—but goes nowhere. It was built on the assumption that the BRT would one day be awarded rights for a line to Washington Heights, a route which John Francis Hylan preempted for his municipal subway. The unused tunnel heading will soon be put to use, however; it will be tied into the MTA's new East River tube at the foot of 63rd Street.

After some small talk and introductions to waiting motormen, Frank and I were squeezing into the cab of another R-32 unit and heading back downtown to pick up homewardbound passengers.

The return differed from the inbound trip in that the express tracks along Broadway did not offer us any opportunity for high-speed running. Trains ahead were delayed. We ran to Canal Street with yellow and red signals perpetually in view. Although we didn't have to stop between stations, Frank was never able to "unlimber" his charge. We were running with a full load of seated and standing passengers—approximately 2,000 human beings on one eight-car train. Collectively, 2,000 passengers weigh about 150 tons, a plus factor that was most apparent when we later assaulted the grade on the Manhattan Bridge. Empty, a train of eight R-32 units weighs 280 tons. Thus, our Brooklyn-bound trip took much longer to crest the bridge than did our earlier Manhattan-bound crossing with fewer passengers aboard.

Perhaps the most unnerving feature of the ride was the sight from the cab window as our train pulled into stations jammed to the platform edge with waiting rush-hour passengers. In accord with the transit behavioral patterns New Yorkers have developed over the years, the passengers were clustered only at those points where they expected the doors to be when the train stopped. Indeed, of all the minor and major annoyances that form the warp and woof of life in Gotham, few can touch off the displays of temper that routinely accompany a motorman's stopping a few feet off his mark.

One nostalgic note: Back in the salad days of the BMT three express services operated over the Broadway line: the Sea Beach, the West End and the Brighton. Each service had its own stopping marks. Strung out along the length of the platforms were seventy-five small circular signs neatly indicat-

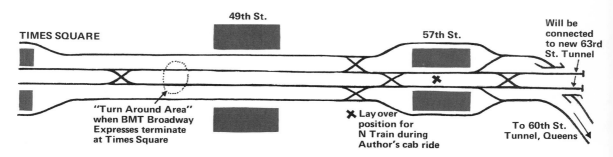

TIMES SQUARE — 49th St. — 57th St. — Will be connected to new 63rd St. Tunnel

"Turn Around Area" when BMT Broadway Expresses terminate at Times Square

✘ Lay over position for N Train during Author's cab ride

To 60th St. Tunnel, Queens

*Left: Stopping marks at a BMT subway platform. (Author)*

*Opposite page: A placid moment at the busiest station on the entire system, West 4th Street in Manhattan, a two-level stop handling well over a thousand arrivals and departures each day. And no wonder—not only the F train but the D, B, A, E, CC, AA and JFK (airport express) trains stop here as well! (Tom Nelligan)*

ing where the doors would be for each of the three routes, white on red for the Sea Beach, white on green for the West End, black on white for the Brighton.

I later asked Frank as tactfully as I could if he had ever suffered the misfortune of having a passenger fall in front of his train. He replied no, but said that once, when entering Bay Parkway station on the West End line late at night, there was a man sitting on the tracks. Frank stopped in time. As the inebriated gentleman was escorted away by two transit policemen, he loudly denounced what he regarded as very poor subway service.

Soon enough we were leaving the Sea Beach's open cut at 86th Street in Brooklyn, heading toward Stillwell Avenue. Trains were moving into Coney Island Yards off to our left for servicing by night maintenance crews. We rumbled over Coney Island creek, up the ramp into the terminal, and through the complex switchwork. We were back on Track 1 where our journey began almost two hours earlier. The return from 57th Street had taken fifty-eight minutes, eleven more than the schedule calls for.

### A Summing-up

After we had a cup of coffee in the crew room I bid "so long" to Frank Ruffino, but before catching an F train back to Manhattan I stood for a few minutes against the steel railing of the overpass and watched the action below. Off to one side, Christmas lights rimmed the windows of second- and third-floor apartments on Stillwell Avenue; to the north, the night sky periodically lit up with sharp flashing blue arcs of subway trains moving about

the yard—a spectacular man-made aurora borealis. All sorts of thoughts raced through my head.

Consider this: New York is beset with problems and difficulties of such magnitude that it is not unusual to hear doomsday prophecies of no future at all for the city. But defeatism is alien to the can-do traditions of the subways. Confidence inspired the Dual Contracts; the men who built transit lines into uninhabited sections of the Bronx and Queens were optimists, not pessimists. Somehow I couldn't but feel that the MTA will shoulder the burden and help New York through its present years of crisis to a new era of urban growth and tranquility.

Then a whimsical thought came to me. In 1904 when August Belmont's Interborough Rapid Transit opened for business, it did so as a minor and merely locally consequential addition to the American electric railway industry. Long gone are the interurban cars that raced the wind across the flatlands of Indiana, trolley cars survive in little more than memory, and the New York stock exchange took down its last electric railway listing decades ago. But the successor to the Belmont empire is not only alive and passably well, but looking forward to better years.

How to sum it all up? The subway is an anti-hero by popular standards. The system is criticized in letters-to-the-editor, ridiculed by stand-up comics, and lambasted by campaigning office seekers. But this incredible city, this arbiter of world style and creator of national opinion, this center of the arts and focus of commerce, this entire pulsating metropolis simply could not exist without its under-the-sidewalks rapid transit network. How sad it is that the subway's vivid history and solid accomplishments; its technological triumphs and social significance; its unique, if fleeting, aspects of beauty and —always—its vibrant "presence" go disregarded by so many eyes.

I turned up my coat collar, walked away from the railing and quickly headed down a flight of stairs to where an F train of R-40 units was waiting to leave for Manhattan.

*Tom Nelligan*

### Notes to Epilogue

[1] The "4" became "N" in 1967 when the Chrystie Street connection was opened and the BMT's number system was changed over to the IND's letter system.

[2] Both the R-44 and the R-46 units feature a single handle for controlling both power and brakes, an arrangement that most other U.S. transit systems employ. Also, the term "air handle" is somewhat anachronistic, as cars now feature a combination of air and dynamic brakes.

[3] In pre-unification days, the BMT issued a system map for its passengers. The map's legend distinguished "elevated lines" and "subway lines." Open cut construction on both the Sea Beach and Brighton lines was shown in the "subway" style.

[4] Descending the Manhattan Bridge has always been the ultimate test of a motorman's skill. The air handle has to be worked continually to hold back a heavy train on the steep downgrade, and time signals will not clear unless the motorman is below the prescribed speed limit—15 mph. When the Boeing-Vertol State of the Art Cars were testing in New York during 1974, they provided dramatic evidence of how modern electronic technology can ease a motorman's lot. Descending the Manhattan Bridge, the SOAC motorman simply set the train's "top speed" for 15 mph, and then proceeded downgrade on full power. The train's sophisticated electronic controller made certain 15 mph was never exceeded.

[5] Charing Cross on the London Underground is a potential challenger.

*Above, a typical Manhattan skyline greets the subway patron mounting these stairs on the way to work in the morning. Such vistas remain, but the old IRT kiosks have all been replaced by less ornate structures. Gone, too, are the New York* Herald Tribunes, Suns, World-Telegrams *and* Daily Mirrors *from the piled up newspapers on the sidewalk. (NYCTA)*

## APPENDIX 1

PASSENGER EQUIPMENT ROSTER

*Interborough Lo-V motor car. (NYCTA-Interborough collection)*

*Absence of marker lights on IRT car No. 4838 indicates that it does not have operating controls, and cannot serve as the lead car of a train. It is a motorless trailer built by Pullman in 1916. (NYCTA)*

*Shorty! Car No. 66 much resembles a conventional IND R unit, except it's much shorter and has fewer windows. It's a revenue collection car. (Phil H. Bonnet)*

**A:** Equipment purchased by the Interborough Rapid Transit Corporation prior to the 1940 unification

| Car Number | Name or Designation | Builder | Date | Notes* |
|---|---|---|---|---|
| 3340 | *August Belmont* | Wason | 1902 | 1 |
| 3341 | *John B. McDonald* | Wason | 1902 | 1 |
| 2000-2159 | Composites | Wason, St. Louis & Jewett | 1903 | |
| 3000-3339 | Composites | Wason, St. Louis, Jewett & Stephenson | 1903–04 | |
| 3342 | First steel car | PRR | 1903 | |
| 3344 | *Mineola* | Wason | 1904 | 1 |
| 3350-3649 | Gibbs Hi-V | ACF | 1904–05 | 2 |
| 3650-3699 | Hi-V deck roof | ACF | 1907–08 | 3 |
| 3700-3809 | Hi-V motors | ACF | 1910–11 | |
| 3810-3849 | Hi-V motors | Standard Steel | 1910–11 | |
| 3850-4024 | Hi-V motors | Pressed Steel | 1910–11 | |
| 4025-4036 | Lo-V Steinway motors | Pullman | 1915 | 17 |
| 4037-4160 | Lo-V Fliver motors | Pullman | 1915 | |
| 4161-4214 | Lo-V Fliver motors | Pullman | 1915 | |
| 4215-4222 | Lo-V Steinway motors | Pullman | 1915 | 15, 17 |
| 4223-4514 | Hi-V trailers | Pullman | 1915 | 16 |
| 4515-4554 | Lo-V trailers | Pullman | 1916 | |
| 4555-4576 | Lo-V Steinway motors | Pullman | 1916 | 15, 17 |
| 4577-4699 | Lo-V motors | Pullman | 1916 | |
| 4700-4770 | Lo-V Steinway motors | Pullman | 1916 | 17 |
| 4771-4810 | Lo-V motors | Pullman | 1916 | |
| 4811-4965 | Lo-V trailers | Pullman | 1916–17 | |
| 4966-5302 | Lo-V motors | Pullman | 1917 | 4 |
| 5303-5377 | Lo-V trailers with compressors | Pullman | 1922 | |
| 5378-5402 | Lo-V trailers | Pullman | 1922 | |
| 5403-5502 | Lo-V motors | Pullman | 1922 | 4 |
| 5503-5627 | Lo-V motors | ACF | 1925 | |
| 5628-5652 | Lo-V Steinway motors | ACF | 1925 | 17 |
| 5653-5702 | Lo-V World's Fair cars | St. Louis | 1938 | 17 |

All of the above noted equipment has been retired from passenger service, although selected cars have been retained for non-revenue service.

*\*See following pages 168, 169*

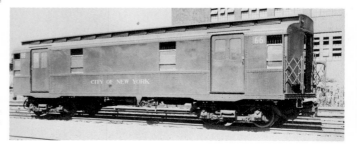

**B:** Equipment purchased by the New York City Board of Transportation and the New York City Transit Authority for service on the IRT Division

| Car Numbers | Contract | Builder | Year | Notes |
|---|---|---|---|---|
| 5703-5802 | R-12 | ACF | 1948 | 5 |
| 5803-5952 | R-14 | ACF | 1949 | 5 |
| 5953-5999 | | | | |
| 6200-6252 | R-15 | ACF | 1950 | 5 |
| 6500-6899 | R-17 | St. Louis | 1955–56 | 6 |
| 7050-7299 | R-21 | St. Louis | 1956–57 | 6 |
| 7300-7749 | R-22 | St. Louis | 1957–58 | 6 |
| 7750-7859 | R-26 | ACF | 1959–60 | 6 |
| 7860-7950 | R-28 | ACF | 1960–61 | 6 |
| 8570-8805 | R-29 | St. Louis | 1962–63 | 6 |
| 8806-9345 | R-33 | St. Louis | 1963 | 6 |
| 9346-9769 | R-36 | St. Louis | 1964 | 7, 18 |

*R-33 unit. Destination board reads "6/ LEX-PELHAM." Car of this class could have served as the hijacked vehicle of the novel and movie,* The Taking of Pelham One Two Three. *(NYCTA)*

*A "married pair" of two R-36 units, painted blue and off-white for service to the 1964-65 World's Fair on the Flushing line. (NYCTA)*

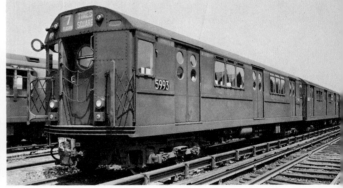

*A.C.F.-built R-15 units. These cars were delivered in 1950, and their basic lines were continued on all New York subway cars for almost twenty years. (NYCTA)*

**C:** Equipment purchased by the Brooklyn Rapid Transit Corporation and the Brooklyn-Manhattan Transit Corporation prior to the 1940 unification.

| Car Numbers | Name or Designation | Builder | Year | Notes |
|---|---|---|---|---|
| 2000-2599 | Standard motors | ACF | 1914–19 | 4 |
| 2600-2899 | Standard motors | Pressed Steel | 1920–22 | |
| 4000-4049 | Standard trailers | Pressed Steel | 1924 | |
| 6000-6120 | Triplex | Pressed Steel | 1925–28 | 4, 8 |
| 7003 | *Green Hornet* | Pullman | 1934 | 9 |
| 7029 | *Zephyr* | Budd | 1934 | 9 |
| 7004-7013 | Multi-section units | St. Louis | 1936 | 9 |
| 7014-7028 | Multi-section units | Pullman | 1936 | 9 |
| 8000-8005 | *Bluebird* | Clark | 1938, 1940 | 8 |

*6000 series Triplex displays the special sign for the BMT's service to the '39-40 World's Fair via a connection at Queens Plaza. (NYCTA)*

All of the above noted equipment has been retired from passenger service.

*March 8, 1932. This R-1 unit posed in a BMT tunnel prior to IND's opening that September. (NYCTA)*

*Framed by massive steel girders, an R-38 car on the GG route service sits in the station at Smith-9th Streets in Brooklyn. (Author photo)*

**D:** Equipment purchased by the City of New York for the Independent Subway System

| Car Numbers | Contract | Builder | Year | Notes |
|---|---|---|---|---|
| 100-399 | R-1 | ACF | 1930–31 | 4 |
| 400-899 | R-4 | ACF | 1932–33 | |
| 1300-1399 | R-6(1) | Pressed Steel | 1936 | |
| 1150-1299 | R-6(2) | Pullman | 1936 | |
| 900-1149 | R-6(3) | ACF | 1935–36 | |
| 1400-1474 | R-7 | ACF | 1937 | |
| 1475-1549 | R-7 | Pullman | 1937 | |
| 1550-1599 | R-7(a) | Pullman | 1938 | |
| 1600-1649 | R-7(a) | ACF | 1938 | |
| 1650-1701 | R-9 | ACF | 1940 | |
| 1702-1802 | R-9 | Pressed Steel | 1940 | |

All of the above noted equipment has been retired from passenger service, although selected cars have been retained for non-revenue service.

### NOTES

(1) Did not run in regular passenger service; non-revenue equipment otherwise not included in this roster.
(2) Car No. 3352 preserved at Seashore Trolley Museum, Kennebunkport, Me.
(3) Car No. 3663 preserved at Branford Trolley Museum, East Haven, Conn.
(4) Several representatives of this class preserved by the TA for historical purposes.
(5) Single unit cars; cabs on both ends.
(6) Coupled into two-car sets; one motorman's cab per car.
(7) Permanently coupled into two-car sets, except Nos. 9306 through 9345 which are single units.
(8) Three-section articulated units.
(9) Five-section articulated units.
(10) R-10 units in the 1800 series re-numbered into the 2900 series in 1970.
(11) Rebuilt under contract R-34 in 1964–65.
(12) Some of these cars air conditioned.

*Five of the Board of Transportation's Budd-built experimental cars that were designated the R-11 units. Later these cars were rebuilt and are now known as R-34s. An end view of an R-34 reincarnation is at the left. (Both photos NYCTA)*

**E:** Equipment purchased by the New York City Board of Transportation and the New York City Transit Authority for service on the BMT and IND divisions.

| Car Numbers | Contract | Builder | Date | Notes |
|---|---|---|---|---|
| 1808-1852 |  |  |  |  |
| 3000-3349 | R-10 | ACF | 1948–49 | 10, 5 |
| 8010-8019 | R-11 | Budd | 1949 | 11, 5 |
| 6300-6499 | R-16 | ACF | 1955 | 5 |
| 8020-8249 | R-27 | ACF | 1960 | 6 |
| 8250-8351 |  |  |  |  |
| 8412-8569 | R-30 | St. Louis | 1961 | 6 |
| 8352-8411 | R-30(a) | St. Louis | 1961 | 6 |
| 3650-3949 | R-32 | Budd | 1965 | 6 |
| 3350-3649 | R-32(a) | Budd | 1965 | 6 |
| 3950-4149 | R-38 | St. Louis | 1966 | 12, 6 |
| 4150-4549 | R-40 | St. Louis | 1967–68 | 12, 6 |
| 4550-4949 | R-42 | St. Louis | 1968–69 | 13, 6 |
| 100-399 | R-44 | St. Louis | 1971–72 | 13, 14 |
| 500-1278 | R-46 | Pullman | 1974–78 | 13, 14, 19 |

NOTE: In 1954 30 ex-Staten Island Rapid Transit cars were purchased for service on the BMT. Of the total, 25 were motor cars, and they were numbered 2900-2924. Five trailers never were used in passenger service by the TA. All were built by Standard Steel in 1925 and have since been retired.

(13) Air conditioned.
(14) Includes cars with full width cab on one end, no cab on the other end; also cars with no cabs at all.
(15) Converted from trailers to status shown in 1929.
(16) Nos. 4223-4250 converted to Hi-V blind motors in 1952.
(17) Designed for steep grades of Steinway tunnels; would not m.u. with other cars.
(18) None of the post war IRT cars were built with air conditioning. Retrofitting began in 1975.
(19) Nos. 1228-1278 include even numbered cars only.

Compare this silhouette of an R-10 unit, A.C.F. 1948-49, with the R-1 on page opposite. (NYCTA)

The TA's newest equipment – beginning with the R-44 units – features equipment and operation significantly different from older rolling stock. (MTA)

Above: Last of the BMT experimentals was this lightweight train of 3-section articulated units built by Clark Railway Equipment Corp. on the eve of World War II. Design drew upon the PCC streetcar. At right: A sidelight to the subway story is the fact that the PCC trolley car first rolled on the rails of BMT's surface subsidiary, the Brooklyn and Queens Transit Corp. PCC No. 1016 was one of the nation's first production run of these cars, and is operating on B&Q track on the site of famous Culver Depot, in this 1954 view. (Roger J. Cudahy)

| Vehicle | BMT Standard | R-36 | R-38 | R-46 |
|---|---|---|---|---|
| Quantity | 950 | 424 | 200 | 754 |
| Year First Purchased | 1914 | 1962 | 1965 | 1974 |
| Builder | ACF & Pressed Steel | St. Louis | St. Louis | Pullman |
| Service | BRT/BMT | IRT | IND/BMT | IND/BMT |
| Length | 67' | 51'4" | 60'6" | 75' |
| Width | 10' | 8'9½" | 10' | 10' |
| Weight | 95,000/99,000 | 72,600 | 68,500 | 90,000 |
| No. of seats | 78 | 44 | 50 | 56 |
| No. of motors | 2 | 4 | 4 | 4 |
| Status | Retired | In service | In service | In service |

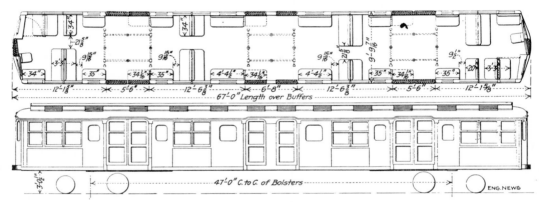

*Above drawing shows the unusual three-two transverse seating in the famous BMT Standard subway car. Longitudinal seating (left, below) has virtually always been the rule on narrower IRT cars and, for a time, was the practice on wider BMT-IND equipment as well. Newer cars have returned to the more comfortable transverse seating, as in the R-44 unit interior (right, below), albeit only on the ten-foot-wide vehicles. (Photos by author and GSI-St. Louis)*

# APPENDIX 3

## SUBWAY SIGNALING

THE NEW YORK SUBWAYS have not been 100 percent free of collisions over the years, but the record is remarkably good. Credit on this score goes to many factors, not the least of which is the automatic signal system that protects the various lines and routes.

The signal system in use today is a simple one—simple, that is, compared to the many different kinds of indications and aspects a person must know to pass a book-of-rules examination on any standard American railroad. Excluding early BRT/BMT el operations, the BMT and IND have always used roughly similar signal codes. While the Interborough employed a different and more complex system through most of its history, including a generous reliance on semaphore-type signals, it is now being brought into step with the system used on the other two divisions.

There are two principal kinds of signals—automatic block and interlocking. Block signals contain green, yellow and red indications, although in certain instances a fourth indication is used in conjunction with one of the three colors to inform a motorman of some special condition. Red means stop, and if a train doesn't, a raised arm next to the signal at trackside exercises a simple but effective form of automatic train control. The raised arm trips a switch located on the lead truck, emergency brakes are applied automatically, and the train stops. All TA lines and trains are equipped with this fail-safe mechanism. (The term "fail-safe" is used advisedly; the circuits are designed so that any short circuit or malfunction in the system immediately throws the signal to red and raises the trip arm.) Except for some local tracks on some early lines—and most of the els—all rapid transit ever built in New York featured automatic train stop signals as original equipment. The new Second Avenue line in Manhattan, as well as other new routes, will introduce a more complex and varied form of automatic train control. Plans call for coded electronic impulses to be transmitted to a monitor on board the train, providing a full range of speed controls, and not just simple stop protection. The R-44 and R-46 subway cars are equipped to run on such lines.

Once a train pauses at a red block signal, the trip arm automatically lowers and the train *can* proceed. However since 1970, the book of rules does not permit the motorman to do so. A red automatic block signal now means "stop and stay"; in past years it meant, rather, "stop and proceed," prepared to find the next signal also showing red, or possibly even finding the block itself occupied. This maneuver—stopping at a red signal and allowing the trip arm to lower automatically—is called "keying by." The terminology dates to bygone days on the Interborough: When a motorman paused at a red signal he had to get out of his cab, descend to trackside, and crank down the track trip with a key-like device. Keying by a signal still happens in the subway, but only after a motorman has been given radio clearance by the dispatcher to execute the move.

*Below is the automatic trip arm that serves as the subway's first line of defense against mishap. Trip is shown in the raised position to intercept the train valve that applies emergency brakes. At right, a wall-mounted conventional IRT automatic signal. Both BMT and IND Divisions have similar devices. (Both photos, NYCTA-Interborough collection)*

*Husky operator heaves at a switch lever in the system's last manually operated interlocking plant, Rockaway Parkway on the BMT's Canarsie line. At one time, of course, all switch towers featured such hand-operated gear. Today, electronic equipment such as that installed at the Euclid Avenue Station interlocking plant (right) is the rule. Operator controls "A" line switches with push-button ease. (Photos from NYCTA)*

A yellow block signal means "slow," since the next signal may be showing red, and green means "proceed." Variations occur chiefly in what is called "time signal" territory. Here block signals do more than protect trains from each other, they force motormen to observe permanent speed restrictions. Approaching a downgrade, say, on which the maximum allowable speed is 15 mph, a motorman will see ahead nothing but yellow and red block signals. Often the red signals will also show an extra lunar white indication in time signal territory to distinguish the aspect from a conventional "stop" signal. The motorman must reduce his speed. If he is traveling at or under the allowable limit, the signals ahead will clear and permit the train to continue—but only at a rate that will require the motorman to remain below 15 mph.

Interlocking signals are the second major species found at trackside. They contain two separate red-yellow-green signal heads, and frequently other indications as well. They protect all junctions, and can often be found at places other than junctions where a towerman or dispatcher might want to be able to exercise con-

*Left: Interlocking signals with two separate signal units on each mast control approaches to turnouts. Right: A typical yard dwarf signal. (Photos by author and Tom Nelligan)*

trol over a train. A standard automatic block signal cannot be set at "stop" from a remote location, whereas an interlocking signal can.

A double-red indication on an interlocking signal means "stop and stay." No keying by is, or ever was, permitted in the face of such an indication. Interlocking signals also indicate the route for which an approaching switch is set. Green-over-green and yellow-over-green are the "proceed" and "proceed with caution" indications for the straight set; green-over-yellow and double-yellow are the equivalent indications for the diverging track.

Until the DeKalb Avenue reconstruction in 1958 eliminated its need, the BMT employed a special blue signal on an interlocking unit. It was used approaching a unique three-way switch, and allowed the motorman to know which of three routes was set.

There are other kinds of signals and indications used in the subway system. Small ground-level dwarf signals are often used at switches to allow for occasional movements against the ordinary flow of traffic. They are manually controlled from a tower, generally do not include trip arms, and are not really part of ordinary operations. In some yard locations on the IRT, semaphore signals are still used to control traffic.

The Transit Authority maintains total respect for its signal system. For in addition to obvious considerations of safety, it is a smoothly functioning signal system that permits optimum performance on any subway line. Passengers on the IRT may have been impressed by the new subway cars that were purchased for the old Belmont lines during the 1950s, but TA engineers were just as concerned about that part of the IRT Improvement Program which called for total replacement of all older signals, so that the new equipment's full potential could be realized.

A simple but dependable signal system—now backed up by two-way radio—plus a management that insists upon near-religious observance of the book of rules: These are the elements that combine to produce safe and dependable transportation for four million passengers each day.

## Underground Films

*Hollywood unit production manager Wes Thompson (left) confers with producer Ed Montaine while filming the made-for-television movie,* A Short Walk to Daylight. *(NYCTA)*

WHILE THE SUBWAY is often criticized as a passenger-carrying railway, it performs in admirable fashion as a ready-made movie set. In a typical year more than fifty camera crews visit TA property to film everything from major Hollywood productions to 10-second television commercials. These ventures afford a tidy profit to the always cash-strapped Authority and generate interesting promotional exposure as well.

In bygone days when authenticity was not the vital concern it is today, Hollywood directors often settled for some stock footage of trains, and then posed their actors aboard a Pacific Electric interurban in southern California, or possibly just a studio mock-up of a subway car. Today, however, cameras, technicians, supporting cast, and stars themselves must venture into the caverns under New York and perform on location.

The Academy Award winner, *The French Connection,* brought subway trains into the plot in two separate sequences. The first involved the IRT's Grand Central-Times Square shuttle. Two full days of shooting were required for a scene that lasted perhaps three minutes on screen. Far more complicated was the now-famous chase scene on, and under, the elevated structure. It involved fourteen days of shooting between January 18th and March 12th, 1971. The movie-makers chartered R-42 units Nos. 4572 and 4573 for the two months and installed their equipment inside. The cars were placed under a special 24-hour guard at the TA's Coney Island yard when not in use. The numbers of these two cars were the only ones ever visible on the screen; during shooting they were coupled to six additional, but not specially rigged, sister units to form a typical eight-car train. The extra cars came fresh off a morning assignment, and were back at work for the evening rush hour. The movie extra, of course, could only roll during midday hours when the system was not busy.

All interior scenes were filmed on the BMT West End line in Brooklyn, as were most of the exterior shots of the train speeding along. One little bit of artistic license was taken, however, and one scene was actually filmed out in Ridgewood along the Myrtle Avenue line. A further deviation from absolute authenticity

was an incorrect marking on the train. The proper letter code for a West End train is a black and white letter "B." When equipment for the movie was selected in January, car washers were out of service because of the cold weather. A clean group of cars was a must. The units chosen were normally assigned to the N line, had no B line signs, and therefore operated during the movie with an orange and white "N" in the front slot.

Although *The French Connection* presented subways in a supporting role, when Hollywood turned John Godey's best-selling novel, *The Taking of Pelham One Two Three,* into a film, the IRT's Lexington Avenue local became a virtual co-star. The plot was about the hijacking of a subway car and the holding of its passengers for ransom. The book and the movie both successfully captured the pace and texture of day-to-day subway operations under the Transit Authority.

Contemporary films, such as *The French Connection,* while interesting, do not provide the challenge of a period piece. Film makers are not adverse to the expense of refurbishing some of the older rolling stock maintained by the TA for a production. For instance, when *The Class of '44* was filmed, an old BMT train from the 1920s was used to depict the stock of the era. Even the appointments of a station, this time on the Sea Beach line, were restored to the style and hue of an earlier time. Regular passengers who didn't remember the former fixtures and paint scheme simply shrugged off the cosmetics as a new decorating pattern, but old-timers were seen to walk into the station, look around, and appear uneasy, possibly convinced they had stepped into some sort of twilight zone.

*On the Bay-50th Street station of the West End line, actor Gene Hackman fires at a fleeing suspect in the film,* The French Connection. *(NYCTA)*